You're in Game!-2

More LitRPG Stories Set in Your Favorite Worlds

Vasily Mahanenko
Andrei Livadny
Alexey Osadchuk
Pavel Kornev
Andrew Novak
Dan Sugralinov
Eugenia Dmitrieva
Michael Atamanov

Magic Dome Books

You're in Game!
Copyright © 2018: Vasily Mahanenko, Andrei Livadny, Alexey
Osadchuk, Pavel Kornev, Andrew Novak, Dan Sugralinov, Eugenia
Dmitrieva, Michael Atamanov
Cover Art © Cover Art © Vladimir Manyukhin 2018
English translation copyright © 2018: Andrew Schmitt, Krystal
Diehl, Irene Woodhead, Neil P. Mayhew
Editors: Barbara D. Jenkins, Neil P. Mayhew
Published by Magic Dome Books, 2018
All Rights Reserved
ISBN: 978-80-88231-94-3

TABLE OF CONTENTS:

ARCHIBALD

A TALE FROM *DARK PALADIN* SERIES

BY VASILY MAHANENKO

A PIERCING ICY WIND struggled to penetrate a protection dome, trying to get to a player who was skulking astride the bough of a tree, keeping a watchful eye over the country estate of the person he habitually called his *foe*. Not an enemy, mind you: to earn this name, Iven would have to do something truly extraordinary. By the same token, he wasn't a friend, either.

You could tell that the estate defenses had been built by professionals. A large fenced-off area and a deep moat half-filled with water were supposed to dissuade any stray NPCs. An enormous wall thirty feet high fitted with motion detectors ran all around the estate, offering protection against an unexpected albeit inexperienced trespassing player.

His comm vibrated. Archibald opened it, checked the picture and nodded, content. The estate was fortified against any air attack, as well. The image sent by the spy satellite was blurred and fuzzy.

This was going to be an interesting day.

Archibald waited. Judging by the marker, Iven was now at Gerhard's. Apparently, Iven was naïve enough to think he was the only player on planet Earth not having a marker. He was right in a way: Archibald's own marker was impossible to detect with any of the current technologies. Even the trackers and cleaners brought from the previous era which Gerhard used in his reception room couldn't detect the bug.

Yes, the first-era technologies were nothing short of perfect. Also — something that Archibald loved — the appliances were magic-free. He didn't care whether magic was explained away as "cargo rays focused with the help of the prism of Éowyn, one of the three Creators" as some better informed creatures claimed.

Archibald waited. Entering the grounds now wouldn't be a good idea. After his rapid rise through the ranks, Iven spent money like there was no tomorrow. You might think he kept the Emperor himself prisoner in his cellars, charging the Game a daily fee for not hurting him.

Archibald might still have to look into this. It looked like the granis-burning upstart had commissioned one of Nord's defense systems —

and Nord used to be one of Archibald's best students. With the rise of the third era, Master must have decided to turn the perfect assassin and executioner of his will into a true professional.

Just imagine that a certain Gerhard von Brast used to think you could make the world better simply by eradicating violence! How wrong he'd been. You can't change the world without sacrificing all of yourself to it at the moment of transformation. This was something Master didn't want. He still couldn't forgive himself for his first restart and the following five thousand years spent trying to piece his memory back together.

The method of consciousness transfer developed by Archibald couldn't hold Master's entire identity. Archibald had had to split it into separate components, then entrust them to several separate creatures, two of whom he'd never managed to locate. Master would never be the same.

Archibald waited. Every time Iven met with Gerhard, he had to unwind afterward. This seemingly calm and unmoving paladin was in fact a very edgy and thin-skinned creature.

Dozens of mutilated bodies of local NPCs had to be buried at the nearest graveyard every time Iven came back from Master. Once, Archibald had even had to seek the services of a local necromancer in order to interrogate one of the dead bodies. Iven personally tortured his victims, reveling in their suffering and the sight of blood. Master only shrugged, telling Archibald that everyone was free to relax in whichever way the rules and the person's own conscience allowed. Still, Archibald was pretty sure that Iven wasn't going to make it to the next era which had just been activated.

A happy smile crossed Archibald's lips when he thought about the restart. He'd played a fine game setting up that bunch of unlawfully elevated mages. Master had kept him on his toes with his constant errands but the result was worth it. He'd found the Immune one, found a way to bring him to Earth, then erased his memory, turning a perfect being into an imbecile. Then he'd fed the mages a story about their supposed rise to power after the Immune one's execution, forcing them to risk everything and bribe the Councilor. He'd made an arrangement with the Councilor about the initiation of both the Keymaster and the Guide. He'd also arranged for the restart to begin with one of the Guide's incarnations. He'd had the Keymaster's incarnation ready and made an agreement with the ogres to protect her. Basically, he'd made everybody believe they were doing it all on their own free will, ensuring everybody happened to be in the right place at the right time.

Or rather, at the time which was right for Archibald.

The only thing he hadn't taken into account was that there was yet another incarnation of the Guide in the Academy. Still, he'd been lucky.

Three hundred years ago, Archibald had found an incarnation of the Keymaster and implanted it with the consciousness of Madonna which he'd hosted all that time. The only thing that had saved him then from Gerhard's wrath was the fact that the latter liked the girl. Still, Archibald hadn't escaped punishment. Gerhard had warned him there and then that as soon as his Doll regained her own consciousness she'd destroy Archibald, simply because a Keymaster's mind should remain whole until the moment of its reincarnation — and it's not supposed to host two identities. Madonna would not like it: she was sure to demand sacrifice.

Still, that had only been a warning. By way of punishment, Archibald was supposed to mentor Dolgunata, as well as every Paladin of those randomly chosen on Earth every month. Two hundred years later, however, Master had adjusted his punishment. Now he got to choose Archibald's students personally, simply because none of the Catorian's students had left the Academy alive.

That didn't help, either. Archibald's students kept dying one after another, releasing him from the burden of mentorship, while Master wasn't in a hurry to let Dolgunata join the Academy.

The arrival of Yaropolk had changed everything. This petty NPC had done what many experienced players had failed: he'd destroyed Devir. Still pretending he didn't single out his new student amongst the others, Archibald broke the rules, using the mental block ability against the NPCs and granting him a certain immunity against being frozen out by the Academy.

His student hadn't let him down. Not only had he managed to survive the Academy and restart the Game, but he'd also entrusted the Head of class with the right to form the list of players allowed entry into the new era. Everything had worked out just fine.

His comm vibrated, informing him that Iven was back in his lair and would be quite busy for the next couple of hours. Archibald stretched his never-stiffening neck like a boxer, then jumped softly to the ground. You had to give Master his due: he'd created a perfect race. Speed, excellent reflexes, immunity to poisons and radiation, strength, intellect and a gorgeous tail — the product of the first era, Archibald was nothing short of perfect. Later, he'd given birth to other races such as the Catorians — the result of mixing with humans, — as well as half-Elven Delganians and half-cynocephalian shapeshifters.

Archibald heaved a sigh. He habitually considered himself a Catorian. He used to have much more freedom in the past. Forever stuck on Earth and receiving a new name with every new restart, Master used him as his eyes and ears in other worlds. For tens of thousands of years Archibald used to be his voice as well, seeing as the Game had severely punished this restart-defying renegade by erasing him from memory, both his and the other players'. Every time Master had to start all over again, clawing his way back to the top.

Archibald shrugged off the memories and headed toward the entrance. His shimmering force field concealed him from any prying eyes or detection devices.

A system message flashed before his eyes,

Object identified. Entry granted.

The automatic gate slid aside. A few armed guards stared in confusion at the gate and the empty space behind it, trying to fathom out what might have caused the system's malfunction. Still, they were anything but reckless: Iven had trained his men well. Their commander scanned the empty space with an advanced analyzer, trying to detect the trespasser.

What Archibald really liked, Iven had turned out to be just as stupid as the hundred thousand players before him. You shouldn't always aim for the best: the result might not be what you expected. The stinking-rich paladin had splurged on the best defenses for his place, seriously thinking he could secure it against every possible threat.

His lack of experience in these matters was obvious. Despite all his fabled objectivity, Nord couldn't have very easily refused his own mentor's request, fitting each and every of his defense mechanisms with a friend-or-foe system which granted Archibald admin rights and the keys to the guarded object.

Which was why the manor now recognized Archibald as its owner, opening its doors to him and completely ignoring petty obstacles in the face of its own guards. As Nord used to say, "If they want a defense that works, they'd better make it themselves." Whoever counted on a third-party product was bound to pick up a handful of trojans.

Archibald raised a quizzical eyebrow. Iven's manor was too much even for him, and he thought he'd seen it all. A picturesque garden — which was the exact copy of the Viceroy's — started immediately behind the wall. It had everything, even a few Garnians: a fireball-shaped energy beings hovering in mid-air, a product of the third-era experiments with lightning. Then, a tragic accident had turned out to be a blessing in disguise, transforming the unfortunate researcher struck by lightning into the first Garnian. The player researchers loved the result and decided against destroying the creature. A similar story had happened to the hedge which was now staring at Archibald with millions of its green eyes. None of these things were natural: they had either been built or created.

The first obstacle serious enough for Archibald to start paying attention to appeared by the entrance into the main building. Two guarding statues watched Archibald's every movement, betraying their ability to see him.

Archibald stopped a few paces away from them. His tail twitched nervously. It's not that the statues could do him any harm: they remained silent, considering him a "friend" as long as he remained outside in the yard. But within the few split seconds in which he might need to kill them, they'd inform the entire estate about the trespasser. The fact that Archibald had entered the grounds meant nothing to them: he hadn't been granted access to the building itself.

Archibald looked at the ground-floor windows. There was an identical statue posted next to each. And he'd have hated to blow his cover now.

Which was why he had to act out of the box.

Archibald unstealthed, walked over to the statues and said in his best pompous voice, "Gerhard van Brast's latest incarnation desires to secretly visit his vassal. Request maximum access level."

"Status confirmed. Maximum access granted," one of the statues replied in a mechanical voice, gliding aside to vacate the path. The other one did the same.

Master was going to hate this. Archibald shouldn't have used his name again. Still, he couldn't see any other way of infiltrating the building. He had to make it quick before his students did something they might later regret.

Actually... if Lady Lecleur's estate indeed had a Reverse, he might need to find out who'd made it.

"Take me to Iven's personal office," Archibald said.

The statue momentarily zoned out. The front door opened, letting out a Garnian hovering in mid-air.

"Do follow me, Sir Avatar," the fireball said before floating unhurriedly back into the depths of the building.

Archibald made a mental note to erase all information about his visit. Nobody should know anything about his own nature, least of all Iven.

One of the main conditions of the Game's restart was that all of its initiated participants had to be located on Earth as the first era's main Game world: the world which harbored the Game's very mechanism. This was exactly what had inspired Gerhard to create Archibald, also during the first era, and to turn him into his own "voice".

As for the remaining restart participants, they already had Madonna even though Gerhard didn't want to initiate her prematurely. Already during the past era Master's Doll had become too jealous and power-hungry, taking pleasure in humiliating every female being that chanced to be near her sweetheart. If she learned about Master's orgies, the resulting scandal might be mind-boggling... and Archibald just might be the one who lost the most in this. Because Madonna just plain didn't like him.

Which was exactly why he'd implanted the

Keymaster with her identity and why'd he'd taught Dolgunata everything he himself knew. Naturally, Dolgunata wasn't as powerful as Madonna but at least this Druid girl knew something that Madonna had always been trying to avoid: clawing for victory to the last. Two beings as dramatically different as they would be too busy fighting one another, which might give Archibald a decent survival chance. They were bound to strip him of his Paladin status once again, as had happened during the two last restarts, but that was nothing.

If only he knew what Merlin was up to! The nasty old guy had always managed to get initiated first, then spent all his time in hiding trying to last as long as he possibly could. In this respect, the Guide was Archibald's only hope. He had either already come across Merlin's new incarnation or would do so shortly. This was how restart worked.

He absolutely had to use Gerhard's influence to gain access to the library's limited-access section which contained the clue to the location of Merlin's diary. Archibald doubted that Yaropolk could talk the librarian into leaving for a self-imposed exile.

"His Lordship's office," the Garnian said as yet another door opened before Archibald.

You wouldn't call is exactly ascetic. Pompous and pretentious, rather, like that of a penniless lottery winner who hurries to shower himself with expensive stuff not bothering whether his new possessions go well together, as long as the price tag is humongous.

Archibald sat down in front of the laptop and began studying its contents. He had to get to know his "foe". He needed to work out how he'd gotten his money and whether Lecleur's estate indeed had a Reverse.

You never knew, it could be one made by Marcus.

TRANSLATED FROM RUSSIAN BY IRENE WOODHEAD
AND NEIL P. MAYHEW

THE DARK KNIGHT

A TALE FROM
THE NEURO SERIES

BY ANDREI LIVADNY

WINTER HAD ARRIVED early. The piercing wind bore down at the city towers, lashing them with torrents of snow.

A group of maintenance robots emerged from the snowstorm. Their cybernetic bodies had no fear for subzero temperatures.

The man who was watching them, however, had frozen solid. He lurked behind the rows of flybots parked on the street, stoically waiting for his trap to go off.

The sky was already darkening. The cold was getting fiercer.

The robots quickly located the cable he'd severed. Having promptly replaced it, they began testing the nearby devices — including a large manhole.

Friedrich White curved his lips in a smile. The nano comp bracelet on his wrist (the only thing he still had left from his past life) had successfully intercepted the maintenance access code.

The robots soon departed to do more repairs elsewhere. Limping, White scrambled to the precious manhole and activated it using the code he'd just received.

The hatch opened, breathing heat in his face. He crouched, warming his frozen fingers in the air current until they began to prickle.

At last. The wretched existence of a street bum he'd led since last year should be over tonight.

A vertical ladder disappeared into the darkness far below. White began to climb down. With a humming noise, the hatch overhead rattled shut.

He soon grew warm in the rising air current. He even broke into a sweat climbing down toward the dimly lit panorama of the metropolis' underbelly.

There, nested amid the city's powerful support framework, its reactors breathed their hot breath. Recycling plants and food factories toiled non-stop. Automated to perfection, the city's substructures appeared perfectly autonomous.

Still, even this realm of dead mechanisms had provided shelter to a few human beings.

Two of them approached White as he jumped off the ladder.

"Is it cold up there?" a skinny young guy asked him.

"It's flippin' freezing," White replied, brushing flakes of rust off his hands. "Did you have a raid again?"

"Just some police bots. They left half an hour ago."

"Did they catch anyone?"

"They got Max. And the new girl, whatever her name is. We managed to disable two of them but we couldn't do too much, as you can imagine."

"Pointless trying to fight machines."

"Why, you wanna back out now? That's not how you used to speak," the guy spat at his feet.

The girl next to him turned away without saying a word. She too was skinny and pale.

"I know," White said. "I haven't chickened out if that's what you mean. You know very well I'm here looking for my daughter."

"And?"

"I'm leaving tonight. I'm going to the Crystal Sphcrc. I'm afraid you'll have to make do without me."

"You're freakin' mad. You gonna sell out to the corporation, is that what it is?"

"Sorry, Frank. That's none of your business. You want a piece of advice?"

"Depends on what it is."

"Go virtual."

"Are you crazy? What do you want me to do there? You really expect me to lie in one of those coffin things? I don't think so! Rachel and I can manage very well on our own, thank you very much. Let those bots catch us if they think they can. I'm not implanting myself with anything!"

"It doesn't hurt, by the way. They attach the implant with nano needles. You won't feel a thing. All they do, they press the implant to your temple and-"

"You sure you're not working for them? Where've you been these last few days?"

"Doesn't matter. Take this," White offered the young guy a fully charged first-aid kit.

How was he supposed to explain to them who'd been born underground that the world overhead had already changed irreversibly? These days it was ruled by Infosystems' new technologies. Without an implant, you couldn't get a job. They wouldn't even issue you a social code number without one. Very soon, humankind would leave the real world for good, entrusting their mortal bodies to the care of complex machinery.

White had no idea what stood behind it. Those revolutionary virtual technologies seemed to have sprouted out of nowhere. He didn't know what to think — but he fully intended to find out.

Frank took the first-aid kit from him and put it in his pocket. "So you've made up your mind, then?"

"I'm afraid so."

"Well, good luck to you, then. Enjoy your

virtual dreams. Come on, Rachel."

✳ ✳ ✳

THE STEEL DOOR opened with a long creak.

After the gloom of level zero, the dim lighting of the corridor assaulted White's eyes. He cringed and held his breath, unable to inhale the effluvia which passed for air in this low-grade capsule hotel.

He walked down the narrow corridor until he came to some sort of reception desk manned by a heavy-set guy of indeterminate age.

"What is it?" the man grumbled without looking up at him.

"I need to get to the Crystal Sphere."

The hotel owner gave him a sideways glance. With a theatrical sigh, he ticked something off in the document he'd been filling in and closed the holographic computer windows. He then touched his nanocomp bracelet, switching it to sleep mode.

Finally he turned to his new customer, sizing him up with a faked indifference. "So what do you want me to do?" he raised a sarcastic eyebrow.

"I need to get to the Crystal Sphere," White repeated, suppressing his strong dislike of the man.

"For how long?"

As a dealer, Herod had a very bad name with the city's underground. His practiced eye must have already taken in White's worn clothes which once must have cost a lot of money. His eyes glistened with greed promptly replaced by nonchalance. His new customer must have robbed some rich guy, as simple as that.

The only problem was, the clothes — a posh business suit and a tattered cashmere overcoat — seemed to have been made to measure. You could see it was bespoke stuff. The customer himself was a tall, lanky guy — another man's clothes would have looked funny on him.

"I said, how long do you need access for?" he repeated. "A day, a month?"

"No idea," White replied in all honesty. "It could be a day. Or it could be one-way. If you can't do it, just say so," his voice rang with determination.

The dealer's shifty eyes glistened with the anticipation of an easy profit. Ripping this rich idiot off would be a piece of cake.

"Don't even think about it," White said, reading the dealer's face as if it were an open book. "I know prices."

The hotel owner choked mid-word. "Very well. I can see you've been around the block a few times. How come I've never seen you here before?"

"I've never been here before."

"I bet you haven't. Come to rough it, have you?" Herod gave him a meaningful look.

"That's none of your business."

"It might be, in case you have other intentions."

"I'm looking for my daughter. She's gone missing. I've spent most of my savings looking for her and now I've found out she's gone virtual. No idea where her capsule is stored. Now you know why I need to get to the Crystal Sphere. Happy now?"

"I see, I see. It's all right," Herod blew a long breath and leaned back in his tatty office chair.

Nothing new there, he thought. Developed by Infosystems Corporation, the new virtual world of the Crystal Sphere had already swallowed several generations of young gamers, luring them in with the previously unheard-of 100% authenticity of experience. A lot of people had gone there with the intention of never resurfacing again. Shame about the old man, though.

"Very well," Herod said. "Give me your implant number. Come back in a couple of hours. I'll sort it out for you. A hundred credits for a Crystal Sphere account and another hundred for the in-mode capsule rental. After that, you can either extend your rent of piss off to the communal in-mode center."

"I don't have an implant."

The dealer's jaw dropped. He gulped a few times, staring at the weird man. "Have you been living under a rock for the last year? These days, you can't even breathe without having one. You can't rent a place or do your shopping, you can't even get first aid if you drop dead on the street."

White perched himself on the edge of a rickety chair. Fatigue was getting the better of him — and with it came apathy, the most dangerous feeling of all. "Do you really think I would be talking to you if I didn't know that? I don't have an implant, period."

"Then you should go to a communal in-mode center."

"I would have if I could. Don't you think you're asking too many questions?"

"You have the money?"

"I still have some savings left, yes."

"But if you don't have the implant, how on earth are you going to pay?"

"Like we always did before," White touched the cybtech on his wrist.

Herod nodded. Poor old man. Kids! They plunge into the Crystal Sphere headlong without even thinking about their parents who're worried sick about them. Herod's own son never left his capsule these days. He found the real world colorless and depressing, he said. He might be right. Still, if everyone moved to cyberspace... the human race would discontinue, that's for sure.

Herod cringed. These kinds of ragged, bitter thoughts didn't seem to hurt him anymore. The world as we knew it was over and done with, anyway. Progress had turned out to be a treacherous companion... it had led humanity into a dead end and left it there to die.

"Very well," Herod said. "An old-style wire transfer, why not. I've got this bit of software that can connect two cybtechs. No implant needed. But," Herod just couldn't shake off the sympathy he felt for the man, "are you all right with having yourself implanted here? I'm not a brain surgeon, you know."

"I'll take my chances. How long will it take?"

"The implant is two grand. How long do you need the in-mode for?"

"And if I buy it off you?"

"Ten grand."

"Maintenance included?"

"Yes. Life support cartridges replaced monthly. You don't have to worry about that."

"Good. I'll also need an incognito-class account."

"That's another five grand."

"You're pushing it."

Herod didn't bat an eyelid. "You might be a wanted man, I don't know. Or a hacker planning to disable the Crystal Sphere. I'm not even sure you have a daughter."

"Okay. Let's do it this way. I pay you seventeen grand. You provide me with a lifelong lease on an in-mode. I'll install the implant myself. If I don't survive it, just burn my body in the nearest garbage disposal, end of story."

Herod didn't reply. The old man must have gone completely nuts with grief.

Reaching into a desk drawer, Herod produced a small flat plastic bag containing a microchip. "Know how to use it?"

"Yeah."

"Good. Now listen to me. An incognito account isn't something you can buy for money — any money. They're issued by an underground clan. They're officially known as the Order of Mercenaries."

"What do they want?"

"You'll have to work for them in the Crystal Sphere."

"For how long?"

"Not the slightest idea. Their fee is a hundred grand in game money. Once you work that off, you're free to do what you want."

White paused, weighing up all the options, then gave a grim nod.

There was no other way for him to get into the Crystal Sphere. Any communal in-mode center would start by checking his biometrics and immediately report him to Infosystems. After he'd located one of their technologists and beaten the truth out of him, he knew that Enea was alive.

Still, he also knew he was on the corporation's wanted list. Infosystems didn't forget things like that. An incognito account was the only possible solution.

"Sounds good," he said, taking the microchip.

✳ ✳ ✳

THE IN-MODE CAPSULE bed looked hard and uncomfortable. For a brief moment, the cramped space inside gave White a surge of claustrophobia.

He suppressed his nausea and climbed in, grunting with the effort. He wasn't a young man anymore.

The bed was just as hard and uncomfortable as it looked. Still, he'd have to grin and bear it. He might get used to it eventually.

He braced himself, waiting for the lithe

manipulator to attach the implant to his temple.

The prickling sensation from the nano needles stopped. His head span. A sharp pain pierced his head.

The light inside the capsule went out. A message appeared in front of his eyes,

The neural implant has been successfully installed.

Please wait for the first time configuration to be completed.

He breathed in shallow gasps. His entire life seemed to flash before his eyes in those few moments as the implant dissected his mind, imbibing his memories and adapting itself to the new user's identity.

After a while, a mnemonic interface appeared in his mental view, complete with a plethora of icons and even a virtual keyboard which he could use by focusing on its keys.

Remembering Herod's last warning, White entered just one word when asked for his social code, *Incognito.*

Account choice accepted. Please confirm your awareness of the incognito-class account requirements.

Your character class will be chosen

automatically once your neural matrix analysis has been completed.

Agree, he entered.

After a brief pause, new messages appeared,

Class, Dark Knight
Gender, Male
Starting level, 10
You will be automatically enrolled in the Order of Mercenaries and will be bound by its rules and objectives. You can leave the Order once you have earned it 100,000 gold coins.
Agree: Yes/No

Yes, he entered. He just saw no other way out.

Choice accepted
Please enter your user name

He'd already thought about that. His name was the only thing he didn't want to change. Anything else would be a sick mockery of his past life.

Friedrich White, he entered.

Please wait while we're checking the

name's availability.

The name is available.

The dealer hadn't let him down. Until now, everything seemed to go just as he'd said it would.

Welcome to the Crystal Sphere!

THE PALE LIGHT of dawn was already filtering through the tufts of mist which trailed amid the mossy tree trunks.

White opened his eyes, then sprang to his feet off the heap of rotting pine needles he'd been lying on.

He looked around himself. His head was still spinning. He felt nauseous. The crude leather clothing was too tight on him and hindered his movements.

A long, thin piece of steel pressed hard in his back. A sword. How was he supposed to draw it? Did he know how to use it even?

An array of system messages flickered across his view,

You've discovered a new region: the Silent Lands.

You've received a summoning mark. Please check your inventory.

The Order of Mercenaries status update!

Current rank, Private

You have -100,000 gold on your account

Please take a moment to review the Order's rules

White looked down at a parchment scroll in his hand. He unraveled it and began reading,

As an Order of Mercenaries member, you're under obligation to respond to any appeal for help or dueling challenge performed by another player via a dedicated scroll.

Having received a dueling challenge, you're obliged to fight until one of you is killed and transported to their respawn point.

Having received an appeal for help, you'll be automatically teleported to the player who's summoned you. You are under obligation to render him assistance for a minimum of 4 hours of in-game time or until you are killed and transported to your respawn point, whichever is the earliest.

In the case of a dueling challenge, you have the right to collect trophies from the defeated player. Victory is accredited regardless of your

challenger's manner of death.

When there is no need for your services, you are free to pursue any plot lines of your choice.

The moment White finished reading, the scroll crumbled to dust.

He took another look around himself, this time trying to concentrate on his sensations.

The leather jacket covered in sewn-on steel plaques was very uncomfortable. Same went for the pants and high boots too. He was itching to peel this ridiculous getup off.

Still, White didn't trust his confused state of mind. He refused to act on impulse.

He stood motionless, casting watchful glances around and taking in the fresh, moist air infused with a multitude of strange aromas.

White didn't belong here. In his opinion, virtual reality was nothing more than entertainment for kids.

His nausea had subsided somewhat. His head seemed to have stopped spinning. He had to get used to this.

He checked the pouches in his leather belt. Empty. How about his interface?

He had no problem locating and opening his inventory. Still, its slots contained nothing of interest apart from a diamond-shaped badge with a weird logo embossed on it. That must have been the "mark" of the Order of Mercenaries mentioned earlier.

White had no idea what he was supposed to do now.

Where was he supposed to go? The small forest clearing was overgrown with low ferns which quivered occasionally. Whatever could be lurking there?

He tried to draw the sword from behind his back but it got caught in its scabbard and refused to budge. It had nothing to do with his lack of practice: the wretched piece of steel was simply too long, much longer than his arm's span.

A faint blue light seeped from a cluster of boulders heaped up at the clearing's edge. It radiated in every direction in a cascade of thin piercing rays which gradually fell apart, turning into slowly expiring waves of circular light.

A girl's outline materialized at the center of the brief but spectacular VFX. "Hi. You coming or what?"

"How do you do," White said mechanically.

"I'm asking, are you coming? Get off your ass, we have too many things to do. I'll be your driver for today. That's your starting bonus from the order. We have no time for noobs."

A system message flashed through his mental view,

Lera, a level-25 Warrior, has invited you to join her group.

"Oh, for crying out loud! What's wrong with you? Just click *Accept*! Is it your first time or something?"

"It is," White grumbled as he focused on the right icon, activating it. "I didn't see you coming. I thought this was some kind of forest backwater."

"There's a portal between the rocks. How difficult is that? And by the way, it doubles as the nearest respawn point. So if you get smoked, that's where you get rezzed."

White curiously accepted the information.

Still unmoving, he studied the girl. She was dressed in a sexy outfit fashioned from a few scanty strips of leather held together with bits of chainmail.

"Quit staring, time is money! What have I done to deserve this? Jesus, just my luck!"

Her arrogance began to grate on his nerves. "You'd better mind your manners, young lady!"

"No way! Are you really so old?" the girl gave him a look of disdain. "Did you model your avatar on yourself?"

"How old do you think I am?"

"Well, I dunno. Seventy? I've never met anyone so old here. Only a few NPCs."

"Come and sit down," he said. "No need to be in such a rush. You're my driver, I understand that. I have a few questions to ask you first."

"Well, you'd better ask them in your spare time. My job is to rush you like ten levels and teach you a few things. Just to make sure you aren't completely useless the first few times you're summoned. Got it? Come on now, we've got some farming to do! I'll tell you all you need to know as we work."

"Okay," grunting, White scrambled to his feet. "How do I draw my sword?"

"You don't mean it."

"Well, you'd better tell me if that's what you're here for."

"So what's your problem?"

"I can't draw the wretched sword. I suppose my arm isn't long enough?"

"Try and bend a little as you do it."

White did as she said. On his second attempt, the sword slid out of its scabbard.

"Much better!" Lera said. "Now cut the bullshit and let's move it! Go go go!"

✳ ✳ ✳

WHITE HATED every minute of it. That day, he learned a lot of things about himself he hadn't known before. Quite unflattering ones, too. Lera was much faster than himself. He couldn't even keep an eye on her as she rushed around making mincemeat out of all the mobs while snapping at him,

"Watch me! To the right! The hare's behind the fallen pine tree! Use a leaping blow to one-shot it! I showed you how to do it!"

The neural implant flooded White's mind with a 100% realistic sensations, just as the game developers had promised. The location's petty NPC inhabitants seemed to ignore his attempts at combat prowess. Despite their cute cuddliness, they bit his feet, scratched him and even went for his throat.

"Wait a sec... I need a breather..."

"Don't be such a noob! You don't need a breather! Forget about your age! There's nothing wrong with you! Don't you understand, here it's who you are inside that matters! Got it?"

"In that case, why are my arms shaking? I ache all over!" White leaned against a rough tree trunk, trying to calm his frantic heartbeat.

"That's because you don't have enough Strength, Stamina and Agility. We need to level them all up. Are you ready? Let's go!"

Without waiting for him to reply, she dove into a thick nut grove. White heard several thumping sounds followed by a scream. An 'XP received' message appeared in his view.

"Where the hell are you?" she shouted.

"I'm coming!"

"I'm bringing a mob! He's yours! You hear me?"

Lera shot past him. The nut bushes crunched, releasing a horrendous creature at least eight foot tall. It was lopsided, with parts of its body overgrown by tree bark. It had fiery eyes and long branchlike limbs which clawed the earth below. White's interface identified it as a "Forest Sprite".

The sprite saw him and went right for him.

White's fatigue was gone in seconds. He ducked to one side, avoiding the incoming damage, then attacked, investing all his strength in a series of slashing blows until his Vitality bar shrank to zero.

You've received a new level!

"What a noob, Jesus Christ almighty," Lera groaned instead of the praise he'd expected. She gave him a light poke. Still devoid of Vitality, White failed to keep his footing and collapsed in a heap on the ground.

He felt hurt and offended. "Why did you do that?"

"This is a sword, not a club," she replied with disdain.

"But I killed the sprite, didn't I?"

"That wasn't a kill, that was blow spamming! You've wasted all your energy on him! Even peasants can use a sword better than you can. If I wanted to PvP you, you'd be dead in two seconds. With such combat skills, no customer will touch you with a barge pole. You're a merc, remember. Until your contract has expired, forget everything else. Your job is to take the customer who summoned you from A to B without getting him smoked."

"But I did kill that mob!" he objected hotly.

"Good boy! Do you really think they'll always wait in line to attack you? The moment you walk into a pack, that's it! First they'll smoke you and then turn to your customer."

White was furious but tried not to show it. All this contradicted his entire real-world experience. "Surely my customers can take care of themselves?"

Lera snorted a laugh. "You can't even imagine the kind of nincompoops we have to work with."

"So what do I do?"

"Just stand and watch. First of all, stop rushing around like a headless chicken. You need to preserve your energy. Second, you should have eyes in the back of your head to constantly be aware of the enemy numbers and their levels.

All the information is in front of you, provided you can read and process it in time. Thirdly, you should keep an eye on your status bars. Your Health and Vitality should never, I repeat, never drop below 30%. That's the worst-case scenario. If you think it's dropping too low, you'd better step back, take a breather, drink a vial. Now, your combat technique. Every weapon has its own special attacks. And I mean every weapon — even peasants' rakes and pitchforks. Oh, yes. They may require more energy but they double the damage — even triple it if you're lucky..."

She went on and on, showering White with terms whose meaning he could barely fathom. "Some blade weapons when used in particular types of special attacks can ignore shields entirely as if they were hot butter. You can figure it all out yourself later. One thing you need to remember now is that all special attacks require a particular stance. This is something you need to learn to do instantly without even thinking about it. Now watch me. You'll know what I mean in a moment. If you don't listen to me now, you'll always remain a noob, no matter what level you are. It's up to you," she turned and headed for the nut grove.

Two sprites leaped at her almost at once. One tried to outflank her while the other attacked her head-on. It went for her like mad, its gnarly arms scything the air like windmill blades. If it reached her, that would be the end of it! The creature would squash her in a deadly embrace, piercing her body with its sharp branches, then discarding it a lifeless, mauled heap.

Lera calmly ducked the blow. The sword in her hands (which was an ordinary weapon, nothing special about it) began to glow, enveloped in a fiery aura. She attacked the mob like lightning.

Bellowing, the sprite erupted in flames. By then, the girl had already rolled over to the second mob in a well-calculated motion. This time she performed a series of stabbing blows, immobilizing her enemy. Four deep wounds smoldered in the mob's body, stun-locking it and rendering it helpless in the face of her lethal coup de grace combo.

"Got it?" she asked.

She wasn't even out of breath.

✳ ✳ ✳

BY NIGHTFALL, he began getting the hang of it. He'd made ten levels, almost catching up with his tutoress. Still, he was so exhausted he could barely stand. Every muscle in his body was aching. He was about to collapse.

"I think that's enough for one day," Lera

smiled. "You've been under Fatigue for an hour already."

"You mean the debuff? I hadn't noticed it."

"You probably can't see it. It's very possible the debuff tab isn't even open. You might need to adjust the interface settings to suit your own needs."

"Thank you."

He was so tired he could barely speak. The full immersion experience was no walk in the park. All he wanted was to drop on the grass and just lie there mindlessly without having to move a muscle.

"Don't thank me yet," Lera walked over to him. In one sharp, powerful thrust she buried her sword in his chest.

His mind exploded in pain. His vision darkened. The world around him disintegrated into snippets of images, than faded.

✳ ✳ ✳

HE CAME ROUND in the dead of night.

He was lying in the same clearing. Moonlight seeped through the foliage overhead. The stars above glowed like silver dust sprinkled on black velvet.

Little flames cast a weak flickering light around. Lera sat on a fallen mossy tree next to the small campfire, staring pensively at the glowing embers.

Why hadn't she escaped the murder scene?

Groaning, White sat up. His head was spinning again. His chest throbbed. Mechanically he touched the terrible wound but didn't feel anything. "What the f-"

Lera looked up at him. "Sorry. Nothing personal. This was part of your training. I'm very happy you've made it. I must be off now."

"No, wait," he croaked.

"Why, would you like to kill me back?" her hand closed around her sword hilt.

"I have questions to ask you. I want the answers."

"Okay," her sword slid back into its scabbard. "Here, take it," she handed him a bundle containing his stuff. "I fetched it myself to save you the trouble."

Only now did White realize he was almost completely naked apart from a skimpy loincloth.

That's right. He'd been killed, hadn't he?

The memory of the experience still smarted. Every now and then he writhed with agonizing bouts of phantom pain in his chest. Lera studied him shamelessly in the moonlight, a gaunt old man with a silver crewcut.

His cheek twitched.

"You've taken it well," she said.

He undid the bundle and began to equip himself. "Why did you kill me?"

"Don't you understand? How much did you pay for your implant?"

"Not much."

"Well, that's your answer. A low quality device with poorly calibrated feedback. Not everybody survives their first respawn. A device like yours can cause a lot of problems on the very first mission. Which is something our bosses don't really need," the girl's voice rang with suppressed hatred.

"What kind of problems?"

"Don't you understand? A guy with a cheap implant and a piss-poor excuse for an in-mode set up in some shabby capsule hotel... am I right?"

He nodded. Pointless to deny the obvious. "Could I have died?"

"Easy. All original factory implants are installed under medical supervision. Specialists fine-tune the pain threshold based on the subject's medical records. But you chose an incognito account. There's no information about you in the system."

"Are there other guys like me here?"

"Virtually everyone who slaves for the Mercs. If they fail to respawn, well, tough."

White sat closer to the fire. "So you

basically did me a favor?"

"You can say that."

"And what if I'd died?"

Lera shrugged. "Your avatar would have become part of the scenery. Like so many I've seen before."

White frowned. "I don't understand. "Full immersion is supposed to be a great thing, at least for the game industry. Now why would they expand it to include the feelings of pain and discomfort? Why take such a risk?"

"I've no idea," Lera admitted. "Sometimes I wish I could kill them whoever invented it. And other times I'm so grateful to them you can't even imagine."

"Grateful, what for?"

"For allowing me to feel all this. To live a real life in a magical world. When I think about it, pain doesn't seem such a big price to pay."

"Ever tried to log out?"

"You serious? The real world is finished. It's on its deathbed. Our future lies here," she said confidently.

"Does it really?"

"Oh yes. You'll soon see. *Cyberspace as the next stage of human evolution.* Sounds awesome, don't you think?"

He didn't know what to say to that. In any case, the girl seemed to be well-educated. She also appeared to have been around the block a few times.

"Okay," she said. "You need to get some rest now. You need to build yourself some kind of shelter, a lean-to or something. Any dwelling built with your own hands will become your safe zone, but only for six hours in every twenty-four. Being a light sleeper gives you a great survival advantage. Understood?"

He nodded mechanically.

He was absolutely exhausted. He wished he could just sit by the fire and do nothing. Still, the circle of light was rapidly shrinking as the embers expired and turned ashen gray. Darkness crept upon him.

"I'm off, then," she stepped toward the portal. "I've shown you all the basics. The new recruits have two weeks to practice so you'd better get on with it. Once you're contracted out, you'll have no time to learn. I suggest you study the guides and practice on the local mobs for a bit."

The eerie blue light enveloped her. She was gone.

White added some twigs to the fire, then scrambled to his feet and headed staggering to the nearest pine trees to cut some branches for his shelter.

✳ ✳ ✳

HE SPENT the next week exploring the area, building a sorry excuse for a hut and reading up on whatever was available, trying not to aggro any mobs if he could help it. So far, his first-day farming marathon had been plenty for him.

The portal resembled an ancient millstone covered in runic writings. Whenever White approached it, it triggered a new tab in his interface. Still, it only listed one available option,

The Order of Mercs Castle
Central Square

All other potential routes were labeled with question marks and identical brief prompts,

We advise you to find other portal stones or purchase a portal map.

White decided against traveling to the castle. Pointless. He couldn't afford more comfortable gear, anyway. As for food, there was plenty of it around. In any case, he had no intention of lingering in the Silent Lands.

He needed to repay the loan ASAP and get on with looking for his daughter. No good him meeting new people — he'd be out of this place very soon, anyway.

In the meantime, his old pragmatism which was firmly rooted in his life's worth of experience had begun to crumble. Virtual reality — which he'd believed to be a pastime for wusses — had dealt his mind a shattering blow. The implant kept flooding his mind with perfectly authentic experiences. His every attempt to reject them led to new blackouts.

For a while, he resisted it, trying to convince himself of the world's fakeness. Until one day he finally broke down.

It felt as if his ill luck had finally decided to give him a break. Now in the ebb of his life, he'd been pulled out of the rat race and jettisoned to these new shores, stripped of everything he'd held dear — and receiving a whole new universe in return.

In the mornings, the first tentative sunrays would filter in through the wicker walls of the humble hut he'd built all by himself. He'd wake up feeling young and fresh, then hurry to the stream and wash his face in its icy-cold water.

He'd stare at his own reflection, noticing the changes. The deep furrowed lines and the dark circles around his eyes were now gone. Just after one week, he looked twenty years younger.

He could finally get a second wind. His heart seemed to have awoken, too, responding to the simplest of things he'd never known before. The sheer splendor of wildlife which had long been extinct back on Earth and which had been restored here in every meticulous detail was mind-boggling.

Eventually White began to realize why an entire generation had made its home here, adamant not to return to the real world.

Slowly but surely, the realism of the experience eroded his perception. The two worlds began to shift places. Soon the surrounding forest felt more real and lifelike to him than his old real-life existence.

He tried to ignore these rebellious thoughts or come to grips with this duplicity. Still, he just couldn't help it.

Whenever he pondered over his past, it only made things worse. The luxury and power he'd been striving for had turned out to be but a tiny island in an ocean of cynical pragmatism.

He'd long lost all of his friends. He used to measure people by whether he could use them or not. He'd even managed to alienate his own daughter by giving her everything money could buy — and believing that love too could be financed.

* * *

HE WOULD NEVER forget his first summoning.

Firstly, because he wasn't at all prepared. Despite Lera's warning, he'd been busy doing anything but leveling up.

Secondly, it had happened too quickly. He didn't get the chance to equip his awkward, uncomfortable leather armor. He never bothered to wear it these days because it rubbed his skin raw. Problem was, he still clung to the notions of the real world. After the cold, hunger and deprivation of real life, he'd succumbed to the blissful existence conjured up by his implant. He behaved like a happy idiot, roaming the area, picking wild berries, and fully enjoying his new wildlife experience.

At some point, he discovered a trail leading to a nearby village. He went there and swapped whatever loot he'd amassed — mainly hare skins — for a homespun shirt, a pair of pants and a jugful of milk.

For some reason, the smaller mobs had stopped aggroing him. Luckily, the area seemed to be devoid of any truly dangerous beasts.

One hot midday, White sat in the shade perusing a *Hunter's Guide*. From his point of view, learning to set traps was much more useful in his situation than chasing after some petty mob with a sword, panting from the heat.

In those early days, he used to have a totally different outlook. He left his armor and weapons in the hut instead of keeping them at hand in his inventory. He'd done no leveling whatsoever. He'd learned nothing about his location.

Also, his first summoning was accompanied by a very bad blunder[1].

White was just about to swipe his eyes across the guide's page, moving on to the section entitled *How to Fish and Make Fishing Tackle,* when a large message flashed before his eyes,

You've received a dueling challenge!
Prepare to be teleported automatically in 3... 2... 1...

The world faded.

He was standing on a crumbling stone bridge.

The dry, scorching hot air made his throat seize.

Wasteland lay all around him, encircled by the flat weathered ruins of what once must have been a castle wall.

---

[1] What follows below is a true story which happened to the author with only a few minor details changed.

The bridge spanned the collapsed moat, leading toward a dilapidated barbican.

White didn't get the chance to get properly scared. A young guy barged out of the gaping gateway — a cleric, judging

g by his gear. He was followed by several very unhealthy-looking mobs. Undead, most likely. They must have once been abnormally large ravens the size of a hunched-up man. Now, however, their feathers had lost their sheen, their skin had split in places, revealing the bones beneath. Their empty eye sockets oozed darkness.

"Help!" the cleric screamed.

White didn't know what to think. This was supposed to be a dueling challenge. Indeed, the guy's name tag was highlighted a fiery red. In order to complete the mission, White had to attack and kill him. And this idiot was screaming his head off, begging for help!

Armed with bone spears, the spooky ravens approached fast. Although they couldn't fly anymore, they were good runners. They also didn't seem to have the kind of moral qualms White did.

Two spears whooshed through the air. One of them pierced the guy's leg.

The hapless adventurer cried out in pain. His Life bar shrank halfway.

The second spear grazed White. Blood splattered everywhere.

His mind went momentarily blank. Then it felt as if someone had flipped a switch in his brain.

The makeshift spear had ripped through his shirt and sliced through his flank before dropping to his feet. Acting on impulse, White picked it up and, blind with rage, swept two of the ravens off the narrow bridge. The others backed off.

"Thanks, man…. Great timing…"

The cleric was bleeding profusely. For some reason, he wasn't in a hurry to use any of the healing spells typical of his class. Instead, he backed off, limping, apparently hoping that the summoned merc was going to make mincemeat out of the pack of undead.

"You got the wrong scroll!" White shouted, desperately fighting off the attacking mobs.

"What?"

"You activated a dueling challenge! I'm not obliged to help you!"

"Oh-" the cleric cussed profusely.

"Heal yourself!"

"I can't! You know it! Magic doesn't work here! And I'm all out of vials!"

White had no idea what he was talking about. Still, their situation looked pretty grim.

Another large pack of mobs appeared by the ruins. The ravens split up, flanking them. They began hurling spears albeit with little success. Fashioned out of long hollow bones, the spears were too light to reach their targets at that distance.

White backed off slowly, trying to contain those already on the bridge. "You got more scrolls?"

"Loads!"

"Use them! Summon more mercs!"

The guy didn't get the chance to do as he was told.

Two more ravens appeared behind his back, the ones White had swept off the bridge. With a hoarse squawk, a mess of stinking feathers rose in the air.

The cleric screamed.

A new flashing message appeared before White's eyes, hindering his view,

Success! Your opponent has been slain!
Prepare to be teleported back automatically in 3... 2... 1...

The world faded again, then White was back by his hut, still clenching the bone spear.

His side bled profusely. The bundle containing the slain player's possessions lay in the grass by his feet.

More system messages flashed through his view,

Achievement received: First Blood

+1 to your Reputation with the Order of Mercenaries.

Achievement received: Berserker

The Achievement conditions are met (engaging in combat without equipping your gear)

You instill fear in your enemies!

-5% to all NPC enemies' aggro radius

Achievement received: Renowned Berserker

The Achievement conditions are met (engaging in combat without having any weapons)

You instill uncontrollable fear in your enemies!
-10% to all NPC enemies' aggro radius

Achievement received: Trophy Hunter
The Achievement conditions are met (using

the weapon you've taken from your enemy)

+1% to your chances of receiving loot from your slain opponents

Task completed: A Dueling Challenge

Your obligation to the Order of Mercenaries has been reduced.
Current obligation, 95,000 gold coins.

You've received a new level!

✳ ✳ ✳

THIS INCIDENT had radically changed White's opinion of the Crystal Sphere.

The incredible authenticity of the experience — the intricate design of every rock and grass blade — had initially rendered him blind to its true purpose. He'd been badly wrong thinking that Infosystems Corporation had created a reality simulator, aiming to bring the lost environment back to humanity which had destroyed it in its race for progress.

This was still a game. You couldn't just live here guided by your desires and your common sense alone.

Now he had to face the ugly truth. Stripped

of illusions, he seemed to have finally awoken to reality. He had to tackle all the questions he should have asked himself from the start.

He could be summoned again at any moment. Somehow White doubted that his incredible beginner's luck would stretch that far, granting him another level.

He set aside his *How to Fish and Make Fishing Tackle* book and began searching for information of a different kind.

With his lifelong logical thinking habit, it didn't take him long to grasp the basics of character leveling. The rest, however, offered a lot of food for thought.

Why had the cleric died, for instance? He'd had plenty of time to heal himself. Still, for some reason he hadn't even attempted to do so.

The answer wasn't long in coming.

Apparently, the Silent Lands weren't on the official Crystal Sphere regions list. This particular territory had been activated six months after the game had been launched as a supplement available for sale.

Whoever had bought it remained a secret.

So what did the players find so special about this particular region?

According to the official story, the Crystal Sphere had been created by the Founders: a mysterious extinct race of all-powerful creatures who'd left behind a still-functional school of uncategorized magic, as well as a great number of ruins and artifacts.

The Silent Lands were supposed to have once been the sacred heart of that ancient magic which had since nourished all modern schools.

Later, however, the Founders had fallen victim to the arrogant new races they themselves had brought into existence. Believing themselves equal to their creator Gods, the newcomers had defied their own makers.

This had resulted in a great battle which had destroyed the region's prosperous cities, razing them to the ground. But what was even worse, the Founders in their desire to teach the coming generations a lesson, had cast a Veil of Silence over these lands, surrounding them with an impenetrable barrier which was still active until present.

Here, amid the ancient city ruins and deep down the perilous tunnels below them, one could still discover a great many unique scrolls and items which granted their owner power beyond human imagination.

Problem was, the Veil of Silence was still active too, stripping all wizards of their magic skills.

The only portal connecting the Silent Lands to other regions of the Crystal Sphere was located in the ruins of a castle which had long become the seat of the Order of Mercenaries.

White chuckled. Their little business scheme was painfully obvious. Any wizard would have loved to lay their hands on some of those uncategorized spells and artifacts which could increase their power manifold. But how were you supposed to get them if the Veil of Silence rendered you helpless in the face of some of the most dangerous mobs in the Crystal Sphere?

That was exactly how the Order of Mercs had come to prosper. It charged 5,000 gold for a so-called "summoning scroll" which allowed one to hire a merc and turn to his or her services whenever needed. The Order's employees accompanied their wizard customers on their perilous journeys, clearing their path for them.

Another interesting requirement (created specifically for this purpose) stipulated that in order to retrieve any unique scrolls or magic items — even those dropped by a mob — a player had to have 50+ pt. Intellect. None of the mercs could boast Intellect numbers that high. They were warriors, after all. Which in turn prevented them from farming rare artifacts for themselves.

The region's mysterious owner had thought about everything. He'd bought the place, then paid the game developers to create the kind of balance and content he wanted.

White had ventured as far as the Mercs' Castle's outskirts where he'd had a few discussions with other incognito account holders. Apparently, the Order's owner kept the mercs on a short leash. Those who were about to pay off their obligations and quit were given impossible missions which they predictably lost, returning to the Order's ranks of slave labor.

The place was impossible to escape. The barrier separating the Silent Lands from the rest of the Crystal Sphere may have looked like a wall of murky air but it was harder than rock.

The only access to the rest of the world lay via the Mercs Castle's long-distance portal. Still, in order to use it one had to be in possession of the artifact key.

This looked like a Catch 22 situation. An incognito player couldn't file a complaint with the developers about all the abuse taking place here. An incognito account had neither a face nor a name to put to it. Which meant that its owner was helpless against any amount of lawlessness and oppression.

That didn't mean that White was going to give up. Oh, no. Still, he had enough courage to admit that leaving these lands might cost him a lot of blood, sweat and tears before he could even begin looking for his daughter.

There had to be a way out, he tried to

convince himself. There was bound to be.

* * *

HE APPROACHED the task with his habitual thoroughness and determination. And by doing so, he made another mistake. A successful merc was bound to attract unwanted attention.

He still lived in the forest, only these days he practiced till he dropped, studying every bit of information he could lay his hands on and developing his own combat style. He also went on missions, which were usually successful.

His obligation to the Order had shrunk to 40,000 gold. Apparently, this fact had begun to worry someone on top.

Immediately afterward, he encountered a bad streak. No matter what he did, his customers kept dying. His debt began to grow again, and he was absolutely furious about it.

Now, too, as soon as he received this new mission, he could see it wasn't doable. His summoner was heading for the ancient city ruins. In his simple-mindedness, the customer had chosen the mountain route believing that he would encounter fewer mobs that way.

Big mistake. The only surviving mountain pass which used to be part of a caravanning route had long since become home to a demon.

No one knew where it had come from. Even stripped of its magic, the creature of Inferno had preserved all of its physical strength and murderous attack abilities.

White had heard about that particular mob but he'd never had to tackle it before. Now he quickly realized he wouldn't be able to smoke him on his own. Without waiting to be killed, he retreated wisely, trying to work out his next step.

He'd been toying with one particular idea already a month. His plan was admittedly daring but he'd never had the chance to try it in action.

He opened the location map and checked it against his friend list.

He had nothing to lose.

After his memorable first dueling-challenge mission, he'd kept the cleric's possessions which included a few summoning scrolls. Even though officially mercs couldn't buy them, there was no rule that said that an Order's employee couldn't use one.

That must have been an oversight on their part — which White now fully intended to put to good use.

He produced a scroll and broke the seal, waiting intently to see if it worked.

After a few moments, a transparent circle formed on the ground. A familiar avatar materialized at its center.

"Hi," he waved.

Lera looked around herself. "White, are you freakin' nuts? That's against the rules! Where did you get the scroll from?"

"Mind showing me the rules?" White chuckled. "Hello to you too."

"Oh really? And who's gonna pay for my contract?"

White shrugged. "It's already paid for by whoever bought this scroll. So don't sweat."

She frowned, then forced a laugh. "You think you can cheat the Order? How many scrolls have you got? And where did you get them from?"

"Just by chance. I have no intention of cheating, if that's what you mean. I'm just curious if we can do it together."

"And even if we can, so what?" she asked. She seemed to have known all about the demon. "What's your plan?"

"My plan is, we can help each other out. Only when needs be. Without scrolls, you're right. It's too risky. I'm pretty sure the Order tracks them all down."

"So what do you suggest?" she asked, apparently interested.

"There're several popular locations where most artifacts are farmed. Mercs can do whatever they want in their spare time, can't they? There're plenty of local portals around — enough for us to team up really quickly when necessary. By doing that, we won't be breaking any rules, will we?"

"No, we won't," Lera mechanically reached down, picked a blade of grass and began chewing on it. "Why can't you smoke the demon yourself?"

"I can't do it on my own," White replied. "No way. He's as strong as hell. He focuses on me straight away and starts using Fierce Attacks. I can dodge them but I can't attack him myself. I need a partner who could outflank him and deal damage while he's aggroing me."

"Yeah right. All he'll do he'll aggro me, end of story."

"Exactly. We have to think out of the box here. You deal him damage and just as he begins to turn to you, you dodge or parry his attack or just roll out of his reach while I attack him instead. He turns his attention to me and you in the meantime attack him again."

She paused, pensive, then nodded. "Very well. It actually might work."

"I'm surprised no one has thought about it before. How many people have died here in this pass? Is cooperation such a crazy idea here that no one's thought about it yet?"

Lera ignored his question. She walked over to the mouth of the gorge and checked on the demon, taking in the surrounding space. Once she'd decided they had plenty of room to maneuver, she waved to him.

"Let's do it!" she said, drawing her sword.

✳ ✳ ✳

THE TACTIC SUGGESTED by White worked in the end. Between the two of them, they finally smoked the beast. It had cost them a lot of sweat and all of their elixirs; the pain from their wounds was excruciating — but still they'd done it, albeit on a wing and a prayer.

White's wizard customer crossed the gorge casting wary glances at the defeated monster. White and Lera lingered behind, intending to check the demon for any loot.

"Oh. The mission's not closed yet," White said. "That's strange. I did help the wizzy get through. What the hell?"

His jaw dropped as he read a new system message. "Excuse me? Mission failed? Reference: the Mercenary Code Clause 7.12? That's bullshit! I read the code! There's no such a clause in it!"

"There is now," Lera stretched out a demanding hand. "Can I have the remaining scrolls, please? And remember: any cooperation between mercs will not be tolerated. It's bad for business. Thanks for informing me about this oversight. It might count toward your pay obligation one day."

He couldn't believe he was hearing it. "Is that you? No way!"

"Why not?"

"You can't be the location's owner, surely? Do you mean you work for your own company training newbs?"

She shrugged. "There aren't so many incognito accounts around. Much safer to meet them all personally and see what they have to offer. It can even be funny. Especially the respawn test. Please don't get me wrong. You're a nice guy. But no one's gonna rip me off, is that clear? If that wizard couldn't cross the pass with one merc, let him buy twenty scrolls and hire twenty people. That's cooperation the way I see it. If you don't like it, just log the hell out of here. It's not my loss."

Her avatar transformed. Instead of a young warrioress, he was now looking at a rather ordinary middle-aged woman with a hungry, predatory gaze.

He just couldn't help himself. "You bitch! I've known mobs with nicer characters! I work for you the best I can and you keep sending me on impossible missions?"

She ignored the insult. "The mobs are controlled by neural computers property of Infosystems. Honestly, I've had their so-called revolutionary technologies up to here. No need to get mad at me. I told you already: if you're unhappy, just log out. Only you won't. I know you won't."

"Why not?"

"You're a funny old fart, aren't you? Who do you think buys incognito accounts?"

He shrugged.

"Even convicts are obliged to have social code numbers these days," the fake "Lera" said. "That grants them access to their human rights. Incognito accounts are for those who've been blacklisted by Infosystems. Hackers, cheaters, repeatedly banned users, that sort of thing. Plus a small percent of society dropouts who were born outside the system. Underground dwellers, mainly. So please give it a break. You can live a good life here. If you keep generating revenue, I can make it worth your while."

With those words, she vanished into thin air.

Mission update: Mission failed!
Reference: the Mercenary Code Clause 7.12
Your obligation to the Order has increased. You have -55,000 gold on your account.

White kicked the demon's carcass and headed back toward the portal.

He wasn't going to give up. Still, at the

moment he just couldn't see how he could do it. He had to calm down first. Then he'd have to give it a good think.

At least now he knew the lay of the land.

✳ ✳ ✳

THREE MONTHS LATER

WHITE LAY IN AMBUSH on top of a small hill. The tall grass provided enough cover as he studied the surrounding area, pinpointing the mobs and analyzing their levels.

The group of three wizards who'd hired him were waiting in a relatively safe zone further down the slope.

His new suit of armor was light and comfortable, its steel plates covered in an intricate silver design. White had procured it on one of his missions. These days, he was never without it.

Green meadows lay ahead, studded with occasional NPC villages: a peaceful bucolic vista, so rare in this part of the world. A bit further on, past the neat squares of ploughed fields, rose the first rocky outcrops of a mountain ridge.

No ancient ruins here. No idea where those three were supposed to look for the Eye of a Dragon, one of the Founders' most powerful artifacts. The wizards seemed to be pretty desperate to get it.

"And?" one of the casters approached him.

"Please sit down. You're hindering my view. What is it your manuscript says?"

"*The Breath of a Dragon will show you the way,*" the wizard quoted from memory. "Can you see those dark spots over there?"

"Up in the mountains, you mean?"

"That's right."

"And what do you think they are?" White asked.

"I think they're the caves where the dragons live."

"Are you sure? You really think peasants would build their homes so close to dragons' nests?"

"They're used to it, aren't they?"

"How do you know?"

"I read a lot," the wizard replied. "One thing we do know is that the Eye of a Dragon is hidden somewhere underground. This must have been an ancient dragon city once. The dragons who used to guard these lands, I mean. The city must have been destroyed during the war, and its ruins buried under mudslides. Take a look at those shallow rock ridges over there. Don't you think they look a bit too regular? Almost like street blocks."

"You really think you can dig the whole place up?" White said. "That'll take you a year, provided the locals give you their permission. You have any idea how many workers you might need? You can't even use magic to help you. Or do you have a particular location in mind? Or some kind of a mark to go by?"

"No, I don't," the wizard replied. "But we've got an offer to make you."

"Spit it out."

"We know what's going on here."

"Meaning?"

"The Order. These Lands will never let go of you."

"And?"

"We have an idea," the wizard switched to a hushed whisper. "The dragon might help us. But to do that, we need to lure him out first. You think you could aggro him?"

"How's that gonna help? He'll just kill me. The level gap is too big."

"You don't need to fight him! All you need to do is attract his attention and draw his aggro to yourself. Then just run downhill as fast as you can. We can give you some Stamina potions."

"And? Can you speak any clearer?"

"The dragon will scorch the whole area to cinders! Once the top soil is gone, we'll be able to see the ruins. And we'll know how to tell the ancient temple among them, trust me."

"You can't do it. Magic doesn't work here, remember?"

"But what's Fiery Breath for you if it's not an ability?" the wizard said hotly. "Listen, man. We understand your situation. We can be grateful. How much do you need, a hundred grand? I have the right to offer my own price for the contract. I can enter the sum in it right in front of you. Just between the two of us, you're not the only one. It happened before. You think nobody knows how they drive you all into the ground?"

"A hundred and twenty-five grand," White said, "counting the failed missions."

"That's not a problem. The Eye of a Dragon is worth millions even if we wanted to sell it."

"Okay. Give me a minute to think about it."

The wizard didn't insist. "If you wish."

He hurried back down the slope, rubbing his hands. He probably thought he had White in his pocket now. Still, that wasn't what White was thinking about.

The temptation was just too big. But as he stared at the surrounding fields and villages, squinting his eyes against the sun, he unwittingly triggered his Piercing Vision ability which he'd only received just recently.

Distances disappeared. Now he could see

everything around him in every detail. Like the peasant children playing by the village gate.

His daughter... Enea...

His heart raced, thumping anxiously in his chest.

This was his chance to escape and finally do what he'd come here for: to search for Enea. It sounded too good. Still, something in him kept resisting it, screaming at him, 'Don't!'

Why?

He wasn't afraid of being burned alive. He knew he could overcome the agony and respawn. The price was worth the risk. He'd better start thinking about how to aggro a dragon — or a couple even, just to be sure.

Should he use a bow? Not a bad idea. If he fired an arrow from the village gate, it just might hit one.

Still, his heart was growing heavier with every second.

Why? After all, none of this was for real! Those were only NPCs! Why should he feel sorry for them? They would respawn, anyway!

They would. Question was, what would become of them?

From a seasoned gamer's point of view, White's arguments were rambling and highly academic.

What was going to become of these villages

and their populations? White's imagination helpfully offered a picture of the upcoming fire attack and its consequences.

He saw houses burning, fieldfuls of corn going up in flames; he saw villagers running, trying to escape the fire; children squirming in the heat and turning into little scorched corpses; old people dying helplessly in their homes under the weight of collapsed ceiling beams crumbling to embers...

The world of the Crystal Sphere was controlled by neural computers. Its main difference from its predecessors was in its incredible interactivity. Here, every action had a consequence. The villages would be reduced to heaps of charred sticks. Just as the wizard had suggested, the top soil layer would burn away, revealing the ruins of the ancient dragon city.

And as for the villagers... they would most definitely respawn, only they wouldn't be peasants anymore. Stripped of everything they'd had, burned to the bone, their minds crippled by their agony, they would add to the ranks of the undead. They would pick up their fire-polished scythes and become the ghosts of this scorched wasteland: insane, malicious and devoid of mercy.

Later, these lands might be purged of them. The wounded earth would rebloom. Many years from now, new peasants might settle down here to work the land until yet another treasure hunter arrived in order to check out the old flat hills just to see if they concealed any ancient ruins.

That was exactly what they'd done to planet Earth, White thought. They'd been devastating it time and time again, destroying cities and killing all wildlife, leaving behind endless crowds of refugees fraught with grief.

He was crazy. This wasn't real life. This was nothing but a digital space.

Did it make any difference?

But why should he bother? This world was against him too, wasn't it? When a mob charged on him from the forest, would he just stand there ruminating and let himself get killed?

No, he wouldn't.

Then what was the difference?

He squinted into the distance.

A peasant girl of about ten years old was running carefree along the dirt road, laughing.

White's cheek began to twitch.

For a while, his gaze followed the girl. Then he put his bow away and walked down to the wizards awaiting his decision by the foothill.

They seemed to be arguing, exchanging excited whispers.

"Here, take it," White handed them his

contract.

"Have you made up your mind? Which sum do you want us to enter?"

"Just write, 'Mission failed'."

"What did you say?"

"You heard. I'm not doing it."

"Why? You can't handle pain, is that it?"

"It's not about that. Dying is not a problem."

"What is it, then?"

White looked him in the eye. "I'm afraid you won't understand."

He turned around and walked away.

✳ ✳ ✳

IT TOOK HIM until sunset to reach his hut. He was angry and jittery.

He went to the stream and tried to wash away the fatigue. It didn't help. Still, the cool water had refreshed him somewhat.

The failed mission had added another five grand to his debt.

So what had he achieved? The wizards were going to hire someone else, as simple as that. Someone who wasn't so scrupulous. The result would be the same — the only difference being, he'd missed his chance.

"Oh, give me a break!" White snapped. He

hadn't even realized he'd been arguing with himself all along.

He returned to his hut, reluctantly had a meal and lay down on a heap of hay trying to get some sleep. He kept tossing and turning long after the stars had filled the sky.

A crashing noise came from outside. Tree tops rustled as if disturbed by a hurricane.

He jumped to his feet. This promised nothing good.

The walls of his hut creaked, about to collapse. Before he could do anything, a giant skull covered in bony spikes broke in through the roof. A fiery breath escaped its open jaws, scorching him and extinguishing his mind.

※ ※ ※

WHEN HE CAME ROUND, he was suspended in the air. Earth floated past far below, flooded with moonlight.

Fear overcame him. He began to shake uncontrollably. He couldn't even move in the clutches of whatever creature had captured him.

As he tried to overcome the perfectly natural panic, the monotonous wingbeats overhead began to slow down. The creature began to descend, soaring soundlessly toward the impenetrable wall of murky mist which separated the Silent Lands from the rest of the Crystal Sphere.

One more wingbeat, and they'd crossed it.

The giant wings rustled as the creature slowed down. Its talons slackened.

White hit the ground hard, tumbling over. In a well-practiced motion, he jumped to his feet, drew his sword and assumed a combat stance.

A black dragon towered above him, leaning back on its feet and tail.

The creature's yellow eyes studied him. A fiery breath escaped its nostrils and half-opened jaws.

You're free now, a voice roared through his mind.

White cast a doubtful glance at the swirling wall of mist behind which lay the Silent Lands.

There's nothing we can't do, the dragon answered his unasked question. *We know all about everything. Humans created us as complex neurosystems. They don't yet know they've long lost control of our neural matrices. Here's your contract with the Order.*

A scroll materialized in the air and exploded in flames, crumbling to ashes.

White chose not to ask any stupid questions. He sheathed his sword and lowered his head in respect for this mysterious creature and its boundless power. "How can I ever repay you?"

A wave of unbearable heat scorched him.

"Whatever you do, don't forget you're human," the dragon gasped.

TRANSLATED FROM RUSSIAN BY IRENE WOODHEAD

AND NEIL P. MAYHEW

THE TERROR SLAYER

A TALE FROM
MIRROR WORLD SERIES

BY ALEXEY OSADCHUK

THE SHRILL SOUND of a phone ripped through the silence of the office.

Anton startled. Grunting like an old man, he swiped his thumb across the screen, then pressed the Conference button.

"You know what time it is?" his wife's voice sliced through the speakers. "It's nearly ten! If you don't get away from that blasted computer now, you can spend the New Year in your car!"

"But listen, sweetie, I-"

"Enough! I already called your workmates. They're all home with their families! And you just have to be the eager beaver, don't you?"

"No, but-" Anton offered unenthusiastically, trying to concentrate on the program code he was working on.

"I don't want to know! You can work on your game some other time!"

"Please, you need to understand..."

"Darling," her voice softened. "It's New Year's Eve. We don't see you at all as it is. This job of yours..."

"I know, sweetie," Anton said, giving in. "One last test, then I'm coming."

He hurried to hang up before she could continue and returned his tired, bloodshot stare to the monitor. His long piano-playing fingers fluttered over the keyboard, adding more numbers, letters and symbols to the growing columns of code.

He screwed his face into a crooked grin, remembering the expression on his nine-year-old son's face when Anton had shown him what a famous online game looked like from the inside. No Elves, no dragons — just line after line of program code running across a black computer screen.

The memory made his heart warm. His wife was right. What was he doing here? All his workmates were already cracking open the champagne while he was stuck here doing their dirty work for them.

"Never mind," he mumbled, glaring at the screen. "One last location, then I'll be off. Let's take a look now. Aha, there it is... sector five."

He glanced at the clock. If the truth were known, that particular sector required a good dozen mobs at least. Still, time was an issue. More mobs meant more lengthy calculations.

Not tonight. One would be plenty for the time being. Once the celebrations were over, then he would add all the remaining ones.

Anton opened a potential mob's stats and chuckled. Standard issue. Intellect, 9 — wasn't that a bit too rich for a Dwand? Should he change it to 6, maybe?

What happened next was about to radically change Anton's career as a game designer.

The phone rang again, shrill and insistent. Anton startled, shifting his attention to the phone's screen. His left index finger twitched on the key, pressing "6" twice.

"Yes, sweetie. I'm coming. Honest. I've already turned the computer off."

Anton rose from his desk and had a nice stretch. He cricked his neck and staggered toward the door.

✳ ✳ ✳

THE WORLD CAME DOWN on the Dwand like a ton of bricks. It blinded him with sunlight. It deafened him with a multiple cacophony of strange sounds. The first breath he took brought a plethora of new scents.

He spent a few moments just lying on his back with his eyes closed. Then he dared take another look.

The blue sky was the first thing he saw. Somehow he knew that the thing above him was the sky and he recognized the color.

Tall, old trees towered all around him. The green grass. The bushy undergrowth.

A new knowledge escaped the depths of his

subconscious.

"Forest," was his first word.

He hugged his scrawny knees with his skinny arms and attempted to sit up.

His hand looked unusual. Green skin. Long fingers topped off with sharp pointed nails.

He tried to see the rest of his body. He had a sinewy torso and a sunken belly. His stomach growled, confirming his suspicions. He was hungry.

Immediately his mouth filled with saliva. Mechanically he licked his lips. His teeth felt remarkably sharp.

Good, a thought came out of nowhere.

He continued inspecting himself. His only clothes consisted of a filthy loincloth fashioned out of an animal pelt. He had nothing else on.

A stealthy rustle behind his back made him swing round.

A four-legged creature froze just a few paces away from him. It was covered in grayish brown hair. A long trickle of saliva dribbled from his mouth onto the grass.

Its intentions were pretty clear. The creature was about to attack him.

I wonder who you are? he thought. *How should I fight you?*

As soon as he thought about it, weird symbols materialized before his eyes,

Name, Forest Rat
Level, 2
Status, Aggressive
Strength, 5
Agility, 5
Intellect, 1
Damage, 9 to 12
Skills, none

As he struggled, open-mouthed, to read the mysterious signs, the rat charged.

The world around him faded. Darkness enveloped him.

✳ ✳ ✳

HE AWOKE WITH A JOLT. He drew in a deep fitful breath and jumped to his feet, casting wary glances around. The rat wasn't there. He was surrounded by trees and undergrowth.

How weird, he thought. *Had it been a dream?*

Pensively he touched his throat where the rat's teeth had ripped through it. Had it been a dream — or what was it?

Dream or not, this place wasn't safe. He had to find shelter.

He looked around himself, searching for somewhere to hide. An ancient tree towered deep in the forest. It had a broad trunk and a thick heavy canopy supported by sturdy boughs.

Perfect hiding place.

Trying to step noiselessly and looking watchfully around, he started off toward it. As soon as he'd left the clearing and entered the giant tree's shade, more symbols appeared before his eyes,

Warning! The object #2234 <Forest Dwand> (1) has left Sector 5 <Forest Clearing> and relocated to Sector 23 <Ancient Oak Tree>

Objective, To avoid confrontation with other aggressive objects

Rewards:

+1 to Intellect. Current Intellect, 67

+10 to Experience. Current Experience, 1 (100/10)

So it wasn't a dream, then, he thought as he walked around the Ancient Oak Tree looking for the best spot to climb it.

For some reason, the fact that he could read and understand the messages hovering in his view didn't surprise him. The only thing that worried him at the moment was his safety. The rest he could sort out later.

Climbing proved to be a challenge. His muscles refused to obey him. His arms and legs slid from the trunk. It might not be such a good idea, after all.

He tried to use his claws. That way it seemed to be working. As he climbed, he saw more of the strange symbols but by then, he'd already learned how to make them disappear.

"Sorry, I'm busy," he croaked, climbing doggedly upward.

Sweat seeped into his eyes. His arms and legs shook with exertion. Several times he was about to stop but every time he forced himself to soldier on.

Halfway up, he decided to stop and see what the strange symbols had been trying to tell him. He also remembered what they were called. Letters and numbers.

Object #2234 <Forest Dwand> (1) has activated the Tree Climbing skill. Current skill level, 1

Rewards:
+1 to Strength. Current Strength, 6
+1 to Agility. Current Agility, 7
+1 to Stamina. Current Stamina, 3
+70 to Experience.
The object's current level, 1 (100/80)

He reread the message several times until he realized that it must have concerned him. It looked like he was doing pretty well.

He also found proof of the fact that he hadn't dreamed that rat up. It had indeed killed him — but for some reason, he'd come back to life.

He discovered it purely by accident. As he read the previous message, he noticed a tiny blue dot flashing below the text. At first, he thought he had something in his eye. Still, no matter how long he rubbed his eyelids, the speck remained in his mental view. He finally resigned himself to the fact that it was there to stay.

But what was it supposed to signify? The moment he wondered about this, a new message appeared before his eyes,

Would you like to see the logs?

He shrugged. "I suppose so."

The logs turned out to be quite a revelation. They told him in every detail how Object 4592 <Forest Rat> had killed him by ripping out his throat. There were more stories there but he didn't have the time to read them. Fear drove him up the tree trunk.

First he needed to find shelter. Then he could start looking into these strange stories.

Ever since he'd received the Tree Climbing skill, he didn't find his ascent so challenging. He even laughed at his initial weakness.

Having climbed almost to the very top of the tree, he breathed a sigh of relief. No rat could get to him up here.

And even if it did, it would have to look hard in order to notice him here. The green of the foliage and that of his own skin were almost identical.

His heart clenched with pleasure as he realized he was virtually invisible to any prying eyes.

The object #2234 <Forest Dwand> (1) has activated the Camouflage skill. Current skill level, 1

Reward:
+30 to Experience

The object #2234 <Forest Dwand> has received a new level. The object's current level, 2 (200/ 10)

Rewards:
5 characteristic points
2 skill points
2 ability points

For your information: Autonomous point distribution requires 50 pt. Intellect

He made himself comfortable and began studying the writings.

* * *

HE'D FORGOTTEN he was hungry. He didn't care about the time. Nor the rat. The new world of words and numbers fascinated him. He'd learned a lot and realized even more. And what was even more important, now he had a plan.

As it turned out, he shouldn't have been afraid of the rat. He should have been wary of it, true, but not afraid. Otherwise he might just as well have spent the rest of his life cowering at the top of the oak tree.

He'd also learned another thing. According to the logs, the rat hadn't been the only creature that had killed him. In fact, he'd died lots of times. He'd been killed by wolves, bears and lynxes, as well as some "users", whatever that was supposed to mean.

He'd learned quite a few new words such as "the system", "the logs", "Intellect", "a skill" and "the interface". He also knew what they were supposed to mean. He'd learned a lot of new words like those. Really a lot.

Strangely enough, most of his new knowledge came in the process of studying the rat. He realized that before the fight, their stats had been virtually identical. With one difference. The rat had had 1 pt. Intellect against his 66 points. Not that it had done him any good at the time. The gray predator had defeated him anyway. Still, a few things had changed. Primarily, it had made him leave the place where he'd died countless times before.

And even so he had a funny feeling that the change in him had begun much earlier.

He actually could understand the rat's motives. It couldn't have acted otherwise. It had been driven by hunger. Because if you failed to quench your hunger, sooner or later you'd die. Such was the law of this world.

The thought made him realize he hadn't eaten in quite a while. He had to climb back down and search for food.

But prior to that, he had one more thing left to do.

The object #2234 <Forest Dwand> would like to change his respawn point to Sector 23 <Ancient Oak Tree>.

Request denied!
Minimum requirements to perform this action:
Object's level, 5
Intellect, 70 pt.

Having read the message, he scratched his chin and got thinking. He could have raised Intellect to 70 straight away if he really wanted to. But what would it give him? He would still need to reach level 5 in order to change his respawn point. And he might gain more by investing the available points into other stats. He could improve his strength or agility. Health was important, too.

By now, he knew that each point meant +10 to Life. A small red bar in the top left corner of his interface sported a glowing number "9" — while its maximum reading was "20". No wonder the rat had killed him with such ease! His blue "Energy" bar was at zero. Compared to Life, its maximum reading was 10 points more. It was actually his Energy chipping away at his Life.

"I'd love to know why," he whispered, studying the numbers.

After a while, he smiled, pleased with himself. He'd found it. Every Stamina point added 10 points to the blue bar's capacity. Same principle as with Energy and Life.

He'd already noticed that both Energy and Life had a tendency to regenerate, on one condition: he had to eat.

That's how he learned Law #1: one should not go hungry.

✳ ✳ ✳

DARK THUNDERCLOUDS covered the sky. Despite the early afternoon, the forest submerged into darkness.

Two hours earlier, he'd returned to "his" forest clearing. A large bush next to the forest's edge had largely shielded him from any prying eyes.

Before climbing down the tree he'd invested one point into Camouflage. Better safe than sorry. He'd decided against improving his Tree Climbing skill. You never knew when a spare skill point might come in handy. Now that he'd raised his Strength to 7 and Agility to 8, climbing down the tree trunk had proved much easier.

He'd brought Life up to 50 by investing 3 pt. into Health. Now the rat would have its work cut out for it.

Talking about which... there it was, his rat, as large as life and twice as ugly.

He tensed up. His breathing slowed to a halt. Now he could study his enemy in detail.

No wonder it had killed him so easily. As far as rats went, it was big. If it reared up, it might have been almost the same height as himself.

His back crawled with fear. Goosebumps erupted on his skin. He had to shake himself up and get a grip. He focused on the creature's stats.

Agility, 5. Strength, also 5. Intellect... he chuckled. The rat's Intellect was dangerously close to zero. Maximum damage, 12 — against his 25. No abilities: in this they were equal. The creature's Life and Energy, however, were both at 30, full to the brim. The rat must have just had its kill and its dinner.

He looked around. He seemed to be alone. With a deep sigh, he slowly climbed out of his hideout.

The rat was sitting with its back to him a mere twenty feet away. It looked drowsy — almost asleep. Even its ears had stopped twitching.

The timing was good. Stealthily he began shifting his feet toward it.

Why the rat, might you ask, when there was no shortage of more harmless game in the forest?

For several reasons. First, he needed to eat. The rat might not be the safest of options but it was still food.

Secondly, he just wanted to get even with it. It had killed him yesterday, hadn't it? In fact, it had killed him many times before. It was about time he broke its lucky streak.

And last but not least, he wanted to see how he'd fare in combat. In theory, the rat's stats were weaker in every respect. Time to see how it worked in practice.

He took three more short stealthy steps, moving silently like a shadow. Or was it his imagination? In any case, the rat didn't seem to notice him.

A new message popped up before his eyes. He nearly jumped.

Rrrgghh! he mentally growled. All this message-flashing was getting a bit annoying. It was the second time it had happened to him — and every time it seemed to occur when the rat was nearby.

The object #2234 <Forest Dwand> (1) has activated the Stealthy Step skill. Current skill level, 1
Reward,
+30 to Experience (200/40)

That was all good and well but it couldn't go on like this forever. Surprises like those could be lethal.

Somehow he seemed to know how to collapse the messages into a small square box in the right-hand bottom corner of his interface. This way he could still stay informed of new developments without all those pop-ups scaring the hell out of him.

Changing the settings had only taken him

a few seconds but they felt like hours. Luckily, the creature still seemed to ignore him.

He had three paces left to take when the rat finally sensed him. Its muscles rippled under its grayish brown fur. The creature tensed, about to turn round.

Time was an issue. He crouched, straining his every sinew and preparing to dart forward.

He put his trust in his agility and bolted off.

He took a long leap while the rat still continued to turn round.

Another leap, long and powerful. His muscles quivered with exertion. His joints crunched. His stare sank into the animal's neck like a claw.

The rat had turned around just in time. Unfortunately for it, its prey had become the hunter. One who was stronger, more agile. And fast.

It all ended surprisingly quickly. Two blows, that was all it had taken. The rat's cooling body lay on the grass with its throat ripped out. His claws had proved to be a terrible weapon.

The Dwand stood tall and strong over his defeated enemy. His chest heaved. Hot blood dripped from his shaking fingers onto the ground.

He'd won!

He'd beaten his enemy with its own tactics. He'd stolen onto the rat just like it itself had done earlier . He'd leapt onto it and assaulted it. And he'd won!

The object #2234 <Forest Dwand> (2) has defeated the object 4592 <Forest Rat>
Rewards:
+40 to Experience
Rat steak, 1
Rat's tail, 1
Rat's fangs, 4

He froze, breathless, as he watched his enemy's gray-brown corpse disappear into thin air until finally it was gone, leaving behind a chunk of meat, a long bare tail and four sharp teeth.

Would you like to collect the items?

He nodded. His jaw dropped in disappointment as all the items disappeared from sight.

"What the-" he exclaimed, peering around in search of his trophies.

He couldn't see anything on the green grass. Even the blood was gone. Nothing suggested the fierce lethal combat which had unfolded here only moments ago.

The Dwand heaved a sigh and slumped onto the ground.

Why? he asked himself. *All that risk for nothing?*

To add insult to injury, his stomach rumbled, reminding him of itself. What a bastard!

Just to take his mind off it, he decided to check the logs. But first he had to find a new hiding place.

The Dwand made himself comfortable in the depths of a fat nut bush and opened the logs,

The object #2234 <Forest Dwand> (2) has activated the Leap skill. Current skill level, 1
Reward:
+30 to Experience

He chuckled. So that's where the extra experience had come from. Good. What was next?

+1 to Strength. Current Strength, 8
+1 to Agility. Current Agility, 9
+1 to Stamina. Current Stamina, 4

His green face stretched into a smile. Even the disappointment of losing his prey had subsided somewhat.

The damage messages, too, were good

news. As it turned out, he'd very nearly killed the rat with one blow. The second 5-pt. blow was a "coup de grace", whatever that was supposed to mean.

Once again his skin erupted in goosebumps. He was proud of winning the combat. He'd done everything right!

As he closed the logs, he noticed a little flashing square box in the top right corner of his interface. The picture on it depicted a small bag marked *"Inventory"*.

Should he take a look?

He gasped at the sight which opened up to his eyes. The interface had split in two. In its left half stood a scrawny little green figure with pointy rat-like ears, large jaws and a mouthful of sharp little teeth. The creature had a narrow chest, a sunken belly and knobbly knees. Its ribs were sticking out.

An inscription above the creature announced,

The object #2234 <Forest Dwand> (2)

Then he knew it.

"So that's what I look like, is it? No wonder everyone in this forest is trying to get rid of me!"

The little figure was surrounded by empty square boxes. Only one of them was filled. It contained his tattered loincloth. He studied its stats. Apparently, the only purpose of his single piece of attire was to cover his nudity.

But that wasn't a problem. The abundance of empty square boxes (which were called slots) meant that he could fill them with more useful items.

He switched his attention to the right half of the interface and smiled a happy smile. It contained five slots. Two of them were empty while the remaining three contained all of his recent loot.

His stomach grumbled its enthusiasm. The rat steak!

✳ ✳ ✳

SINCE THEN, the fiery ball in the sky had set and reappeared six times in a row. The Dwand had made level 7. Now he was considerably smarter, stronger and faster. He'd received three abilities and activated over twenty useful new skills. By now, he could swim, fish, climb cliffs, run really fast and even see in the dark. He could also tell useful plants, berries and mushrooms from bad ones.

Still, hunting remained his main occupation. It had brought him the bulk of his Experience. It was his love for hunting and his craving for self-improvement that finally made him leave his location.

He had to move on. He'd first realized it the day he'd received neither loot nor experience for the killing of yet another rat. He then killed two more, with the same result. Nothing.

He scrolled through the logs, looking for an explanation, and finally found an interesting tendency. The rats had stopped to drop trophies as soon as he'd made level 4. After that, killing them had become a waste of time.

So he'd moved on to the next clearing where he'd discovered new prey, namely level-5 Vipers.

He met the dawn of day six with a broad smile on his lips. Last night, he'd made level 7. Which meant that it was time for him to set off in search of new adventures.

If the truth were known, the vipers had been boring. Despite their levels, they were quite easy to kill. Still, he hadn't wasted his time. Apart from all the experience gained, he'd also learned a very useful skill, Immunity to Toxins. In order to acquire it, he'd very nearly died from a snake bite — but luckily, his high Health numbers had kept him out of trouble.

He'd used the snake skin to make himself a new bag for ten extra slots, a belt and a jacket with a bonus to Strength, and a pair of pants and moccasins with a bonus to Agility.

He also used the snakes' teeth to make himself new claws for each hand. Smeared with venom, they turned into lethal weapons. Now killing the snakes had become a walk in the park — because as it turned out, they weren't immune to their own venom.

True, his new clothes didn't look like much and only added one point each to the aforementioned stats. But that was the start of a new life. The day he made his new clothes, he'd made a point of discarding his old loincloth.

The scared scrawny creature he'd been only a few days ago was gone. Only the weird name still reminded him of his old self: object #2234 <Forest Dwand>.

✳ ✳ ✳

HE CAME ACROSS a Dwand village by midday. At first, he hadn't even realized those creatures were his brethren. And when he did, his heart very nearly jumped out of his chest with joy.

His first impulse was to walk out of the woods toward them. Still, he suppressed it almost straight away. His newly-acquired hunting habits warned him against any rash actions. He had to take a good look around first.

By the evening, he was glad he hadn't

revealed himself to those creatures which had at first appeared so familiar and so dear.

They were indeed Forest Dwandes like himself. Or at least that was how the system had identified them. Green hide, pointy ears, a large mouth — everything about those scrawny creatures was identical to himself when he'd been level 1. Actually, that's what most of them were, levels 1 and 2. Their stats, too, were similar to what he'd started his new life with. Their low Intellect readings were the only difference. Only 5 points — and many of them didn't even have that.

Their village was located on a small clearing surrounded by sparse undergrowth. They lived in holes which they called "earth houses".

They built them without any system — each Dwand just dug his own wherever he pleased. They also had clumsy wickiups made with sticks and animal hides.

The Dwand smirked with disgust. He didn't even want to compare his own comfortable wickiup on top of the Ancient Oak Tree with those hovels.

The wickiups were occupied by those of the Dwandes whose levels were higher. Two of the huts were especially big. A new system message informed him that one belonged to the tribe's chief and the other, to its shaman.

The Dwand didn't like either of them. Conceited bastards. They treated their tribesmen so cruelly that he clenched his fists in helpless fury.

Both the chief and the shaman were level 10. With only 8 pt. Intellect, the chief wasn't particularly bright. The shaman, however, was full of surprises. He had 15 pt. Intellect.

The Dwand also made another discovery. Apparently, apart from almost identical descriptions and system numbers, all of those creatures also had *names.*

And as for the shaman himself — an old man dressed in tattered animal skins hung with birds' skulls and strings of animal teeth — the system identified him as *Junior AI <Grryrgh the Shaman>.*

The Dwand gulped anxiously. This was the first creature he'd come across which wasn't an Object.

He immediately knew who was the true leader of the settlement.

✳ ✳ ✳

HE SPENT ONE MORE DAY watching the tribe's comings and goings. His level-3 Camouflage made him invisible for the Dwandes busy living their village lives.

Their daily routine was quite uneventful. Lowly community members worked to provide for the senior ones: the shaman and the chief as well as their entourage. They even had their own guards: the level-5 and 6 Dwandes he'd noticed earlier. Their clubs and punches helped to keep the community in check.

Judging by their emaciated bodies, the tribe was starving. Quite a few of them had died before his very eyes. What outraged him even more was that the children had to work just as hard as the adults. The little ones had to go into the woods to gather roots, berries and mushrooms under the watchful gaze of the guards who made sure the children didn't eat their humble pickings. The woods around the village were poor.

The Dwand smirked. No wonder! The chief, the shaman and their clique ate like there was no tomorrow, demanding more and more food. And the villagers were too scared to venture deeper into the woods.

All the villagers but one, that is.

✳ ✳ ✳

ON THE THIRD MORNING, he decided to move on. The more he watched the tribe, the clearer he realized that they had no place for him. He wasn't going to obediently serve the spoiled chief, anyway. And he had no desire of joining the ranks of his sidekicks. Did they expect him to watch over the hungry children, forbidding them to eat a few berries? The mere thought made him sick.

Oh no, he'd seen enough.

With that thought, he left his lookout and continued on his journey through the woods. It was time he did some hunting. His supplies had almost run out.

He'd left the village far behind and finally came to a small stream. Had it not been for his level 3 Observation Skills, he would have found himself in big trouble.

He was about to step out of the cover of the undergrowth when he glimpsed a spotted yellow animal secreted within the foliage.

He froze, breathless.

Name, Forest Lynx
Level, 7
Status, Aggressive
Strength, 19
Agility, 26
Intellect, 10
Damage, 33 to 67
Skills, Paw Swipe

That was one hell of a serious opponent. Only why wasn't it attacking him?

The lynx lingered, then stepped forward.

He tensed. His claws, smeared with venom, were ready for combat. With any luck, he might win this fight.

The lynx took another step forward. Finally he could see its head in detail.

What he'd seen surprised him. Apparently, it wasn't him the creature was hunting. Its gaze was focused on the far bank of the stream.

He heaved a mental sigh of relief and began backing off, slowly and warily. The lynx completely ignored him, so absorbed was it by what it could see on the bank.

He was about to swing round and run for his life when something made him trace back the lynx's gaze. He stood on tiptoe and drew a branch aside, peering in the direction of the bank.

What he saw almost made him cry out in despair.

Stupid child!

Oblivious to the world, a tiny Dwand sat on the bank peering at something in the water.

Level 1. This *was* a little boy. What was he doing so far from the village?

Stupid question, really. He was trying to catch some fish. *Trying* being the operative word. The boy was so starved he'd lost all fear.

As the Dwand racked his brains for a solution, the lynx emitted a guttural growl and charged.

The bushes rustled. The boy turned to the sound.

To his own surprise, the Dwand rushed out after the feline, shouting, "Run! You idiot! Run, quick!"

The boy, however, froze in place open-mouthed, staring curiously at the scene.

Trying to prevent the inevitable, the Dwand darted across and stepped in the animal's path.

The lynx had heard him shout and swung round, then went unhesitantly for its new prey.

The Dwand dropped to the ground and prepared to meet its attack. Out of the corner of his eye, he could see the boy still standing there, his mouth open even wider.

He decided to ignore the child for the time being and concentrate on the enemy.

If I live, I'll box his ears for him, he thought, dodging the lynx's lightning leap.

His opponent was fast — but not fast enough. In one smooth motion, the Dwand flowed to the right like a droplet of mercury. In doing so, he ran his venomous claws across the cat' ribs. The lynx yelped in pain, swung round and attacked again — this time not as hastily.

He was prepared for this turn of events. His

lithe body leapt through the air, landing directly onto the animal's back. His hands worked fast, ripping through the hapless hunter's back, neck and head. He watched the snake venom work, gradually depriving the lynx of Life.

He showered the animal with a series of well-aimed blows.

Everything was over in seconds.

Unable to offer anything against this unexpected new enemy, the lynx vanished into thin air, leaving behind a beautiful spotted pelt, a set of fangs and a small steel ring with +1 to Strength.

Pleased, the Dwand slid the ring — which was his seventh already — on his finger and sent the remaining trophies into his inventory.

"How did you do that?" the child's excited high-pitched voice made him turn round.

The boy stared at him in disbelief.

"It's impossible!" he exclaimed, jumping around him. "You've killed the Terror of the Forest all on your own!"

"Some Terror!" the Dwand grumbled. Admittedly, he liked the lynx's name. "Why didn't you run when I told you to? Are you deaf?"

The thundering voice of a strange warrior who'd single-handedly killed the most dangerous predator in this part of the woods made the boy lower his head in silence.

"Answer the question!"

"I was scared," the boy replied softly. Then he looked up at his rescuer, "And who are you? What's your name?"

"I'm a Dwand like yourself. And as for my name... you know what? I don't have one."

The boy looked puzzled. Then his face dissolved in a beaming smile. "If you don't have a name, mind if I give one to you?"

The Dwand frowned. Before, he'd never used to care about what he was called. But now...

He shrugged. "Go ahead, then. Just make sure I like it too."

"I know! How about Grrorgh? It means Slayer! Grrorgh the Terror Slayer! What do you think? Do you like it?"

The boy's green eyes filled with hope.

Really, why not? The Dwand smiled. "I like it a lot. I accept it."

The boy shrieked with delight and leapt high in the air. "I gave a name to a great warrior! I gave a name to a great warrior!"

He soon calmed down and proffered his hand. "My name's Cro. It means Mite."

The freshly-baked Grrorgh smiled and shook the tiny hand.

"This is only my nickname," Cro hurried to explain. "After the initiation, the Shaman will give me a proper grown-up name."

"I see. You'd better tell me what you were doing here."

Cro's face fell. His stomach rumbled, betraying his hunger. "How can I explain... We need to find food and bring it back to the chief. Then he wisely shares it between all the tribe members."

Grrorgh cringed. He already knew all about their chief and his "wise" sharing practices.

"The warriors who defend us from the wild beasts don't allow us to stray away. They are worried about us."

Yeah right. They just want to make sure their forced laborers don't do a runner or eat their own offerings, Grrorgh thought.

In the meantime, Cro continued, "There's nothing left to gather near the village. Everybody knows that. So I decided to go to the river and catch some fish. Lots of fish here."

Grrorgh felt sorry for him. Once in a lifetime the kid had tried to get a full stomach. He was just a bag of bones with sunken eyes and protruding ribs. His Energy bar was virtually empty.

"Do you know how to fish?" he asked, already knowing the answer. He could see the boy didn't have the Fishing skill.

Cro shook his head. "Not really. I just wanted to see if I could catch some."

"Instead, you very nearly became somebody else's lunch."

The boy's large eyes welled with tears. Grrorgh hurried to add, "But the fact that you did it is already a lot. Well done! Fishing isn't all that difficult, by the way. Would you like me to teach you?"

Cro opened his mouth, then began to nod, twitching his ears in a most peculiar way.

"Come on, then," Grrorgh said and headed for the river.

The boy hopped and skipped in his wake, showering him with questions about his weapons and armor. And when he heard that Grrorgh had made them himself, the boy very nearly choked in his admiration.

Grrorgh walked along the river for a while until he came upon a calm discreet backwater. Just what he needed.

He pressed his finger to his lips. "Quiet now."

The boy grew silent. He was anything but stupid.

"Look," Grrorgh said, pointing at the fat scaly backs basking on the surface. "Those are carp. It's a juicy fish, very tasty."

He reached into his inventory for the trident he'd made the other day, then walked over to the water's edge.

He chose a target, brought his arm back, then launched his weapon into the water. Pierced by the trident's sharp teeth, a shiny fish thrashed in the air.

To say Cro was happy would be an understatement.

"Wait up. Don't eat it quite yet," Grrorgh stopped the boy who was about to sink his teeth into the fish. "Let's catch some more and then I'll cook them for you. Ready? Your turn. Take this," he lay the trident in Cro's trembling hand.

The moment he did so, he received an unusual system message,

The object #2234 <Grrorgh the Fear Slayer> has shared his Fishing skill with the Object 5908 <Mity Cro>
Reward,
+200 to Experience
Current Experience, 700/340
+2 to Intellect
Current Intellect, 93

How much? It was impossible. What an eye-opener! It felt almost as if he'd looked up, expecting to see the sun, and discovered it was blue with red stripes! +200 Experience just for passing his knowledge on! And +2 to Intellect!

He opened his skill list and gave a mental

whistle. Just think how much Experience he could get back for all this!

And what if he could also share it with other tribe members?

His skin erupted in goosebumps. The mind boggles!

The first inklings of a plan were forming in his head.

But first I might need to double-check quite a few things, he thought, watching the boy who'd frozen with the trident raised high in his hand.

"Cro?" he whispered to the boy. "Can you hear me?"

"Yes," the boy whispered back without taking his eyes off the water's surface.

"Do you have family in the village?"

"No. I don't have no one. Just-" he faltered.

"Just what?"

"Nah," the boy sounded embarrassed. "There's this girl..."

Even better. "What's her name?"

"Tari," the boy replied breathlessly.

The Dwand smiled. "Does she like you?"

The tips of Cro's ears darkened with embarrassment. He fell silent.

When the Dwand began to wonder if he'd overdone it, the boy finally spoke,

"No, she doesn't. I don't think she even knows I'm there."

"Why not?"

"Because she has a crush on the chief's younger son!" the boy blurted out, then added grimly, "He's quick and strong. And he's handsome. Unlike me. All the girls are in love with him. And now that I've escaped the guards to come here, they'll flog me in front of the whole tribe. That's a disgrace. And I'd rather die than live disgraced in her eyes..."

"It's okay, kiddo," Grrorgh said softly. Then he added in a conspiratorial whisper, "Would *you* like to become smart, quick and strong? You could come back to the village wearing a suit of armor just like my own. And you could bring them lots of game — not those stupid berries and mushrooms, but proper game, with lots of good meat and animal pelts from beasts they've never even seen before?"

The boy swung round. His eyes glistened with interest and hope. "Yes," he said in a stifled voice. "Oh yes, I'd like that very much."

"In that case, I'm gonna teach you everything I know," Grrorgh said with a smile. He nodded at the water, "There's your fish, over there. Kill it. You have lots of things to learn today."

✳ ✳ ✳

"SO HOW DOES IT feel now?" Grrorgh asked calmly. "Mind telling me?"

"What was I like before?" Cro asked him instead.

They stood at the edge of the forest in broad daylight, watching the comings and goings of Cro's fellow tribesmen.

"Well," Grrorgh paused, "you were a bit like that level-1 kid digging over there who's helping his mother to make an earth house. Your ears were just as big. And you were just as scrawny."

"And just as hungry," the boy whispered.

Grrorgh pretended he hadn't heard him.

It had been barely two weeks since they'd met — but it felt like it had been at least a year. So much had happened in those several days!

Watching the village's miserable state of affairs from behind his student's back, Grrorgh suddenly realized the full scope of the change within the boy.

Cro was now level 20. He had six abilities and over thirty skills. His Intellect, Strength and Agility were sufficiently high. A set of armor made of the scaly hide of Rock Pangolins hugged his lithe body. The bow slung behind his back was his own work. The two short swords on his belt were loot he'd received after defeating the Salt

Cave Boss.

Since their first meeting, they'd been through thick and thin together. Grrorgh had taught his new student a lot of what he himself knew. The kid wasn't hungry or emaciated anymore.

The Dwand suppressed a smile. His student! The boy who'd given *him* a name...

Grrorgh hadn't lagged behind him very much, either. By teaching the boy, he too had been developing his own skills. Mentoring him had proven to be the best leveling tactic. They hunted and built new items together. They took turns cooking and studied the world around them.

Cro had turned out to be a smart and curious boy who soaked up knowledge like dry moss soaks up moisture.

Grrorgh had become very attached to him. If ever he had a son, he'd like him to be like Cro.

Everything had been going well. The two had been preparing to depart on a long journey when Grrorgh began to notice sadness in the boy's eyes. The kid was homesick. He missed his tribemates, that's what it was.

It was time to fulfill the promise he'd given the hungry boy he'd met two weeks ago. After a brief discussion, they'd decided to pay the village a visit.

For the rest of that day, the kid had been fidgety, getting ready to face the tribe. He caught a Prairie Antelope — a true delicacy whose meat was especially tender and juicy. He must have imagined his neighbors enjoying his best dish — Antelope Roast, the pride of his recipe collection.

Cro had packed the skin of Snow Leopard into his bag: a gift for the chief. Next to it, he stowed a small bag of rare mountain herbs as an offering to the shaman.

He then packed a tunic made of the softest skin of a Prairie Antelope. He'd made it specially for Tari, the girl he was still in love with. He also packed the necklace of sea pearls he'd made for her. And a mother-of-pearl comb fashioned out of a fine sea shell. Plus a plethora of little gifts which were bound to please her.

Grrorgh had watched the boy's preparations with a skeptical smile, imagining his and his tribemates' reunion.

So now they stood at the forest edge, watching the villagers potter about doing their business. Little had changed in the settlement in those several days.

Having said that, it actually had. Things were even worse now.

Cro was a sorry sight. His face betrayed disappointment, disgust and even offense.

The clearing was still riddled with wickiups

and earth houses. Emaciated villagers in scruffy loincloths walked in files, toiling under the fat guards' watchful supervision.

The chief and the shaman hadn't changed, either. Time seemed to have stood still here.

"Do you see that guy with a scar across his face?" Cro asked. "That's Rruroch. I used to think he was our best warrior. But now I can't believe I was born here. It's all so... so pathetic. I can imagine how you felt when you first saw it. No wonder you decided to leave."

Although Cro spoke about the warrior, Grrorgh sensed there was more to it than met the eye. "Can you see her?" he asked what was probably the most important question.

"No," the boy whispered. "I wonder if something has happened to her?"

His voice trailed away. Grrorgh lay his left hand on Cro's shoulder.

It's all right, boy. This too shall pass, he thought.

"Let's go, then," Grrrorgh said instead.

"Yes, teacher. I must do it."

"I understand. Let's be off, then."

✳ ✳ ✳

THE VILLAGERS FINALLY noticed them when the two were only a couple of dozen feet away.

The riot that ensued! Cro stared in bewilderment as his fellow tribesmen ran around in panic, screaming.

Grrorgh chuckled. "What else did you expect? You left this place a scrawny snotnose. All they can see now is two strangers. Who are very well armed, as well."

In the meantime, the panic had grown. The villagers shrieked, rushing around the settlement like headless chickens. Grrorgh and Cro had to stop by the village gate for fear of being trampled.

Grrorgh chuckled. You had to give the shaman his due: he'd already talked some sense back into both the chief and the village guards. He wasn't a Junior AI for nothing.

Grrorgh had already met five of those AI creatures. They all differed from Objects quite a lot. Unfortunately, they were also monsters only capable of killing and stuffing their faces.

But this shaman... he was different. Doubtless he loved to eat and had no qualms about sacrificing someone to the tribe's bloodthirsty gods but he was also different in another way. This was the first sentient AI he'd met.

Grrorgh chuckled and rolled his eyes. Sentient! Okay, maybe not quite but still.

In the meantime, the screaming, wailing crowd had finally restored some order. A small group headed toward the newcomers: the chief, his entourage, and the shaman who kept a low profile lurking behind the others' backs.

Grrorgh chuckled. Very clever of the AI.

Cro was about to step forward but Grrorgh stopped him, shaking his head. No need to jump the gun.

The crowd stopped a few paces away from the newcomers. Up close, the chief's face seemed even more inane. He didn't seem to understand what was going on around him. His glare burned with anger at the strangers who'd had the audacity to disrupt his perfect day schedule (which consisted of stuffing his face and having his servants flogged, in no particular order).

The villagers' faces betrayed fear and curiosity. And admiration.

Grrorgh cast a sideways glance at Cro. His student must have realized it too because he'd stood tall with his shoulders spread wide. No wonder! The girls' admiring gazes were all over him.

Grrorgh felt out of his depth. He too seemed to have attracted female attentions. Judging by the looks on the older ladies' faces, they found him every bit as attractive as his student.

The chief's guards curiously studied the strangers' weapons. They seemed unable to wrap their heads around the fact that a young Dwand like their visitor could be hung with so many precious items — while they, respected family men that they were, had to wear ripped pants and moth-eaten fur vests, and use clubs and spears with stone tips as weapons.

It wasn't hard for Grrorgh to read their minds. He chuckled under his breath.

"Who are you? What do you want?" a voice came from behind the guards' backs. Its sound reminded Grrorgh of the grating of two grindstones. It was the shaman entering the stage.

Grrorgh stepped forward. "My name is Grrorgh the Terror Slayer," he said, trying to sound as calm and friendly as he could. "And this is my apprentice. We've come in peace."

He nodded to the boy. Avoiding any sudden movements, Cro slowly pulled the bag off his back, just as Grrorgh had told him to do. He lowered himself to one knee.

The tribal warriors tensed. Then they visibly relaxed, watching what the so-called "apprentice" was doing.

Cro kept reaching into the bag, heaping up gifts on the grass by his feet: chunks of meat, animal skins and rare herbs. He explained the purpose of each item as he pulled it out.

"What do you want?" the shaman repeated.

His threatening tone wasn't so insistent this time. The shaman's beady gray eyes focused on the pouch with the rare healing herbs.

"We've come to find a wife for my apprentice!" Grrorgh announced in a solemn voice. "And these are his offerings for the great chief, the wise shaman and the girl's parents!"

The crowd seethed with indignation. The men protested, shouting that outsiders couldn't marry the tribe's women.

The women fumed too. Why only one wife? And why only for the apprentice? Shouldn't the great Terror Slayer have a harem of his own? Say, ten wives to begin with?

As the crowd vented its anger, the shaman and the chief spoke between themselves, casting suspicious glances at the two strangers and eyeing greedily the heap of valuable gifts at the boy's feet.

Finally, they seemed to come to some agreement.

The old shaman raised his hand, calling for silence. "The laws of our ancestors prohibit outsiders from marrying our women," he began.

His words triggered a twofold reaction. Men nodded victoriously while women sighed their disappointment.

"Normally, we never forgive such brazen arrogance. Any such suitor would have been slaughtered on the spot," the shaman squinted craftily. "But seeing as you've come in peace and brought us your modest offerings, we forgive you. You're free to go back to where you came from."

Cro stared at his mentor, his wide-open eyes filled with disappointment and incomprehension. Until that moment, he'd kept his gaze firmly on a dark-haired girl who'd openly admired the handsome boy.

Grrorgh laid a soothing hand on the young man's shoulder. "Just cool it. I know we can easily take what we've come here for by force. But we need to obey their laws. Don't worry. You won't leave without a wife," Grrorgh gave him a wink, nodding at the girl. "Is that her?"

"Yes," Cro mouthed. His ears darkened with embarrassment.

Grrorgh slapped the boy's armor-clad shoulder and turned to the shaman, "O ye wise commander of spirits," he began. "We have the deepest respect for your laws. Still, our request doesn't contradict your customs. My apprentice is no stranger to you!"

The crowd gasped in surprise.

"Only two weeks ago, you all knew this boy. His name was Cro. It so happened that he escaped one of the guards and very nearly became victim of the Terror of the Forest. Luckily, I happened to be near. Together we defeated the beast."

As he so spoke, he thought to himself, *While you were doing nothing, stuffing your faces and making others do your work for you, my Cro was fighting the forest's most dangerous monsters! You — what do you know about true terror? You who nicknamed a humble lynx the Terror of the Forest! You've no idea!*

Grrorgh turned round and gave his disciple another wink. The boy modestly lowered his eyes.

To say his tribemates were shocked would be an understatement.

"Cro?" one gray-haired old woman asked another. "Do you remember anyone of that name?"

"Impossible," a one-armed old man shook his head.

Grrorgh slapped Cro's back. "Your turn to front this show."

Cro took a confident step forward and turned to the tribe's best warrior,

"Rurrokh! Don't you remember me? You saved me when I fell into the ditch last year. Had it not been for you, I'd have been dead now."

The warrior's face cleared with recognition.

"And you, Smyrrkh? Don't you remember how you shared your dry mushroom with me?"

A young Dwand gulped, then nodded.

"And you, Mother Zarkha? Don't you

remember the thrashing you gave me and Grrymkh when we piled up earth against your front door?" Cro peered at the crowd. "Grrymkh? Where are you?"

"I'm here!" a voice replied.

"Don't you remember how your backside smarted from Mother Zarkha's rod?" Cro shouted into the crowd, grinning. "We spent half the night sitting in a puddle of cold water to soothe the pain! Don't you remember?"

"Of course I do! I remember everything!"

Cro kept calling out names, reminding everyone of stories from their past. His tribemates listened in disbelief, struggling to recognize the starved little boy in this lithe and dangerous warrior.

Finally, Cro approached the dark-haired girl. "Tari... I've come for *you*. Here," he reached into his bag and produced the soft tunic fashioned from the skin of a Prairie Antelope.

And the pearl necklace. And the mother-of-pearl comb. And lots of other pretty little things.

"I made them all for you," he said, flustered. "Do you like them?"

Grrorgh chuckled, watching the girl's emerald eyes light up. *Of course she does! She's never seen anything like it!*

A scream of agony came from within the thick of the crowd. People stirred.

What a nuisance. Everything had been going so well!

Another cry came, and yet another. And again...

The tribesmen looked around themselves in bewilderment. Even the shaman froze, open-mouthed.

While they tried to get their wits about themselves, Grrorgh already knew what it was. Someone had attacked the tribe.

"Cro!" he shouted to the boy who was shielding the girl with his body. "Archers! They're shooting from the forest! Take her away! I'll cover you!"

Cro changed instantly. He scooped his fiancée up in his arms and ran into the village.

Grrorgh growled at the warriors, directing them toward the attackers, then leapt toward the trees.

He noticed the first archer standing at the very edge of the wood. He stood with his legs wide apart and, unhurriedly and methodically, loosed off arrow after arrow at the very thick of the fleeing Dwandes. He didn't seem to care that there were women and children in the panicking crowd. His powerful bowstring kept snapping, showering the tribe with arrows.

When Grrorgh was within a few paces of the archer, he finally saw who he was dealing with.

User name, Wurp Ironballs
Level, 5
Class, Archer
Race, Alven

Was that it? What about his stats?

The user named Wurp Ironballs died before he could even notice. One moment he stood there loosing off arrows and feeling on top of the world. The next moment his body dissolved into thin air.

Naturally, he dropped no loot. The level gap was just too great.

Grrorgh discovered two more archers sitting on a tree.

"Come on, smoke the bastards!" one of them was shouting. That one was also a user, a humble level-4 Alven. "You need to get as much XP as you can before the rogues get to the village!"

The other user, a level-5 human, was aiming his weird bow, tongue between teeth with the effort. His weapon resembled an ordinary bow, only that it had a cross-bar attached to the center of its handle.

A new system message helpfully informed Grrorgh that this was a "crossbow".

Don't you even dare, Grrorgh thought,

pulling his own bow.

Two arrows hit both users in the eye. They died instantly. Grrorgh picked up his spent arrows and continued his advance.

In total, having completed a full circle around the clearing, he'd killed fifteen archers and five crossbowmen. All of them users, their levels almost identical. They had all sorts: Alves, humans, orcs and dwarves.

What kind of tribe was that? Grrorgh pondered on his way back to the village.

There, a battle was in full swing. Grrorgh saw from afar that the invaders' attack had failed. Firstly, they were left without their archers' support. And secondly... secondly, Cro was there. Like an ancient god of war, he was chopping the attackers to pieces left, right and center. The blades of his swords glistened in the rays of the setting sun, claiming the lives of the hapless plunderers.

Cro the Death Bearer! The name suited him fine.

Never mind his strongest opponent was only level 7. Grrorgh still had every reason to be proud of his apprentice.

The battle ended as unexpectedly as it had started. The attackers were no match for either Grrorgh or Cro. The villagers, however, had been badly hurt. The chief and the shaman were nowhere to be seen.

Grrorgh sniffed his contempt. The bastards must have legged it.

However, the villagers had celebrated too early. As if mocking their efforts, new attackers emerged from the woods.

Grrorgh and Cro exchanged wary glances.

"Take the survivors into the woods," Grrorgh said. "I'll try and hold them here."

"But master-" the boy tried to object.

"Don't argue," Grrorgh said. Then he added with a smile, "Don't worry about me. Go! I won't be long."

His gaze followed the escaping Dwandes. He breathed a sigh of relief and turned round.

There were four attackers. All of them users. Two Alven girls in borderline skimpy clothes, one of them an archer, the other holding a weird long stick topped with a large red stone. The third one was a human with an axe in both hands, his bare torso covered in weird blue writings.

A giant troll with a gnarly club in one hand towered in front of them, shielding the other three like a great rock.

Their levels were 26 to 31. Strangely enough, the troll had the lowest level. The Alven girl with a funny stick had the highest.

Grrorgh wasn't happy with the fact that

unlike the earlier attackers, these four didn't seem to be in a hurry. Calmly they took up their positions opposite him.

This doesn't look good, he thought.

"Lita," the human turned to the Alven girl with the stick. "Please no stupid tricks this time. The location boss is level 40. Wait for him to aggro Bulldozer."

Hearing his name, the troll took a heavy step forward. The Alven girl smirked.

"Well, if you all know what to do, then off you go!" the human shouted. "Watch it!"

Having received the go-ahead from their commander, Bulldozer lowered his head and barged at Grrorgh.

Or so he thought. With Grrorgh's Agility numbers, he might have just as well stayed where he was.

Grrorgh leapt aside. The troll's enormous bulk careened past him. Grrorgh pulled out a knife smeared with the venom of a Scarlet Spider and threw it at the troll's back.

The poisoned blade sank deep under the troll's shoulder blade. Grrorgh nodded his satisfaction. The troll might need some help to pull that out.

He swung round and leapt forward.

The human and the two Alven girls froze in disbelief.

"Ragnar!" the archeress called, her voice ringing with panic. "Why didn't he aggro our tank?"

"I didn't cast anything, I swear!" Lita added in a similar vein.

"I know that!" the human growled. He froze in a combat stance, the two axes crossed before him, and awaited the approach of this weird "location boss".

Grrorgh cracked a mental grin. Very clever. Did the human really think he would distract Grrorgh, allowing the two women to stud him with arrows and God knows what else?

No way. The human could wait. The other two were priority targets.

Still grinning, the Dwand ducked, diving out of the paths of the flying axes, and found himself opposite the archeress.

The girl looked lost. Fear filled her large blue eyes.

"Fear is good for you," Grrorgh growled.

The girl screamed.

The other girl joined in the shrieking match. That was good. Your enemy's fear is always good news. They start making mistakes. They forget how good they normally are.

The two sharp swords that Grrorgh had procured in the Valley of Oblivion flashed through the air, glistening in the sun. The girl's screaming stopped. Lita survived her friend but by a few brief moments.

"Now we can fight," Grrorgh said calmly, turning to the human who watched in disbelief as the bodies of his team members disappeared into thin air.

Ragnar gulped. "Who are you?"

Grrorgh shrugged. "I'm your death."

He leapt forward.

You had to give the human his due: he stood his ground. Not for very long, though. As he died, he spewed curses, blaming some "admins" and accusing Grrorgh himself of being a "bug".

Grrorgh didn't care. He turned and walked toward the troll with the soft, noiseless gait of a hunter.

The troll stood on his knees mumbling something. Drool trickled from his jaws. He couldn't even raise his hand.

"That's spider's venom," Grrorgh commented, looking into the troll's petrified eyes. "It paralyzes you head to toe in a few heartbeats. Doesn't feel nice, does it?"

Even kneeling, the troll still towered several feet over Grrorgh. The creature kept mumbling its protest but Grrorgh didn't listen.

His sword whooshed through the air. Hot blood gushed from Bulldozer's slit throat.

Grrorgh didn't wait for the last body to

disappear. He needed to catch up with the rest. They had a lot of work to do.

With a cunning smile, he stepped forward and disappeared into the foliage.

✳ ✳ ✳

"THE BOSS WILL SEE you now," the CEO's secretary said indifferently to Anton.

Anton mumbled his thanks, knocked on the door anyway, then sheepishly stepped into the inner sanctum of their department.

He approached his boss's desk on rubbery legs, lowering his head like a guilty teenager at the principal's office. He decided to remain standing for a while. Safer that way.

"Good morning, sir," he said in an unsteady voice.

"Morning, Anton," his boss replied without taking his eyes from the monitor. "Please take a seat."

Anton obeyed, perching himself on the very edge of the chair.

With a long, agile index finger, his boss rolled the mouse wheel. His unkind gray-blue eyes followed the events unfolding on the monitor.

Anton didn't dare breathe for fear of distracting him.

The future of his family depended upon this man alone. It was up to him whether they could pay the bills. And the mortgage. And the car loan. And whether Anton could take his family on vacation this coming summer. Whether he could buy a new computer for his son and a new coat for his wife.

Lots of things depended on the man in front of him. Especially in the light of recent events.

"I suppose you already know why you're here?" the director broke the silence.

"Eh, yeah, I.." Anton mumbled. "I'm sorry. I've no idea how it happened. I worked too much. It must have been a momentary lapse."

"I've found a few forum posts for you to take a look at," the director said, ignoring his bleating. "They're the nicest ones. Do you mind if I read them to you?"

Anton heaved a sigh. He'd already spent the entire morning reading forum posts.

"*The admins are rip-off merchants!*" the director read out loud. "*First they announce a cash event and expect everyone to pay good money for new gear. And it turns out to be a freakin' wipeout!*"

His long finger rolled the mouse wheel some more. "Now listen to this. *Can someone explain to me the friggin' purpose of a level-40 NPC in a newb location? How are you supposed to kill him?"*

The director kept reading. Each of the posts he quoted felt like a new nail hammered into Anton's coffin. His forehead erupted in perspiration. A cold trickle of sweat rolled down his spine.

Finally, the director drew his gaze from the monitor and looked Anton in the eye,

"I wonder what happened? Maybe you could you tell me? How come that a newb location which doesn't have provision for players over level 11 has turned into a gauntlet teeming with high-level mobs?"

His voice was perfectly calm. Not a good sign.

When Anton had first heard about the disaster and realized he was the cause of it all, he hadn't known what to do with himself. As he'd driven to work, he'd come up with a thousand excuses, some of which were rather plausible. But now as he sat pinned by the director's steely gaze, he decided to tell him the truth.

"It's not what you're thinking, sir," he began in a timid voice. "I didn't sabotage it on purpose. None of our competition asked me to do that. And had they done so, do you think I'd be sitting here in front of you? I'd have been long gone by now."

The director chuckled. "Oh really? Where to, may I ask? Back to your parents in Siberia? Or to your sister's country cottage? You're a game designer, not James Bond. Please continue."

"Yes... yes, of course you're right," Anton replied, bathing in cold sweat. "There's nothing to tell, really. I tested a mob and thought his Intellect a bit too high. I decided to bring it down to 6. I was entering it when my phone rang, so I must have pressed it twice by mistake. I never noticed it, so I launched the New Year's patch..."

"So it happened a few hours before the New Year?" the director asked.

"Exactly."

"And then we all had a few days off..."

"That's right."

"I see," the director murmured, pensive.

After a while, he shook himself awake. "Very well. Now I understand. You can go now."

Anton's heart fluttered in his chest. "Are you firing me?" he asked weakly.

The director shrugged. "Why should I? Who's gonna work if I fire my workers for every blunder they commit? All this hoo-ha is actually good for us. Now get back to work. From now on, this location is our main priority. Find yourself a few assistants and start planning the launch."

"The launch of what?" Anton asked, dumbfounded.

"Didn't I just tell you? The new event. How should we call it, let me think... How about Terror Slayer?"

TRANSLATED FROM RUSSIAN BY IRENE WOODHEAD AND NEIL P. MAYHEW

REALITY'S EDGE

A LitRPG short story

by Pavel Kornev

The planet of Hephaestus

Exclusive economic zone, property of Geo Resources Corporation

WE ALL CAME ROUND simultaneously. The assault module's touch-down impact kicked the well-choreographed landing algorithm into action. The side hatches opened all at once, releasing us into the soft humid twilight of a rainforest.

Shadows lurked in the midnight blue of the foliage. The only available light was seeping through the breached gap in the tree tops left by our troop carrier.

It took my eyes a while to adapt to the weak light. I crouched, taking cover behind a gnarly tree trunk. The sergeants' voices echoed in my head,

"All clear at Alpha."

"All clear at Bravo."

"All clear at Charlie."

"No enemy activity detected at the landing zone," the AI concluded. "Frequency scanning initiated."

The Lieutenant decided not to wait for the scan results. "Units Alpha and Bravo, advance to your positions and control the perimeter. Unit Charlie, remain behind and guard the modules."

Unit Bravo — that was us!

The area map materialized in my mental view. Our current positions were marked in green. A blue rectangle indicated the location of our future base camp.

"Go!" the Sarge barked.

The sound adapters finally kicked in albeit with a bit of latency. The rustling of branches echoed in my ears, drowning out the wheezing sounds of my labored breath. The spongy, moist layer of fallen leaves squelched underfoot. It must have harbored lots of nasties like snakes and venomous slugs. Still, our light landing suits offered adequate protection from even a considerably more serious enemy. Local beasties were no threat to us.

Let's move it!

We trotted after the two first men on point, trying not to lag too far behind the storm troopers in their heavy armor and the heavily loaded flame thrower operators.

Almost straight away, we came across a clay ravine with a murky yellow stream running along its bed. Judging by the footprints left in the mud, the scouts had waded right through it. We didn't bother to cut the trees to bridge it, either, but crossed the shallow stream in our stride despite its viscous bottom. It had barely slowed me down.

The moment I climbed up the ravine's opposite bank, my helmet's visor became covered in the sticky whitish pollen of the rampant undergrowth. I had to slow down and wait for the ultrasound wipers to clean the armored glass. Immediately the green marker of my assigned position blinked, shifting slightly aside.

"Bravo Five, this is Bravo One," the unit commander spoke. "Advance to your position. Bravo seven, give fire support to Bravo five."

"Affirmative," I replied. I then began climbing the ravine slope sideways, crawling under the creeping vines and wind-fallen tree trunks. Here, trees grew so densely that they couldn't actually fall to the ground. A foot soldier trotted slightly behind me, stepping noiselessly over the thick moss and scanning the area with the short muzzle of his impulse gun.

Glimpsing a blurred movement in the foliage, I took cover behind a tree trunk and raised my modular carbine. After a brief delay, its smart thermal sights sprang into life. A target description appeared in my view,

A gray sloth

Danger status, negligible

I waved to the soldier and continued on my way. Once I'd reached the top of the hill, I dropped onto the acid-blue moss and crawled gingerly to the edge where I froze watchfully, carbine at the ready. Bravo Seven remained behind me, controlling the rear.

Gradually the dots on the map marking the soldiers of our two units aligned with the markers showing their assigned positions.

"Stage One completed," the AI's deadpan voice reported in my head.

"Charlie One, advance," the Lieutenant ordered.

I continued to survey the area. Our landing zone was on the edge of disputed territory. If our employers' competitors got wind of our arrival, they were bound to take countermeasures. And until we set up base camp, a couple of assault bots could make quick work of us.

Soon we heard the strained roaring of the tractors' motors. Two building drones got to work flattening the terrain, scorching all the vegetation and drilling holes in the ground. Controlled by the AI, the robots began by setting up an early warning station, followed by anti-aircraft systems and lastly, the fire support turrets.

The lid of one of the containers opened,

releasing a flock of drones. I glimpsed a new message,

Perimeter control established.

All personnel report to camp," the Lieutenant commanded.

I heaved a sigh of relief. We'd done it by the book.

Bravo Seven began moving back down the slope. He waved his hand, attracting my attention. I gave him a small nod but didn't follow. Instead, I opened my current status.

Mars 5 Private Military Company
Duty location: 2nd Platoon, B COY, 1st Space Marines
Mothership, Galileo Galilei
Code name, Bravo 5
Rank: Class 3 Private
Specialization, Marksman
Implants, 0/5
Salary account, 0

To my disappointment, neither the landing nor the setting up of the camp had counted as action.

Therefore, no bonuses. Damn.

I cussed and requested an environment report.

Planet, Hephaestus
Gravity, 0,95 G
Temperature, 85 F
Humidity, 93%
Atmosphere, provisionally breathable

I didn't like this "provisionally breathable" at all. Still, I tentatively tried to lift the visor. I couldn't.

The air analysis is in process.
Now searching for harmful organisms.

Probably, that's why it was marked provisional.

Picking up my carbine, I climbed back to my feet from the springy moss and began descending toward the camp. Two spider-like building droids scrambled past me, apparently tasked with setting up a supplementary firing position on top of the hill I'd just left. All the other machines were now busy planting the living module and the hospital block into the ground.

As soon as I walked out into the open, Max stepped toward me. "Hi there," he slapped my shoulder. "I thought you'd got yourself stuck in the bog!"

I slapped him back. "Don't hold your breath."

Max and I had trained together as rookies. I knew nothing about the other unit members, only their code names.

Air quality adequate for breathing

I didn't bother to check all the columns of data that followed. I lifted the visor.

The air was heavy and moist. It had an unpleasant smell reminiscent of wet rags with a sickly floral undertone.

Max cringed and lowered his visor, sealing it back again. I decided against it. Air filters were costly. If it got blocked too soon, I'd have to buy a new one with my own money. Which, in my situation, was an utterly unnecessary expense.

The holographic camo dome opened up overhead.

"Fall in!" the Lieutenant ordered.

As soon as we walked out into an already-cleared area, the communications module which was implanted in my temple emitted a deep, intense alarm buzz.

"The air surveillance has discovered evidence of illegal economic activities seven miles north-west," the AI chimed. "Chances of camp being compromised, moderate. Data analysis in progress…"

Data began uploading to my brain in fits

and starts.

Apart from the surveillance drones, the AI also used the satellite feed, so the resulting picture turned out to be remarkably clear.

Illegal prospectors
Enemy force, 15 light soldiers
Numerical strength:
Locals, 10
Humans, 5

"Orders, stop illegal activity," the AI announced after a pause. "Reward, 50,000 credits. In the absence of irreparable losses, the reward will be paid based on each serviceman's personal results."

The others cheered up. We'd thought we'd be stuck with our meager salaries in the middle of nowhere. None of us had expected a side gig.

"Units Alpha and Bravo are assigned to the op," the Lieutenant decided. "Charlie stays on camp guard duty."

Max emitted a happy howl and threw two thumbs-up in the air.

The Sarge punched him in the ribs good-naturedly, just to bring him down a peg. "Let's move it!"

THE ILLEGALS HAD SET UP CAMP by a bend of the murky stream where it spilled out, turning into a small sleepy river with marshy banks. Here, the rainforest had been scorched. The black entrance of a mine gaped in a nearby hill slope.

The guards posted along the perimeter were humans. The natives, seemingly covered in blue down, carried loaded hand barrows out of the mine, heaping up soil samples.

A man in a protective suit poked the moist piles of earth with a sensor, shaking his head in disappointment. Another man stood behind him holding an assault rifle. I could see the muzzle of a heavy pulse gun poking out from behind a tree trunk.

An Alpha support rifleman and myself took up positions on the opposite bank. The others approached the illegals from the rainforest.

I was thirsty after the forced march. I caught my canteen tube between my teeth, took a swig, then rested my carbine on a small tuft and leaned into the sights.

Immediately a voice resounded in my head,

"Bravo Five, this is Alpha Five. The one with the heavy caliber is mine."

He'd already marked the target on the map. I cussed. The Alphas had got here just minutes before us — but that had been plenty of time for them to choose the juiciest targets.

Never mind. Let's see what we've got here.

I pointed the gun at a miner, triggering the

scanner into action.

Native
Name, unknown
Reward, 100 credits
Range, 160 ft
Armor, none
Kill probability, 98.7%

I didn't even bother putting him on the kill list.

A hundred credits was a joke. Let the storm troopers take the natives out if they wanted.

I moved target to the human guard posted by the water's edge. The reward for killing him was twice as much. Still, I had a few more minutes left before the attack so I decided to check out the others.

The burly man with the assault rifle supervising the workers turned out to have a criminal past. I found his name and service record but nothing of promise. He was just small fry. No chance of anyone having put a hit out on him.

Out of curiosity, I checked out the one with the heavy pulse gun. Shit. He was worth four hundred. Not bad for one shot.

Suppressing a jealous sigh, I checked out the guy in the protective suit, the one analyzing the soil samples. No luck there. Even if he was in the database, the scanner had failed to ID his face behind the polarized visor.

I decided to wait a little. You could call it a hunch, I suppose.

No need to hurry. Just wait.

The other unit members had already distributed most of the targets. I scrolled through the data and after some deliberation decided to take out the guy in the protective suit. There was a high chance of him being in charge here which normally entailed an additional reward.

Dr. Walter Bern
Reward, 2000 credits

Holy shit! I very nearly pulled the trigger.

Dr. Bern must have seriously pissed someone off.

"Fire!" the Lieutenant snapped.

The heavy gunner's head exploded in a cloud of crimson. I fired next. The blinding flash of the electric charge hit the face under the raised visor. The helmet flew off the beheaded body and rolled toward the entrance into the mine.

More shots flashed through the air. Some of the natives fell to the ground. One of the soldiers attempted to flee into the forest, shooting back at us as he ran. Still, the noose had closed. No one had made it out.

I fired a second time, aiming at the soldier with the assault rifle, but he collapsed to the ground just as I shot him. The Alpha marksman had just pipped me to it.

I wasn't too upset. I just chuckled.

"Alpha Three and Alpha Four, advance to mop up the area," the Lieutenant ordered.

Two storm troopers in heavy armor came warily out of the undergrowth and headed for the gaping mine entrance.

A flash of blinding light ripped through the darkness within.

A rocket-propelled grenade flew out of the mine and exploded right in the troopers' faces. Both collapsed to the ground.

"Request casualty evacuation!" the Alpha commander shouted.

As if! A light assault bot shot out of the mine and whizzed over the clearing, the hemispheric turret on its back swinging round and loosing off a long burst of fire which cut the Alphas off from their two wounded soldiers.

I zeroed in on the vague outline of their gunman and fired several charges into the turret. The other marksman did the same. The bot banked into a steep turn, trying to escape our fire. But before it could regain altitude, it was hit by a plasma ball launched from the forest.

The clap of the explosion momentarily

deafened me. The bot disintegrated in the air, showering the river with debris.

"Fire into the mine!" a new command snapped. An explosion echoed through the dark entrance, disgorging clouds of white smoke. The ground shuddered underfoot. The mine's wooden struts collapsed. If there was anyone still left there, they had no chance of survival.

Operation complete, the AI reported after the search group had checked all the bodies.

We headed back to camp.

Gradually we began receiving the first updates. Luckily, both wounded troopers had survived. We'd received no penalties for them. I also got another 900 credits for smoking the gunman. According to the AI, I'd hit him before the bot had exploded. It also applied the heavy armor coefficient and added a prompt emergency response bonus.

All in all, counting my share of the unit's reward, I now had fifty-one hundred credits on my account — a sum which, while not exactly mind-boggling, was still extremely close to awesome.

You've been promoted!
New rank, Class 2 Private

What was it today, Christmas?

I laughed, not yet knowing what awaited us all.

BACK IN CAMP, we received a quick checkup from the Doc, refilled ammo and worked out the duty roster. Both Max and I, as well as most Bravos, were excused duty. Once we'd cleared the disinfection chamber, I finally peeled off the hated pressurized suit.

"Meet you by the bridge?" Max asked.

"Yeah," I replied, then climbed into my bunk and closed my eyes.

EARTH 2

WARMTH. SUNLIGHT pouring in through the window. A happy, cozy morning.

Smiling, I sat up on my bed. The awesome city view had cost me, but I really didn't want to slum it in some basement flat. After all, now I could afford it.

I reached for the tablet on the shelf. I could still get to uni on time. I didn't even have breakfast, just grabbed my backpack and rushed out the door.

I didn't have many plans for today. Two lectures at uni, a dinner and a couple of hours free time. Then it was back to Hephaestus.

The lectures were over in a flash. I spent some more time at uni talking to some students I knew, then bought myself a bread roll and set off to see Max. As I waited for him to arrive, I fed all the bread to a bunch of greedy ducks.

Max arrived twenty minutes late. "So what did they cram into your head today?" he asked without even trying to conceal his sarcasm.

"Advanced math," I replied, brushing breadcrumbs from my hands. "And the theory of relativity."

"Well, whatever turns you on. I personally think it's a total waste of money. You'll never need it."

I shook my head. "I might. Just you wait and see."

"Oh, do me a favor. You should be out having fun. And striking up healthy friendships."

"I can always do that."

He smiled knowingly, "Just tell me you decided to level up Intellect."

I gave him a wink. "And Social Status. That's another important one."

"Yeah right. At least I've been to the gym and spent some quality time on the beach. Both Strength and Suntan give great bonuses to Attractiveness. Now all the girls are mine!"

We walked along the embankment until we stopped at one of the cafés. We ordered a pizza, a pasta dish, two steaks and a bottle of wine.

"Same plan?" Max asked, wiping his mouth

with a napkin.

I cast a pensive glance at the calm expanse of the river and the neat little houses on the opposite bank. "Why not?" I tugged at my cuff and glanced at my watch. "We still have time."

He cheered up. "Hah! Today we have something to brag about! Bravos are the best! I made three grand today, can you imagine?"

I didn't say anything. Neither about the five grand nor about my promotion. It would only upset him. "Come on, then!"

✳ ✳ ✳

THE SOLDIER OF FORTUNE Club was a private establishment by referral only. Even so it was absolutely packed. Still, Max had somehow managed to locate a table and even invited over a couple of giggly girls.

"Nika is a radio operator," he said, introducing a curvy brunette. "Martha's a pilot."

"Which ship?" I asked.

"The Wilhelm Tell," Nika replied. "We've been stuck in that asshole of the world for a month now."

"Well, that's your choice!" Max laughed. "You should have joined the space marines! We're ten percent ceremony, the rest is action!"

"Sometimes I wish it was more ceremony

and less action," I said, motioning for the server to approach.

They brought us a bottle of champagne for the girls and two pints of lager, cool and beaded with moisture, for Max and myself. Conversation flowed effortlessly, whatever we could hear of it over the throbbing of the music. Sometimes we had to lean close in to each other in order to hear what the other one was saying. Not that I minded. I leaned toward Martha, Max toward Nika.

When the champagne was finished, Max whispered something in Nika's ear and drew her away from the table — but not to the dance floor as one might have expected but into a narrow side corridor.

Martha's surprised gaze followed them. Then she giggled, covering her mouth with her hand.

I laced my arm around her waist and was about to kiss her.

Her face froze. Then it deformed and disintegrated into a cascade of interference.

The world around me collapsed, becoming a flurry of white noise.

Loss of network connectivity
Router Not Found
Galileo Galilei: Address Not Found

HEPHAESTUS

I SPRANG FROM MY BUNK. I must have bumped my head on something but I didn't feel it. For a brief moment, the two worlds battled for attention in my head until finally, the bright flashes of signal beacons swept away the intoxicating lure of virtuality.

I was back in the real world. Time to live in the here and now.

Everybody around me was busy picking up their weapons. I suited up and ran out of the living module.

A patch of radiant light slowly spread across the dark sky overhead.

Our AI kept squawking like a headless chicken,

"Loss of network connectivity!"

"Loss of radio contact with Galileo Galilei!"

"Loss of visual contact with Galileo Galilei!"

"Bastards!" Max said in a low voice. "I was just going to take her up to the room and show her my etchings. Loss of contact! It'll be loss of libido if I'm not careful!"

I heaved a sigh. "Please. Your real-world misfortunes may merit a visit to the shrink but we seem to have a bigger problem on our hands."

He turned serious. "What do you mean? What can be more important than loss of libido?"

"It looks like someone has just shot down our mothership," I said without taking my eyes from the fading glow overhead. "From now on, we seem to be on our own."

He shuddered, then raised his visor and spat on the ground. "Five minutes, that's all I asked for."

He seemed much more concerned with his failed virtual date than with the real crisis we now had on our hands.

Ironic, don't you think?

TRANSLATED FROM RUSSIAN BY IRENE WOODHEAD AND NEIL P. MAYHEW

Who Fed the Troll?

A TALE FROM
AlterGame SERIES

BY ANDREW NOVAK

WHO FED THE TROLL?

YOUR PARENTS GAVE you your name, and there's nothing you can do about it. All your life, you will be tormented by that name. But your gaming handle — you get to choose that yourself. You might think that you control your character. After all, you created it, starting with its name. Nope. In fact, it's playing you the way it wants. It all starts with the name.

Let's assume that you're a regular guy, an omega from the ghetto. You live in this crowded and rather pathetic little world, post-Gendemic. You gaze in envy and awe at the glittering towers of New Atrium, separated from the ghetto by the waters of the East River. The alpha-citizens, those powerful, civilized beings, ship containers filled with humanitarian aid and game consoles from there. You're waiting for your sixteenth birthday, after which you'll have the privilege to register in Alterra. And you saved your panbucks to be able to play a Scand, because this race has the best starting combat abilities. At last, you are the Scand, Helidon the Intrepid — a novice Warrior and Adventurer. You complete some inconsequential quests, slowly raising your XP, and dream of receiving a quest from a certain

NPC, one of the big shots in the Royal Court.

An incredible dream sparkles before you in the form of a knight in gleaming plate armor, riding on a white horse. Helidon the Intrepid was a fitting name for a knight on a white horse, so that's what you called yourself in Alterra. Nothing had come of it thus far, but you don't lose hope and keep moving step by step toward your dream. Then you see — in reality, not in Alterra — three bastards dragging a girl kicking and screaming behind some trailers. Suddenly you're no longer a nobody from the ghetto, but Helidon the Intrepid in his gleaming plate armor. Yeah, sure, and on his white horse. A noble knight always comes to the aid of a damsel in distress. It turns out that one of the three creeps has a knife... then it becomes clear that the girl hooked up with them herself, but they hadn't agreed on a price beforehand... and then it was too late. You think you control your game character? That you shape his life, starting with the choice of its name? You wish! It was Helidon the Intrepid that drew you into fighting those thugs, was it not? Would you dare do it on your own? That's the thing.

Then it so happens that your knife is longer and sharper than that bastard's knife. The girl isn't even half bad, if you smooth her hair back and wipe the blood from under her broken nose. Which she won't let you do, until she's dressed your wounds and stitched up your slashed sleeve. In other words, until morning. Indeed, she wouldn't mind if you... Helidon the Intrepid, that is... stuck around.

* * *

JACK THE TRAMP didn't fall for such cheap bait. He had always been Jack the Tramp, both in reality and in the game. Jack never believed that he was any kind of Helidon. He knew from the very beginning that the only way not to become a slave to his game character was to be himself inside Alterra. A tramp. A self-reliant man who could pick up and go at a moment's notice.

Even in reality, he didn't limit himself to the boundaries of the ghetto like most omegas. Jack was a Walker, which meant he made regular forays into the Blighted Wasteland and brought back his finds. The odd little things left by a fallen civilization. But Jack somewhat understood Chris, the guy who called his character Helidon. After all, Jack also had a dream, although it wasn't as clearly formed as a white horse and shining armor. Jack wanted something extraordinary. So extraordinary, that he himself could not describe it. Isn't that how it goes? As soon as you put something into words, it starts to control you. Just like Helidon the Intrepid controlled Chris.

"So, Jack, you coming with me to the Dancing Stones?" Chris asked for the second time already.

Jack put aside his reflections on the odd relationship his companion shared with his game personality and paused to think. Chris was inviting him to do some co-op quest together. The task was beyond his ability and he needed a more experienced player. He had shown up at Jack's trailer with this offer.

"You say you want to go through the labyrinth, kill some savages, and take out their shaman? Right, Chris?"

"Yeah. But the quest objective is to destroy the altar and I should be the one to do it. I got the task from the priest of Victorious Ged. You can take the loot, though. It should be pretty decent. If you're lucky, the shaman will drop a Sanguine Ruby. I asked around, poked around in the guides, and looked at the auctions. Nobody's offering a Ruby, which means there's a high likelihood that one will drop now. The savages respawn every hour, so if we fail the first time, we can repeat it. Again and again, until the shaman drops a Sanguine Ruby. All I need is to destroy the altar. They should give some XP for it. The first time, at least. After that, probably not."

Jack smiled, "Still hoping to reach Knight?"

"Well, that, too," Chris gazed off to the side. "It's still a ways off, I know. This is about something else. It's just..."

"Just what?"

"I mean, Lena keeps telling me, 'Cross over to Havian, and we'll play together.' But she's level twenty-two."

Jack nodded. He knew Lena. She was the kind to get something into her head, and harp on it constantly. Maybe that's why Jack never got with her. He didn't like the yapping. Honestly, a lot of people *knew* her, before she became the beautiful lady of Helidon the Intrepid. Now, of course, everything was different. So Jack tried not to think about his acquaintance with Lena while he was with Chris. He limited himself to a brief observation:

"And your level nineteen will pale in comparison?"

"Yeah. I told her that first I need to clear out my old quests from the kingdom of Maxitor. I'd like to at least reach twenty and unlock my second skill, and then move over to Havian."

"I see, I see."

Jack himself had reached level thirty-two, which was why Chris had come to him. According to him, the shaman of the demon-worshipping savages guarding the altar was level thirty. Chris

— that is, Helidon — had no hope of handling him.

"Where is it?"

"In the Wild Lands, beyond the Chand. Where else can you find demon-worshipper shrines?" Chris shrugged his shoulders.

Well, yes, right there. According to game legend, it was where the domain of the King of Demons Azeroth had once been located and where the savages who worshipped the demons still lived.

"Then we'll have to spend money on a teleport," Jack concluded.

Chris looked dispirited. He didn't have the gold for the expensive teleport spell.

"I'm going somewhere the day after tomorrow," Jack informed him. "I mean, I need to go somewhere in real life. So, this needs to be done tomorrow. All right, I'll buy the two teleports."

"You going into the Wasteland?" Chris perked up. "Wanna take me with you?"

Jack had felt right away that he and Chris were alike, so he agreed. Maybe all people who have a dream were kindred in some way. He'd have to think about that. Jack didn't consider himself to be particularly intelligent, but he liked to spend hours turning obscure thoughts around in his head. The Wasteland was just right for it. It was empty out there. Nothing to distract him.

THE PAIR AGREED to meet in-game in the morning. Both had to reach a chapel, the standard entry and exit point in Alterra, during the night. You could leave the game anywhere, of course, but then you would face a fine. To be on the safe side, Jack logged into the Shell and browsed through the guides. The Shell was a collection of sites and mods for Alterra. There was almost nothing about the Dancing Stones apart from the information Chris had posted. The Dancing Stones were an accumulation of enormous granite columns, which moved and shifted every two hours, changing the configuration of the labyrinth. Inside the labyrinth was the heathen temple of the demon Markod. This rancorous monster vanished during the great war between the demons and the dragons, but tribes of NPC savages still paid homage and offered it sacrifices on their altar. Overseeing it all, was the level thirty shaman, who lugged around a heavy gem on his neck. The Sanguine Ruby.

The shaman fed his gem the blood of his victims and collected their strength. Actually, the Sanguine Ruby was a mana accumulator, holding many times more mana than any elixir. A high-level mage would shell out a nice pile of gold for such an item. The main thing was that the Ruby dropped from the shaman, and it only happened about five percent of the time...

When Jack stepped from the semi-darkness of the chapel into the light, Chris was already pacing in front of the door, kicking some poor rock around out of impatience. He wanted it all, and fast.

Jack activated the teleport scroll and a glimmering wall encircled the travelers. Twenty seconds later, the glow fell away. They were standing in the middle of a small courtyard, next to the towering walls of Astra's temple. Astra was a tender-hearted goddess, the protector of all travelers on their journeys. Game legend went that she created the portal magic and the teleports were customarily tied to her temples. Her sanctuary was in the center of a little town situated on the bank of the Chand. Now they needed to go down to the port and hire a boatman who would transport them to the northern shore of the great river, where the Wild Lands began.

"Hey, Jack! Hi!" A lanky, round-shouldered mage in a hooded robe jogged up to him.

Sam Dotter, Achaean
Expertise: 27

Health: 35

"Ah, hey, Sam," Jack replied.

He remembered this player. Air mage. They had bumped into each other a couple of times in the Rusty Rose, the tavern in Svetlograd.

"Jack, listen, can I borrow five gold? I'm short on gold for a teleport. I'll be back tomorrow, just listen!" the mage rattled on. "I designed this spell... it's going to make me rich..."

He began incoherently explaining to Jack that he was about to be well and truly rich. That he just wanted to get to Svetlograd right away, before someone nicked his idea. And once in Svetlograd, he was going to blow up the magical services market because he'd thought of a new gimmick: banners in the form of words hanging in the air. You would be able to choose any font, make the words move, rotate, float like an info window... really, it was just a superb idea. But to make it happen, he needed to be in the largest city on the continent, which was full of shops and stalls, and not in this hole. So Sam had to get to Svetlograd at once, but he was short five gold for the teleport. Just five gold. After all, if he were to go by foot, it would be such a long hike...

In a nutshell, it was just another man with a dream. Jack figured that the loss of five gold wouldn't make a pauper of him. Moreover, he was also due for some riches.

"Okay, wish me luck, Sam," he said. "And take your five gold."

* * *

IT WAS A TWO-HOUR WALK from the shores of the Chand to the Dancing Stones. Along the way, Jack and Chris talked over their strategy and exchanged the info they had dug up in the Shell. The first encounter should happen at the maze entrance, where four savages stood guard. The trick was to attack them a minute before the stones began to move. The four NPCs themselves were not a problem, but inside there were another dozen lurking in the darkness, and they all aggroed at once. That could cause complications. But when the standing stones began their dance, the path would close and the first four could be handled without interference. The important thing was to start at the right time.

So, they calculated a route that would put them at the entrance of the Dancing Stones just before the moment the maze shifted. The Dancing Stones looked impressive. The enormous boulders, like cliff faces, were rough-hewn stone blocks and cylinders standing upright. They formed a perfect circle. Other, even taller, pillars that formed the inner tiers were visible beyond this outer ring. Only thing was, the guards weren't there. No one and nothing, except the standing stones.

"Maybe someone beat us to it?" Chris offered without conviction. "A group of players cleared the guards and now they're going through the labyrinth?"

"Unlikely. Still a few more minutes 'till the shift. If the competition had gone in before the last shift, then the guards should have respawned. Let's wait and watch the stones move," Jack brought up the menu and looked at the timer, "Another four minutes."

They crouched in the bushes and were waiting when the legendary dance of the standing stones began. But it was a bust. Promptly at the scheduled time, a deep, low hum passed over the Dancing Stones and the crags shuddered, but remained in their places. They stirred slightly for a few minutes, their tops swaying, and then the sound stopped. The labyrinth didn't dance.

"And what does that mean?" Chris asked slowly. "Why didn't the stones move? They wiggled, as if they were trying to shift but something's holding them in place. But what?"

"We won't know until we get in there," Jack concluded. "Let's go!"

The stones at the entrance to the maze

were marked with roughly carved runes. Before stepping into the gloom that predominated the interior, they listened closely for a couple of minutes. No sound reached them from the inside. Jack entered first, ready to leap back out into the sunlight at the slightest hint of danger. But all was quiet and empty between the immobile stones. It gave him the impression that the Dancing Stones had been deserted. It didn't work that way. The NPC tribe was bound to this location. They couldn't just pack up and decamp to another place. He and Chris could only hope that the answer was hidden near the altar at the center. And hopefully, it wouldn't kill them. A game death could reduce your level and Chris, in particular, valued his hard-earned experience. Naturally, Jack didn't want to lose any points either. But they already knew for certain that they weren't leaving until they learned what had happened to this location. This place reeked of a mystery, and mysteries brightened the uneventful life of an omega.

Chris went first. He'd copied screenshots of the most frequently recurring maze configurations from the guides to his character's memory. There were 24 in total, but they were able to navigate using the runes carved in the stone, and Chris quickly announced that he had pinned down which configuration the stones were in. Then he led Jack toward the center with a bit more confidence. Rows of tall stones stretched and stretched. The passage between them sunk into the semi-darkness, because the crowns of the huge blocks were thicker than the base, almost like a canopy, and only occasionally allowed sunlight to filter through between them. Jack checked the timer. Wow, they had been wandering for half an hour already, but Chris was still marching ahead and mumbling that they were almost there. He'd been repeating this for a while already.

"Hey, how much farther?"

"We're almost there. We're walking in circles, moving gradually toward the center. It's a kind of spiral, you see?"

Jack was going to crack a snide joke about this being the tenth repetition of "We're almost there", but somewhere nearby, as if behind the closest rock, someone was snoring heavily. The sound was low and so powerful, that Jack thought even the standing stones wobbled. This was clearly not a person snoring.

Chris lowered his voice and whispered, "There's one more circuit, less even, and then we'll be at the innermost circle. But what was that? Did you hear that sound?"

It was the last loop of the annular corridor, and in the narrow cracks between the stone pillars, he thought he saw red flashes of fire. It was a pyre on the demon-worshippers' sacrificial altar. There was nothing else it could be. Jack pressed into a crack between the stones and scanned the center of the labyrinth, the objective of their quest. In the very middle of a perfect circle stood a giant, black stone — the altar. The upper portions were shaped to look like a beast with powerful, clawed paws and a mouth full of protruding fangs stretched in an eerie smile. This, of course, was the demon Markod, the godling of the local tribe. Flames raged on the black stone in front of it. The altar's base was hidden under a pile of skulls. The stones ringed the round hall and maybe only one pillar was toppled. Jack saw something tremendous stretched out in the darkness behind the altar.

The savages were nowhere to be seen. Only the crudely forged poleaxes, pikes, helmets, and shields scattered across the floor spoke to their former presence. All of it had dropped from the savages after they died. Repeatedly. However, who'd done it? And why didn't they gather their loot? What was here was worth a couple hundred gold.

Another thunderous snort rang out and it seemed that it caused the entire labyrinth to shudder and shift, so much so that Jack at first assumed it was a falling rock.

Chris whispered, "Oh, wow. It's a troll! And a big one!"

Trolls differed from other mobs in Alterra in that they grew. With every character they ate, whether it was a player or NPC, they increased in size just a smidgen. When they were killed, they shrank. But to take down a fattened troll, well, that was a challenging task even for a strong group of players, because magic had a negligible effect on them and weapons at that size wouldn't do much, either. What Jack had taken to be a fallen column was actually the leg of a sleeping troll, which would snort and shift from time to time, as directed by its animation.

He looked the behemoth's limbs and lifted a virtual eyebrow. Now, what could this mean...

"Oh, hell! Are you seeing this?" Jack turned to his companion. "Looks like a troll got in while it was still small. It ate the savages, grew, then something happened in the labyrinth. The stones jammed and the troll could no longer escape. So it just hangs around here, and when the tribe of Markod respawns every hour, it slaughters and eats them. And just keeps growing."

"How do we continue?" Chris asked, bewildered.

"Hmm... I don't see the entrance to the central circle. And even if we can get in, we won't be able to destroy the altar. It'll wake up the troll.

Let's go around and check it out from the other side."

They began to walk along the ring of pillars surrounding the cave with the altar. Jack peeked through every crack, looking for the entrance. But the stones continued, one identical, rough-hewn block after another, and the openings between them prevented anyone from squeezing through. Jack spied a spot in the line of pillars on the opposite side, where the stones surrounding the altar parted, but Chris said it was a dead end. A round, dead-end corridor connected to the round cave and led to the res point for players who died in the encounter with the shaman. It was sort of a hollow squiggle, like the tail on the ass of a fat sow. Though, he had never seen such animals the ghetto before. Only the gaunt, wild pigs with sharp fangs that sometimes ran into the outskirts of inhabited areas from the Wasteland. The thought intrigued Jack, but now wasn't the time to think about it. He set it aside for later.

From this perspective, he could get a better look at the troll. Even sitting, the sleeping behemoth was enormous. If it were to stand... it would just be living mountain.

Something began to stir with a rasping sound inside the cave. Jack froze and stared through the narrow crack between the columns.

Ghostly silhouettes of the demon-worshippers began to appear around the altar, pushing aside the piled shields and axes. There were more than three dozen of the athletic, muscular men covered in tattoos, with tall ridges on their shaved heads.

The troll shook itself awake, pulled its giant feet up and slowly began to rise. The figures were becoming more definite, taking on mass and color. The shaman, a stalwart guy with a sparkling scarlet stone in shapeless, embroidered robes was drawn standing next to the altar.

The troll stooped, its hairy paws dangling, and as soon as one warrior took on his finished form, it snapped him up and quickly shoved him into its mouth. There was tremendous proficiency in its movements. The demon-worshippers gave a cry and rushed, axes swinging, at the giant. Their programming dictated that they defend their altar. They hacked, pricked it with spears, howled furiously... and one by one went into the troll's maw. The shaman cast a concussive spell and sent it at the troll, aiming for its head. As he was casting, scarlet whirlwinds swirled up near the Sanguine Ruby on his chest. The shaman was drawing mana from his artifact.

Then Jack noticed an interesting thing — a dim, golden glow on the stone face of one of the columns. He made his way closer. Chris stayed where he was, fascinated by the carnage. Well, it was carnage for the tribe of Markod. For the troll, it was likely just lunch. Neither the warriors' axes nor the magical hammering inconvenienced it. The troll was concentrating on eating.

Jack didn't watch. He was trying to figure out what was glowing on the side of the stone column. When he was close, he realized what it was — a sword hilt. The blade was completely immersed in the textures of the hewn rock. Still, he could read the floating info window:

Tooth of Markod Sword
One-handed melee, magic
Class: Exceptional
Damage: Variable
Wound type: Stabbing, slashing
Durability: Indestructible
Available after level 30

The hilt was radiating the soft, golden glow, like a magical weapon. And Jack realized what happened. The Tooth of Markod was, by all appearances, linked with some sort of hidden quest. No one had worked it out yet because all the previous visitors had been hunting for the Sanguine Ruby. After all, these little stones seemed to be a very sweet prize themselves. But someone had been lucky enough to dislodge the sword from either the shaman or the altar. Although, it had most likely been the troll. That's it! The troll! How long had no one come to the Dancing Stones? A month? Two? And all this time, the savages had respawned hundreds of times, and the troll killed them again and again. Just now, again... that's exactly what happened. The sword had bounced to the side at the very moment when the columns began to move. Maybe it was a condition of the hidden quest? To take out the shaman just at that time?

But it turned out that the troll had done it. The indestructible magical sword had sunk into the column textures when it was knocked from its place, and had jammed the movement program of the Dancing Stones. So much so, that the inner circle — the cave with the altar — was unreachable. He wondered, was it possible to pull the sword free? Jack ran over to the stone with the lodged sword. He stuck his hand through the crack between the columns and stretched as far as he could. Oh, he couldn't... He squeezed in as far as his character's body and the stone textures would allow. He wiggled, squeezed as much as he could — and yes! His fingers closed around the hilt. Jack thought that the sword had moved a little, and if he pulled a bit harder, then the weapon would break free.

But if he did remove this bug, then the

freed columns would probably complete their dance and open the entrance. Then would they have to deal with the troll and the savages? Or not. The giant was already finishing up with the savages. But how to take it on alone?

"Jack, where'd you go? You won't get through," Chris whispered.

Just then, the troll swallowed the last warrior of the tribe of Markod and bent down toward the shaman, who kept sending lightning at his hulking opponent. Every shot was accompanied by a thunderous clap and the troll would wince, but that was all. It scooped the shaman up with its forepaw and popped him into its mouth. Its giant jaws snapped closed and one last magical blast crashed inside its mouth. The behemoth, wincing, began to move its jaws. Its gaze slid thoughtfully over the columns surrounding the hall. It was about to see them. Jack recoiled, ripping from the stone vice, and retreated.

"Quietly, Helidon the Intrepid," he said. "I think I found the thing jamming the labyrinth. But I don't feel like going inside for some reason. What do you think, why is that?"

Chris — Helidon, rather — sighed heavily. It was very clear why going inside was impossible. On the other side of the stones, the troll snuffled and smacked, and every breath of the giant produced an echo in the cave.

"Or should we risk it?"

"We can't take the risk here," Chris breathed. "The res point is inside the cave, in that section of the labyrinth. I told you, remember? But the only exit from there, regardless of the configuration, is through the ring with the altar. In other words, right under the troll's nose. The whole quest in the Dancing Stones is set up so that you have to finish it in one go. Either pass it, or that's it. Bye-bye, you're stuck. Message your friends, call in the cavalry and give them a share of the loot. What do we do, Jack?"

"We're going to have to get creative. I'll work on it tomorrow in the Wasteland. I'll think something up. You're not reconsidering going with me? Then we'll think on it together."

✳ ✳ ✳

THE WASTES DISAPPOINTED CHRIS. Well, of course. There were no damsels in distress here and, therefore, nothing interesting for the noble Helidon. The truth was, there was nothing here at all. Just dust. Sometimes there were concrete fragments, pieces of masonry, some rusted iron... Perhaps the brave knight had hoped for an encounter with monsters, Wasteland beasts, the wild tales of which floated around the ghetto? But Jack knew that his companion was inexperienced, and he did his best to avoid dangerous encounters. So, nothing larger than lizards crossed their path.

Walking along the dusty plain, they talked over their quest in the Dancing Stones, ran through a few ingenious but hopeless ideas about how to avoid an encounter with the troll. But the round hall with the altar was small, with tall stone walls on all sides. There was no way to protect themselves from the giant, whose long arms were a good third of the radius of the cave. It would just take a step, stretch out its paw — and that'd be it, ciao. Wait until it had eaten its fill and fell asleep? But they couldn't destroy the altar without making noise. Moreover, if they freed the maze rotation, it would raise such a ruckus that the troll would surely wake up.

About two hours later, they had reached their goal — a pile of rubble that had once been a house. People used to live here and, as Jack suspected, one of them had also had a dream. Well, maybe not quite a dream, but something like that. Only, it wasn't tied to Alterra because among the rubble of bricks and rotten boards, Jack had once dug up a guitar. Odd as it may seem, it had been intact. God only knew what kind of miracle had saved the instrument from both the Gendemic and the house's destruction.

No one in the ghetto was interested in music, so after discovering it, Jack didn't take it. Instead, he hid it for a better day. Anything was possible. What if it suddenly came in handy? And sure enough, he'd recently found a customer, even for this seemingly useless thing.

While he was digging the instrument out, Chris poked around the ruins and found a piece of junk. He examined it... and cried out in elation. He'd found a heart-shaped keychain, coated with pink enamel. Obviously, he was going to give it to his fair lady.

Jack packed the guitar in canvas, wrapped it with ropes, settled it on his back so that it would be easier to carry, and they started back. More accurately, back to the customer. Only some peculiar people needed a guitar, and that's where Jack led his companion. To a small settlement on the edge of the Waste. Two dozen omegas lived here, led by Old Brian. Good people, light-hearted, although with a lean toward religion. They were out here waiting on the outskirts for Salvation of some kind. Jack couldn't fathom what they meant by that word.

The hermits had settled in the ruins of an institution. At night, they turned on the intact neon sign, which blazed the word "Joy." Initially, the sign had been bigger. There were more words that were supposed to light up, but after the catastrophe, only "Joy" remained.

What had been here before the Gendemic? Maybe a café, maybe something else... Its former purpose was lost in the past and joy had since diminished, but that one-word sign survived. Jack sometimes liked to drop into the hermit village. Here he didn't have to about his problems at home. There were no gang wars, drug dealers, racketeers or any of the other things that colored the lives of omegas in the ghetto. And they had Alterra here — the signal reached out here from New Atrium. The hermits had planted a garden, grew vegetables, and in the evenings, they turned on the sign over their home that read "Joy" and sang. Strange people, but cheerful. They were cheerful in Alterra, too, as a wandering troupe of actors. They wandered the land in their painted caravans, giving performances. Basically, they were tramps in the game, just like Jack himself, even though they led such secluded lives in reality.

Chris scanned the hermit village in amazement. And, why wouldn't he? He'd never seen anything other than the ghetto in his life. Jack winked:

"You'll like it. Good people live here."

Except there wasn't any merriment in the village. The locals looked uncharacteristically dismal. And were all hanging out in reality. Generally, even if the troupe wasn't performing, but was on the road, a few people remained behind in Alterra to direct the wagons. Jack was promptly surrounded by children. They knew that he always brought funny little objects from the Wasteland that served as toys. But their sweet faces were all glum. Jack sensed right away that something wasn't right. Therefore, he asked directly what happened.

"We're in trouble," Brian replied, "in virt. Did you hear about Baron Fang? No? I'd rather not know anything about him either. He ruined the whole game, that little shit."

"Ruined it how?"

"In real life, he's a kid. Young. His daddy supplies dope to all of Queens and he's got the panbucks, so he gave his son a gift for his sixteenth birthday. Bought him a castle. And that little parasite goes by Baron Fang and amuses himself by attacking anyone who shows up on the road near his castle. It started recently, a couple months ago. We hadn't heard about this baron. He hadn't been there before! Well, now he's attacked our caravan. There were ten people in the game. I lucked out. I was in reality at the time, but those who were caught on the road were taken away to the castle, then sent off to work the silver mines. There's no escaping from there. Even if you allow yourself to be killed, the res point is under watch, so you'd go right back to the mines."

"That sucks," Jack nodded. He estimated that ten people — that was roughly the entire company. In other words, almost all the adult population of this building, standing under the "Joy" banner. "You haven't tried talking with the little baron's daddy?"

"The mines belong to his father," Brian said through clenched teeth. "Now, there's no more troupe. Can't even play at all. But it's Alterra... How can I give it up? This game brightens our lives while we wait for Salvation. There you go. There's nothing left."

"Hey, Martha, turn on the sign or something!"

A woman standing in the doorway of the house nodded and went inside. A minute later, the neon letters lit up with a pop. Joy. Brian spit on the ground and smeared the saliva with his boot.

"That's the joy we have here, now," he scoffed. "Either stick around in reality or slave away in the mines. Sorry, Jack, I just can't pay you for the guitar now. But give me a week. I'll go to the market in the ghetto, then we can settle up. Will you wait?"

Jack frowned, but nodded. He didn't doubt

Brian's integrity. He would give Jack the money as soon as he was able to earn it. Although, of course, it wouldn't hurt to have the coins now. What could he come up with to help Brian start performing sooner?

He glanced back at his companion. Well, he had wanted to cheer Chris up by introducing him to these merry hermits... his quest had fallen apart and now the guy's mood was rotten. But Chris wasn't there. Standing in his place was Helidon the Intrepid.

"Damn it, it's not fair!" the brave knight exclaimed. "Listen, Jack and I will help you! We'll make that little beast release those prisoners!

Brian looked at Chris in surprise, then shifted his gaze deliberately to Jack: Really? What was left to say after a performance like that? The brave knight's voice had been clear, everyone standing in front of the building heard him. Everyone gave a start at his promise. Especially the kids for whom Jack had just been unloading the things from his pockets into their outstretched palms. The youngest of the girls, maybe six years old, took Jack by the hand, and peered upward into his eyes:

"Uncle Jack, will you really save mama?"

Jack instinctively stroked the girl's head. He wasn't looking at the kids. He was staring at the electric sign. Joy. There was a thought turning around in his mind... What if... Of course! He recalled Sam Dotter, the air mage, who had borrowed five gold for his invention — signs with glowing words. It would be interesting to try out his invention on Baron Fang, who was robbing everyone who came along on the large road. He'd need to set it up just right. If this job worked out, then it could help out Old Brian and his troupe. Ultimately, the sooner they were released, the sooner they could pay for the guitar.

"Brian, you won't mind if Chris and I use your set to log into Alterra, will you?" No one was playing anyway.

✳ ✳ ✳

JACK FOUND THE AIR MAGE in the Rusty Rose. Where else? This was where he and Jack had met. They both loved this place.

With a sorrowful air, Sam gulped his beer, which gave a small buff in addition to its pleasant taste. Looked like his banner idea hadn't made him rich yet.

"Hi, Sam!" Jack bellowed as he plopped down on the bench across from the mage.

"Ah, Jack... Great. I'll give you your five gold back, just not today, okay? I need just a little time. I swear."

"All right. How's business with the glowing-word banners? I see you've already earned enough for a beer."

Jack was counting on the fact that things hadn't panned out for Sam, and had built his plan around it.

"Just one beer, no more," the mage's face screwed up into a sour grimace. "These shopkeepers have no imagination. They're stuck on their so-called traditions. Just the NPCs with their programs, not the players. 'It should be a board with letters, you know. But a sign hanging in the air — that's not how we do things!' Dolts!"

Sam clung to his mug, washing his irritation down with the buffed beer.

"Yeah," agreed Jack, "You said it, no imagination. But, fortunately, I do have one. Remember you said that you could make the letters any color? Any size? Can you simulate an info window? Make the letters light-turquoise, like NPC stats? The font and size, as well, to a T?"

"You want to forge stats?" Sam asked warily. "Isn't that a violation of the rules?"

"Unfortunately, no," Jack sighed. "And what a shame! Breaking the rules, well, that'd be the best advertising for your invention. Then everyone would be talking only about that. But this might also be a lot of fun. You'll be famous when they find out who was behind our clever deception. And your signs will be a hit. Well, shake on it? You want to get back at this insipid world, don't you? And show them all what real imagination is?"

The conversation with Sam Dotter about the kind of banners they needed for the job cost Jack three mugs of beer. To inspire the mage. After wrapping matters up, he went to the Wanderer mage's shop. This was the NPC who sold teleport scrolls. More expenses! But Jack had already looked into the matter and now he was ready to spend all his gold, provided it would help them pull off this plan. He couldn't wait to see Baron Fang's mug when the final phase of his plan began. This spectacle was certainly going to be worth the money spent.

The portal relocated him to a city called Lamont, which wasn't particularly remarkable, but was located the neighborhood of the baron's castle. It was this way that Brian's troupe of artists had come. And it was where Jack met Brian and Chris. Those two had their own task: Chris should have scouted the castle and surrounding area, while the old actor was to purchase everything they needed for the performance. A seriously cool show needed excellent props, and all the wandering actors' property had fallen into Fang's hands together with their wagons.

The old man complained that he had spent too much buying the equipment. He was ruined as it was! But he had bought everything they needed. Chris also came with good news. He had managed to discover a crumbling temple in the vicinity of the castle. Alterra was rich in these kinds of picturesque ruins. The developers had generously filled the forests and mountains with them. Firstly, it was supposed to be a testament to the rich history of Stoglav and secondly, it was a provision for the future. They could link a newly created dungeon to any ruin. It was only a shame that they weren't making anything new. Instead, they entertained players with the annual Battle — the guild competition. But when the world of Alterra had first been designed, its creators had been concerned with its further development. Simply put, they had found a temple.

"Well, everything's in order," Jack summed up. "A mage, Sam Dotter, will arrive this evening and supply the necessary special effects. Chris will show me the temple, and Brian will prepare everything there. Tomorrow morning, I'll go straight to Baron Fang's castle and demand that he release the prisoners. And, most importantly, he will surely listen. Maybe not right away, but he'll listen."

✳ ✳ ✳

JACK ALWAYS CONSIDERED himself to be a laid-back guy, but right now, lying in the bushes and watching the castle of Baron Fang from afar, he felt an uncharacteristic sense of impatience. You might even say he was agitated. He would have liked to start sooner, but he had to hold back. They couldn't approach the castle before ahead of schedule. What if they had some artifact there that detected the presence of strangers? For someone who robbed people on the road, that sort of artifact would be ideal.

But the flag had unfurled over the tower. It meant the master was in the game. Now it was time. Jack leapt up, worked his way out of the bushes, and headed to the gates.

About forty paces away, he stopped and shouted:

"Hey, baron! Fang, damn you! You captured my buddies and you're about to regret it! If you value your life, let them go, got it?! Otherwise you'll regret it!"

Faces appeared in the arrow slits above the gate. Then they were gone. Well, they were clearly hurrying to the courtyard, where he had dumped his riding mounts from his inventory... The baron, of course, went nuts at the audacity of it. Someone turning up alone at his castle with threats? Alone?! The baron wouldn't let this go, that was for sure. And it was better not to wait while they were there, behind the walls, gathering their wits. Jack had turned and and began running down the road away from the castle before the creak of the gates announced pursuit. He hastily cast a glance over his shoulder. There were six riders. They were, of course, galloping faster than the unmounted runner could go, but they weren't far now from the ruined temple. They wouldn't have time to catch up.

Every ten experience points, players received a new Skill. After thirty, Jack had gotten Sprint, giving him a 30% increase to speed. This blessing lasted only 15 seconds, so now, running away from the riders, Jack was in no hurry to use it. Only when the stamping of his pursuers sounded just a short distance away, practically on his heels, he turned abruptly and plunged into the woods. The riders slowed, their advantage diminished among the trees. But even in the forest, they were still faster. The distance between them had once again reduced to a point, where it seemed to Jack that he could hear the horses' breath over his ear. It was just a little farther, less than a hundred paces to the temple where Brian and the others were waiting.

Here he activated Sprint, which he had called up earlier in the menu hovering to the right, in the corner of his vision. Sprint worked wonderfully. Jack broke away from the riders, who had already begun yelling, imagining that they had caught the troublemaker. He shot like an arrow the rest of the way and broke into the dark interior of the ruined temple. Several seconds later, the baron and his people were at the entrance. They paused for just a moment, long enough for the riders put their horses away into their inventory, and then they were swarming in after Jack.

It was dark inside and the special effects Brian had arranged seemed all the more vivid. Fountains of fiery sparks whizzed from the altar and the old man himself stood amid the jets of flame, dressed in a white priest's mantle. Brian waved his hand at Jack, who was standing transfixed, as if in awe of the current developments. A pillar of flame shot up from under Jack's feet. It was mostly harmless.

You receive damage!
You lose 1 hit point!

Jack, hidden from view by the fire, ducked and dove into a crevice between fragments of chipped stone blocks that littered the floor of the old temple. He sat and kept quiet. It was supposed to look from their perspective as if the priest had incinerated the insolent stranger. An inscription sprung up over Brian's head that, instead of his real stats, read:

Togon Thunderbearer, servant of Ged
Expertise: 100
Health: 100

The old man hid his actual statistics using an artifact that players called a "wipe". It allowed a player to hide his information for a brief time. Players' stats were written in green letters, while NPCs' were a light turquoise. Brian now looked like an NPC. An exceptionally powerful one at that, who clearly held an important role in the game.

Jack peeked cautiously from his hiding spot. Baron Fang and his men stood motionless, wonderstruck by the appearance of the Thunderbearer.

"Greetings, valiant Fang! Welcome, favored of Victorious Ged!" Brian boomed in his well-trained, resonant voice. "I knew, sooner or later, that fate would lead you to this temple. Step away from your companions and hear the will of the God of the Battle, which I will proclaim to you."

The warriors accompanying the baron quickly dispersed, rushing and shoving one another as they tumbled out of the temple. Jack thought that Fang wanted to follow suit, but didn't dare.

"Valiant Fang, favored of Ged," Brian roared, "A glorious fate has befallen you! The Victorious Ged himself bids you to set forth to the circle of Dancing Stones! Find the altar of the foul demon, annihilate the savages, and then receive a reward worthy of the Gods' chosen one. The frozen ring of stones will part for you, and fortune will favor your sword! If you fail to fulfill Ged's wish before sundown today, his judgement will strike you down! Mighty Ged does not tolerate disobedience!"

Jack tensed. The most critical part was beginning. If the magic didn't work...

But lines of text, mimicking an in-game message perfectly, ran in front of the stunned baron.

Attention! You receive the quest "A Feat for the Glory of Ged."
Allotted time to perform the task: 12 hours
Reward: Divine
Accept/Reject

Baron Fang shoved his hand out, accepting the job. The text crafted by the mage Sam Dotter, of course, did not react to it, but didn't the baron have better things to do than notice such minutiae?

The fire spouting from the altar around Brian started to diminish and the old man crouched slowly with it, so that it looked as if he was sinking into the stone. Fang realized that the narrative had ended and darted to the exit in relief, stumbling on broken pieces of carved stone along the way.

A minute later, the outline of Chris's body filled the bright rectangle of the doorway. His mission had been to observe from the outside. If he was here, then Fang and his men had left.

"Hey, you guys alive? How did it go?"

Jack rose from his hiding spot, Brian came out from behind the altar, and Sam Dotter revealed himself in the corner.

"All good here," replied Jack. "Dotter, why do you look unhappy? Now you'll be able to brag that your signs are just as good as an official message. You were equal to the creators of Alterra."

"I'm not sure I want to risk bragging about that," the mage muttered. "That baron's face was... He won't like it if people start to talk."

"Suit yourself. Chris, what happened outside? Did they buy it?"

"Hell, yeah, they did! They bolted for the

castle. Fang asked all his toadies if they knew about the Dancing Stones. One said that the quest seemed to be down because the maze was buggy. And Fang was delighted. Not a glitch, he said, but the devs had prepared a personal quest just for him, Ged's favored. Then they cleared out. In a hurry, too."

"I bet. They have to do it before sundown. Teleports to buy, preparations to make," Brian added. "Jack, are you sure your idea will work?"

"We'll see, we'll see. But let's not waste time! Chris, step aside. We need room for the portal."

"I was thinking," mumbled Helidon, scurrying after Jack, "You're spending a lot on portals and all that for me... All these expenses... Turns out, I kinda drew you into this, huh?"

"Don't sweat it," Jack winked. "For us brave knights, expenses don't matter when we must come to the aid of the weak and oppressed. Well, you ready? Then let's head to the shores of the Chand. We've got to get there and be waiting in the maze before Fang arrives."

✲ ✲ ✲

THEY DIDN'T HAVE to wait long. When someone promises a divine reward, even the laziest person will rush off at full speed. Jack and Chris beat the baron there by less than an hour. Even then, one had to remember that Chris already had floorplan for the labyrinth, but the baron still had to find his way through the winding, twisting corridors. Jack was sitting in the dark next to the pillar that had the sword lodged on the other side, just listening. Yep, they were here. Fang was speaking loudly and confidently. His voice carried through the empty maze.

"I don't want to hear it! Find the entrance. The NPC said, 'The frozen ring of stones will part for you.' So, look harder."

Jack squinted at the timer. Another five minutes until the demon-worshippers respawned. Too early. Let Fang's flunkies keep looking. Which was a mistake. Jack hadn't counted on the search causing them to walk along the ring around the central cave. Well, one of them stumbled on their ambush. He took a couple more steps simply due to inertia and then froze, realizing that these were intruders in front of him. Jack could do nothing. He was stuck between the stone pillars, ready to snatch the hilt of the magical sword. Chris caught on a bit more quickly and attacked. He managed to land a few blows with his sword while his opponent went for his weapon, but the baron's soldier was stronger and his armor was more powerful. Jack jerked to get out from the stone clutches, then stopped. He probably ought to stay here to release the Dancing Stones. What should he do? He cried out:

"Hey, Chris! Press him to the stone! Now!"

Then he grasped the hilt of the Tooth of Markod and yanked. Chris got the hint and when the columns began to move, he rushed the enemy, forcing him back. The soldier's back struck the pillar. As it moved down the passage, the pillar's rotation caused him to lose his balance and it gave Chris the chance to finish the job. As for Jack, he had nearly been flattened between the columns. He hadn't even considered that possibility...

The pillars clamped down on him, began spinning, pulling him deeper into the vice...

You receive damage!
You lose 10 hit points!

But Jack tugged on the hilt and tried to free the sword from the rock textures. The turning columns pulled tighter.

You receive damage!
You lose 10 hit points!

He had liberated half of the blade and jerked himself backward with all his strength.

The stone columns continued to twirl and retract. Little by little, he crawled backward into the passage.

You receive damage!
You lose 7 hit points!

A message ran across his vision, but he didn't bother to read it. He had other concerns right now. One more tug and he was rolling along the floor with the Tooth of Markod, his real quarry.

You receive damage!
You lose 2 hit points!

Chris hopped up, muttering under his breath. He didn't dare yell when Fang was so close and his voice was drowned by the rumble of the moving rocks. The giant pillars rotated, sliding along the floor. They swayed closer and then separated again. Jack listened. There was shouting on the opposite side of the line of rumbling pillars. Ha! That would be Fang and his men entering the altar hall and noticing the troll.

Maybe they wanted to escape? Not a chance. A favorite of Ged the Victorious shouldn't retreat, right? Jack, squeezing his eyes shut for good measure, stuck the sword into a moving stone. Something scraped and began to squeal under his hands... and the rumble of the sliding columns subsided. The cries from the central cave, however, became clearer. The demon-worshipper NPCs began to res at the very moment when the voices of Fang and his companions woke the troll.

When things had quieted down, Jack turned to Chris and whispered:

"Will you show me where the res point is for these losers?"

The res point was a smaller replica of the central hall. There was no altar here and the fire on the floor barely flickered. Fifteen minutes and players from Fang's team began to appear. They looked around as the realized where they'd gone. And then the baron himself resurrected. Only now was Jack able to get a good look at him.

Fang the Baleful, Scand
Expertise: 29
Health: 40

He was just a regular kid, nothing special. Judging by his appearance, you wouldn't be able to tell that he was the kind of sleaze ball that got his kicks by sending travelers to work in his daddy's mine. But just like Chris, he'd chosen a moniker that determined his fate.

"Hey, darling of the Gods!" Jack called from his side of the stone circle surrounding the tiny hall. "How ya doing, Baleful! Want to get out of there?"

"Who are you?" the baron asked grimly.

Both he and his men peered at the face that appeared in the opening between the stone pillars. Reading his stats, of course.

"You don't recognize me? We just talked to you this morning," Jack replied, surprised. "I promised I'd punish you. The only exit from this corridor leads to that cave with the troll. And the entrance there is closed again. You see how this is going to play out?"

"You! I'll find you! I'll find you in reality!" Fang threatened, though his heart wasn't in it. "I'll contact someone in the game to haul me out of here, and I'll deal with you in reality, got it?"

"So, should I leave? Is our conversation over?" inquired Jack. "I thought you were smarter than that... The stone ring in the game is frozen. No one is coming to help you. You're trapped here. And in real life... Well, just try it. It'll be fun, I promise. Mind you, though, there are no res points in real life. Everything is much tougher there. So, enjoy. Look forward to seeing you in reality!"

"Hey, stop! Wait!" the little baron couldn't stand it. "What are you offering?"

"The same thing as this morning. Release my friends from the mine. Once I get a message from them in the Shell, I'll set the stones in motion again. You wait in the hall where the troll is sleeping. As soon as the path opens, you hightail it to the labyrinth exit. The troll will chase you, but you'll be faster since he's cumbersome and will have a tough time squeezing through the narrow corridors. And, as always, the most difficult part will fall to me."

"What difficulty?" one of Fang's soldiers asked sullenly.

"What do you mean? Watching you guys bolt out of here and laughing at you."

❋ ❋ ❋

THE PLAN WORKED perfectly. While the victims were making their way past the sleeping troll, Jack was trying to contain his laughter with some difficulty. It was damned funny watching them slink by, all their stealth bonuses activated, those that had them, looking askance at the giant, sleeping mob. Then Jack grasped the hilt of the Tooth of Markod and... good. This time it was facing out, not inside the round cave, and drawing it out was easier. The rumble of the dancing stone ring roused the troll, but Fang and his men were already racing through the exit as it opened before them. The troll only managed to catch a glimpse of their receding backs. As expected, they aggroed the troll and it plodded after them, lumbering heavily through the passage, which was now too narrow for it.

Jack finally had free range of the cave. Chris withdrew a hammer from his inventory and pounced on the altar with the demon statue. Jack, meanwhile, rummaged through the savages' shields and poleaxes that littered the floor, searching for Sanguine Rubies. At one point, he even began to doubt whether he had enough slots in his backpack.

After Chris had finished his task and checked his growing experience, he asked uncertainly:

"Let's go, huh? I have something to do in reality."

When they made their way out of the Dancing Stones, just a few minutes remained before the savages respawned, so they rushed to escape. The troll was still visible, though it had left the labyrinth right away. It was just so large, it could be seen from a distance across the deserts of the Wild Lands. Jack thought that times were changing for this area. Such a large troll could change the power dynamics here.

"Chris, listen. If you decide to invite me again to these parts, I'll refuse. Now that that behemoth is free, I won't step foot here again."

"All right, I understand," he nodded. "Listen, are you staying with the hermits now or going straight back to your place?"

"I'll stay with them, I think. Why?"

"Well, you know. I have this thing in reality..." Chris hesitated. "Anyway, I'm going straight back, without you."

It was obvious why. Jack just shrugged:

"Suit yourself. Go on. I'm going to stick around in Alterra. I'm in no hurry."

Before long, they came across a temple where they could leave Alterra after. Chris turned toward it. Clearly, he was going to run from the hermit village to his Lena and give her the heart-shaped keychain with pink enamel. How little it took to be able to call oneself Helidon the Intrepid... Jack the Tramp wanted much more. He opened the archive and re-read the message again that had come when he tore the sword out of the stone textures.

Attention! You have completed the hidden quest "Markod's Tooth".
Reward: 100 gold
Reward: Access to the quest "Mysteries of the Dead Demon"

Attention! You receive the quest

"Mysteries of the Dead Demon".
Locate the tomb of the demon Markod.
Enter and read the inscription on Markod's
sarcophagus.
Reward: Unknown
Accept/Reject

Reject it? Yeah, right. He grinned. If you called yourself Jack the Tramp, it meant that your journey never ended.

TRANSLATED FROM RUSSIAN BY KRYSTAL DIEHL

LEVEL UP
FIGHT SETUP

A TALE FROM
LEVEL UP SERIES

BY DAN SUGRALINOV

KNOCKING HIM DOWN WON THE FIRST FIGHT. I WANTED TO WIN ALL THE NEXT ONES, TOO. SO THEY'D LEAVE ME ALONE.

ORSON SCOTT CARD, *ENDER'S GAME*

D ESPITE HIS SCANDINAVIAN ROOTS, Mike Bjornstad Hagen bore no more resemblance to a Viking than a Chihuahua to a Rottweiler. He was better known as Little Mike, Mike Crybaby, Scrawn or just "Hey you wanker!" One name they seemed unable to call him was *Sir*.

The only time it had very nearly happened to him was when he'd applied for a mortgage. "We're very sorry, *Sir*," the bank manager hadn't even tried to conceal a smirk, "but I'm afraid your application didn't go through."

Had Mike known how to fight, he'd have wiped that smirk off his smug face right there and then. He'd been dreaming of his own place ever since he'd moved in with Jess Hagen. The very Jess Hagen who after this sad event had run off with a trucker from Arizona. Or was it Texas? Didn't matter anymore, anyway.

What did matter was that for the next five years, Hagen had never dated another girl. Not because he was so totally taken by Jess, no. It's just that girls weren't that interested, period. Not even Sheila, the fat tattooed lady who ran the comic book shop across the street. Hagen often popped by for a chat whenever she'd stocked up on new issues of *Rat Queens* and *Extremity*.

One night after a couple of drinks at Chuck's Bar, Mike had mustered up enough courage to ask her out to see the latest Avengers flick.

"What's a gorgeous gal like you doing without a cool guy like me?" he asked.

"A cool guy," Sheila repeated. "You mean, *you?*"

She embarked on a lengthy diatribe which basically boiled down to the fact that even if Hagen was the last man on planet Earth, it would still be no reason to go out with him.

Before she could finish, Hagen zoned out — as he always did when faced with rejection — then left the shop.

That was a defense mechanism he'd had since elementary school, the one he'd used whenever someone called him a loser or a jerk or threw food at him in the cafeteria. The "see no evil, hear no evil" sort of thing.

That time, too, he'd staggered out of the shop and never entered it again. Which meant he had to order his comic books online these days which wasn't the same thing, as you can well imagine.

He didn't bear a grudge against Sheila, God forbid. He just couldn't force himself to face her anymore. He couldn't stand the humiliation.

That night, he'd just come home from work. It was Thanksgiving Friday.

Hagen never cared for all those family celebrations. He'd never known his father. His mother had died a few years earlier. She'd been the only person who'd actually loved him.

Some might say she'd loved him a little bit too much. Baby Mike tended to disagree. She'd been his parent, his best friend and a wise advisor he could turn to in order to discuss his problems. At some point, Jess too had aspired to the role — but then she'd walked out on him, and by the time Hagen had come back to Mom from his first "trip round the block" as Uncle Peter had called it, she was already terminally ill. The doctors had estimated her recovery chances at 30% but what was the point if she and Hagen couldn't afford the treatment anyway? And even if they could, that meant moving to Philadelphia while his job kept him here. If he quit, what would have happened to them then?

Mom had died a terrible agonizing death. For the last few days, Hagen never left her side, holding her hand and choking on his silent tears.

For the first year after her death, he had to learn how to take care of himself. Hagen had to cook and use the laundromat, he even did his best to wake up earlier than usual. Still, no woman seemed to be in a hurry to take Mom's place looking after her hapless son.

That was the second time in his life that he'd been forced to make his own decisions (the first one being when he'd decided to move in with Jess). He fully intended to soldier on and stick it out. He may not have had too many ambitions to show for his age, but he had to learn to live on his own, even if just to go with the flow.

And learn he did. He replaced Mom's cooking with Chinese takeaways, took weekly trips to the laundromat and set his alarm clock every night.

His life seemed to have fallen into a pattern. Still, he missed Mom a lot.

The only other family he'd even known was Mom's big brother, Uncle Peter. An ex-marine with tours of Iraq and Afghanistan to his name, he'd tried to add his two cents to little Hagen's upbringing. On his rare leaves, Uncle Peter had tried to add a man's touch to the boy's meager curriculum, even though it hadn't amounted to much.

In the end, even Uncle Peter had given up on him, limiting his lessons to three major things indispensable for any man: how to fight back, how to help his mother and never to yammer and moan.

He'd failed miserably on all three counts.

Hagen was scared of pain to the point of becoming hysterical. When faced with a chance to fight back, he'd rather flee or surrender on the spot. True, he was dreaming of learning to fight like Demetrious "Mighty Mouse" Johnson, the legendary UFC flyweight champion. Five foot three and weighing in at 125 lb, he'd defended his title eleven times!

Little Hagen often imagined himself stepping into the famous fighter's shoes: Mike "Crybaby" Hagen, five foot two and weighing in at 123 pounds, the new UFC champion. He'd show 'em all!

As for helping his Mom, it had been boring — much more boring than playing with his console or reading comic books. Besides, she'd never really asked him about anything.

And as for not moaning, Hagen had given it his best shot and failed miserably. Tears came to his eyes naturally whenever someone said something demeaning to him. Even now when he was almost thirty, he often couldn't help it. Like with that idiot Mr. Goretsky, the wretched shop customer.

Hagen was the only employee in their whole computer shop who actually knew something about computers. So whenever Mr. Goretsky caught yet another virus while browsing seedy adult sites, who did they call to help him?

That's right, they called Crybaby Mike.

Still, Mr. Goretsky's advanced aggro skills (namely, Bullying and Hostility) allowed him to regularly accuse Hagen of having infected his laptop.

That particular Friday, Mr. Goretsky had come to see Hagen again. He didn't mince words. He showered Hagen with expletives through a heavy halitosis of onions and garlic. "Shit for brains" and "useless prick" were the nicest words in his vocabulary spiced with a wide array of much more offensive epithets.

It's easy for him to bully people, Hagen thought as tears rolled down his cheeks. *It's not a problem insulting someone when you're seven foot tall and your forearms are wider than my thighs.*

Friday or not, it had been one hell of a day. After work, Hagen headed for Chuck's Bar intending to get drunk and hopefully pick up a girl. He even noticed one sitting on her own and downing straight whisky by the glass. Still, after a few half-hearted attempts, he didn't dare approach her. And when he finally lifted his butt from the chair, she was already guffawing at some smartass guy's jokes, a sleazy type in a business suit.

In the end, Hagen pumped himself with liquor and headed home, feeling sorry for himself.

Once back in his den, he played his favorite

fighting game on PlayStation, imagining he was thrashing the shit out of that bastard Goretsky. Then he checked out some horror flick on cable and finally fell asleep.

He awoke just before midnight to take a leak.

That's when it all happened.

The entire route from his bed to the bathroom was a dozen feet at most. Still, Hagen failed to navigate it without tripping several times. True, agility had never been his forte — but this had never happened to him before. He could always make it from his bed to the can, no matter how drunk.

This time, however, as he scrambled to his feet and staggered across the room, the world sort of blinked. For a couple of seconds, he felt suspended at the center of a great dark nothing which was devoid of gravity, sounds, smells or light. The air didn't move as he breathed. He didn't even sense his own body anymore.

When the world finally returned, his body acted on impulse, obeying the flood of panicky commands sent by his brain. He pummeled the air with his arms as he tried to regain balance, gasping and searching for some kind of support, until he finally collapsed on the floor. In doing so, he hit his chin and very nearly bit his tongue.

For a while, he didn't dare get up. The

world around him was spinning — a nasty feeling familiar to everyone who's ever been drunk as a skunk. A flurry of white specks flickered before his eyes, resembling some weird Predator-like symbols.

Finally Hagen quietened down, trying to suppress the bouts of nausea. He rolled onto his back and closed his eyes, patiently waiting to feel better.

Still, the flurry of white specks kept racing chaotically across his field of vision.

He tried to blink them out. He rubbed his eyes. It didn't work. Apparently, the specks' nature wasn't physiological.

After about ten minutes, they finally disappeared. Hagen regained his breathing and scrambled back to his feet. Slowly he made it to the bathroom, gingerly placing one foot in front of the other, until he finally did what he'd intended to do all along.

He returned to the room, peeled his clothes off, dumped them on the floor and collapsed onto his bed.

The next morning he awoke parched. It was Saturday. At least he didn't have to go to work.

He stretched, cracking his joints, then stumbled toward the fridge. He finished off the last carton of orange juice in one gulp. He really needed to do some shopping soon.

Hagen slumped onto a chair in front of the small table, half of which was heaped high with computer parts.

He stared at them blankly. There was something not right with him. And it had nothing to do with the six pints he'd drunk last night.

A tiny object kept hovering in his view ever since he'd awoken. It looked suspiciously like a computer icon.

At first he thought it was just a speck of dirt. He blinked several times but it was still there. In fact, it seemed to have grown.

He needed to rinse his eyes.

Hagen climbed back to his feet and staggered into the bathroom. He washed his face. In actual fact, he could do with a shave.

That was something he didn't do too often. Pointless wasting time and razor blades. Having said that... why not?

Surprised by his own impulse, Hagen poured some gel into his cupped hand and began spreading it on his face, staring into the mirror as he did so.

That's when it finally dawned on him. Two lines of text hovered over his disheveled reflection, making him appear like some goddamn computer game character.

Mike "Crybaby" Hagen

Age, 29
Level, 1

Hagen raised his foam-covered hand and ran it over his head. It went right through the text without sensing any resistance.

What the hell?

He studied the mirror but found no evidence of anyone having tampered with it.

What was it, then? Was he seeing things?

He shrank away from the mirror. The thought made him weak at the knees. Hagen sank to the floor.

Could it be cancer? Just like his mom's? In which case...

Oh no. He wasn't even thirty. He still had his whole life to live. True, he'd known no joy all those years — but at least he'd believed he could always catch up with the others later. He used to think he'd had loads of time: enough to turn himself into the next Mighty Mouse.

And what about women? The only woman he'd ever had was Jess. And now he might never have enough time to bed another one.

At this thought, Hagen dissolved in muted tears.

He sobbed with abandon until finally he wailed, desperate for his Mom's hugs. It felt as if his very life was dwindling with every tear he shed.

Depression overcame him, dark and gloomy. He didn't feel like doing anything anymore. Hagen washed away the tears with the remains of the shaving foam, toweled his face dry and staggered back to bed.

He closed his eyes and stayed motionless until evening. His body had turned numb. His muscles demanded movement. Finally, the thoughts of his impending death had faded to the back of his mind, replaced by thirst, hunger and a sudden teeth-gnashing will to live.

He needed to look into it all.

He sprang from the bed, stretched and sat up, peering into the darkness of his apartment.

Wherever he looked, there seemed to be a small object hovering in the corner of his eye. It looked almost like a 3D theater experience, minus the glasses.

He tried to focus on the flat icon-like object. It seemed to have reacted to his gaze. Slowly it began to rotate like a Christmas tree bauble touched by a curious cat.

The object turned out to be a cube. A picture of a human head was drawn on each of its sides. When the cube turned at a particular angle, the picture seemed to resemble Hagen himself.

Unwittingly Hagen reached out, trying to

touch it. As if accepting the invitation, the cube grew in size, approaching, until it brushed the tips of his fingers.

Hagen sensed its lightweight touch. Immediately the cube twitched and opened up, unfolding to form a computer window.

If this was a hallucination, it sure was a good one!

The entire height of the window was taken up by a 3D image of Hagen himself, bare-torsoed and in boxing shorts, standing in a combat stance. He looked admittedly funny with his scraggy, raw-boned frame and a beastly look on his face.

Below, several lines of text were printed on a small plaque. It was divided into two columns and appeared to be clickable.

The first column said,

Mike "Crybaby" Hagen
Age, 29
Level, 1
Health, 4000 pt.
Ratio of fights/wins, 0/0
Weight, 123 lb
Height, 5'2"

Mike reread the text. As he scrutinized each line, a respective prompt popped up, offering more information. When he focused on his own name, the prompt listed his date and place of birth, nationality, social security number and current address.

The second prompt explained how levels were gained. You received XP for fighting. The kind of fighting didn't matter. It could be a street brawl or a sparring practice. The only restriction was, your opponent had to be an adult. In order to progress to the next level, you had to win as many fights as you'd already done in order to progress to your current level. You didn't get any XP when you were defeated but you didn't lose any, either. A victory over a stronger opponent was supposed to speed up your progress but no details of that were given.

The second column seemed to show his physical stats,

> *Main characteristics*
> *Strength, 1*
> *Agility, 2*
> *Stamina, 4*

Hagen reread the list, focusing on each entry,

> *1 pt. Strength equals 10% of an average human being's physical strength*

Affects the damage dealt

1 pt. Agility equals 10% of an average human being's physical agility
Affects accuracy and dodging chances

1 pt. Stamina equals 10% of an average human being's physical stamina
Affects health and its regeneration, as well as the fatigue rate during physical activity

All this made one thing painfully clear to Hagen: he was lamentably weak, ten times weaker than an average person. He was also five times clumsier and had 2.5 times less stamina.

None of this was new to him, anyway. He'd always known this, even as a snotty toddler.

What was much more interesting, however, was that he only needed one win in order to progress to the next level. The opponent could be anyone. Hagen received one stat point for each level which he could then invest in either Strength, Agility, or Stamina. He also received one skill point.

Which meant that actual athletic practice wasn't the only way to level up his skills and the gym wasn't the only place to improve his Strength.

Having considered that, he moved to the

next tab.

It wasn't active but it too portrayed a silhouette of Hagen attacking his opponent.

Mike unhesitantly poked the screen with his finger. A row of icons appeared, bearing the names of various fighting skills. A punch, an uppercut, several types of kicks, as well as some locks and clinches. Almost all of the icons were gray and marked with the picture of a lock.

The only icon which was colorful and active was the one with the simple punch. The number 1 glowed green at the icon's lower right corner.

Hagen focused on the icon. A prompt popped into view,

Simple Punch
Level, 1
Damage, 100
In order to improve the skill, you need to practice it.

A progress bar below the message was filled 2%.

For a hallucination, this was way too elaborate. Still, it might be a good idea to see the doctor on Monday. A brain scan wouldn't hurt, just in case.

Driven by impulse, Hagen assumed a miserable excuse for a combat stance and began punching the air in front of him. Right jab, left, right, left. He performed about a hundred of those, imagining himself shadow-boxing and very nearly tripping over his gamepad in the process. Sweaty and out of breath, he finally checked the progress bar.

Yes! It had been worth it!

The bar had grown visibly. It now showed 3%.

He kept punching the air until late at night, only stopping to use the bathroom and have a quick bite to eat. His low Stamina levels had backfired on him now: he got out of steam really quickly. New bars had appeared under the icon with his portrait (which still showed level 1),: a Health counter and a Vigor one. Whenever he went down on Vigor, he felt so wasted he couldn't even lift his arms.

Health points weren't fictional, either. Hagen punched the wall just to check it. As he squirmed in pain, a new system message informed him of 100 pt. damage received. The green Health bar seemed to have shrunk a little.

By midnight, Hagen had made level two in Simple Punch. A flame enveloped his hands, looking frighteningly real. It warmed his fingers without burning them.

Hagen didn't even get the chance to become properly scared. Exhausted and dripping sweat, he smiled happily as he watched the flames die. A new system message was glowing before his eyes,

Congratulations! You've received a new skill level!
Skill name, Simple Punch

Hagen opened his stats tab. Indeed, the skill's level had grown.

Simple Punch
Level, 2
Damage, 200
In order to improve the skill, you need to practice it.

The Damage had grown, too. This was incredible.

Now he was consumed by the gaming frenzy so familiar to anyone who'd ever leveled up their char.

The first sunrays had already reached into the room through the half-open blinds to find him still pummeling the air, noticing in exasperation that every 1% he now earned required a hundred more punches. He now needed 200 punches to improve his skill 1%. At level 1, it had been 100. Level 3 would probably require 300 punches.

And that wasn't the only quirk of this weird System (as he'd come to call it) which now presented the world to him through a gaming interface. Earlier that morning, he'd been so starved that he'd rummaged through his empty fridge and ordered two Mexicanas from a 24-hour pizza joint. His exhausted body demanded to be fed ASAP. The moment the door closed behind the delivery guy, he devoured both, purring with pleasure like a cat over cream.

Once he'd emptied both boxes and picked all the loose crumbs and olives, the System offered a new message,

Nutrients consumed:
Calories, 2536
Protein, 7.39 oz
Fat, 6.03 oz
Carbohydrates, 12,86 oz

The Hunger debuff which had been hovering in the top right corner of his vision had now disappeared, replaced by a new one: Lack of Sleep with -25% to Vigor.

By sunrise, Lack of Sleep had reached level 2, with -50% to Vigor. Hagen noticed that his bouts of energy depleted much faster now. He was forced to take frequent breaks in order to restore.

Just as his Simple Punch bar had reached 67%, the Lack of Sleep suddenly jumped to level 4, adding a Fatigue debuff to its effects. Hagen's Vigor plummeted. Although technically the Fatigue debuff didn't detract from any of his stats, it prevented Vigor from regenerating.

At that point, he was forced to finally go to bed.

Not that Hagen was upset about it. His entire body ached. His arms were rubbery. His eyes felt as if someone had rubbed sand into them. The moment his head touched the pillow, he fell into a deep comatose sleep.

✳ ✳ ✳

ON MONDAY, HAGEN went to thc clinic where he complained of seeing weird things. The doctor chuckled, then sent him to have an MRI brain scan.

The scan found nothing wrong with his head. The doctor qualified his condition as overwork, prescribed an antidepressant and suggested he took a break from his job.

Hagen had never taken a single day off before. Surprisingly, his boss took the news seriously and even said he could take as much time off as he needed. For once, Hagen's computer skills did him a good turn.

When Hagen was about to leave the shop, Mr. Goretsky walked through the front door to fetch his laptop.

Hagen watched with a badly concealed gloat as Mr. Goretsky searched the shop with his stare, looking for him. Oh well. He'd have to abstain from visiting his favorite adult sites for a while, wouldn't he?

A prompt hovered over Mr. Goretsky's head,

> *Greg "Buffalo" Goretsky*
> *Age, 38*
> *Level, 4*
> *Health, 16000 pt.*
> *Ratio of fights/wins, 9/6*
> *Weight, 250.8 lb*
> *Height, 6'4"*

Oh wow. He had 16,000 Health points! Four times more than Hagen had! Which also meant that Mr. Goretsky had 16 pt. Stamina.

Hagen tried to check out the man's other stats but failed. When he attempted to open Goretsky's profile, the system offered a weird warning,

> *The current level of your Insight skill is*

insufficient to access the information you've requested.

Insight skill? He'd never thought he'd had any. He might have to look into it later.

He could already see that he didn't stand a chance against the man. Even with his doubled damage, he'd have to deal him at least eighty punches which was highly unlikely.

"There you are, shit for brains!"

Hagen started. Mr. Goretsky had somehow spotted him and was now towering over him.

Mechanically Hagen shrank. Mr. Goretsky must have noticed it as he added with a crooked smile,

"Come on, get my laptop now, chop chop!"

Hagen forced his face into a mask of friendliness, "Good morning, Mr. Goretsky!"

"It won't be so good for you if you don't hurry up! Come on, get my laptop now, I'm gonna check it. This time I'm gonna make sure you've fixed it properly!"

"Sorry, Sir, but I'm off work today," Hagen said. "You need to speak to some other assistant."

He wondered how much Punch Force it might take to knock out that beast. Hagen's math skills were pretty good. The calculation results didn't please him though. Level 160! That would take him ten years of twelve-hour practice, day in day out.

Still, this calculation was based on his current Strength level. And once he'd raised it a little...

"Wassup, you wanker? Can't put your brain in gear? Should I give you a good whack to reboot your head, you moron?"

Hagen came back to reality. He opened his eyes, only to discover Goretsky's distorted face within inches from his own, spitting insults at him.

Hagen wiped his face. All the other shop assistants and even a couple of customers had arrived at the scene, attracted by Goretsky's screaming. They stared at the two with concern without actually trying to intervene.

Someone called the manager.

"I'm sorry, Sir," Hagen invested what was left of his self-respect into his trembling voice, "but I have to ask you to stop shouting at me. At the moment, I'm not working here. Please ask another assistant to help you."

"You *are* an idiot, aren't you?" Goretsky said, faking surprise. "I don't give a shit if you don't work here! You're here now. You took my computer. You were supposed to have fixed it. So you're the one responsible for it!"

"Are you okay, sir?" Lexa the senior

manager flashed Goretsky one of her signature smiles. "Allow me to help you," she motioned Goretsky aside. "You've got the receipt with you, haven't you? I'll fetch your computer straight away."

Goretsky cast her an appraising look. He seemed to be happy with this substitution. "You're one lucky guy to work with these kinds of girls," he said, staring heavily at Hagen.

As Lexa steered Goretsky away from the scene, she turned to Hagen and shooed him inconspicuously away.

He nodded and headed for the exit. His ears burned.

"Not good. This is so not good," he mumbled.

Just his luck to have had Lexa witness his humiliation, the only girl in the shop who didn't treat him like a piece of shit. She really appreciated Hagen's ability to diagnose computer problems and fix them in no time, and always had a kind word for him as she praised his handiwork. She was three years his junior, but she was senior manager already. A very pretty girl. What a shame he had no chance with her.

The moment he stepped out of the shop, he forgot everything about Lexa. He had a new goal now, a digital one and a clear-cut one at that.

One thing he desired most in his life —

even more than he'd desired Jess after their first date — was to learn how to fight. Not fight even, because that must have hurt a lot, but to be able to knock any opponent out with one blow. A bit like Brad Pitt's "One Punch" Mickey did in Guy Ritchie's movie.

Hagen couldn't stand pain, that's for sure. He imagined the furious Goretsky punch his face and shuddered.

When he'd awoken late in the afternoon after his marathon punching practice, he'd ached all over — but he felt surprisingly good. He tried to practice some more but his whole body was seized with agonizing pain. Not knowing what to do with himself, he decided to study the mysterious interface.

By squinting his eyes each and every which way, he'd discovered a few more icons he hadn't noticed before. He managed to focus on them and drag them onto the interface panel.

One of them was called *About This Software*. Hagen clicked it.

Augmented Reality!7.2 Home Edition
Copyright © First Martian Company, Ltd. 2101-2118
All rights reserved
Registered owner: Mike Bjornstad Hagen

S/N L5L-7702B-1412010
One-year single user license
Account type, Premium
Activation date, 24.11.2018 09:00.
Expiration date, 24.11.2019 08:59.

Hagen tried to research the mysterious company. Still, Google didn't seem to know anything about either a First Martian Company, Ltd or an "Augmented Reality! 7.2".

That hadn't baffled Hagen for too long. He'd read too many comic books to be so easily surprised. The answer came naturally to him. This must have been a game from the future which had somehow ended up in his head. How simple was that? A hundred years from now, every person on planet Earth — or Mars, even, judging by the game's name — would probably have such thingies implanted in their brains.

The main thing was, his time in the game was limited. He only had a one-year license. So if he wanted to make his childhood dream come true, he had to act fast.

He spent another hour fiddling with the settings until he set up the interface exactly as he liked it. He'd discovered loads of useful little apps, like an alarm clock which woke you up during your lightest sleep stage which made awakening the easiest, or all sorts of data you could monitor: time, air temperature, heart rate, or calories burned. True, you already had most of these functions in your smartphone, but the inner interface made it so much easier.

Mike also pinned the main stat bars to his inner view: Strength, Agility and Stamina. Overcoming the pain, he then spent half an hour punching the air. All three stats had grown. True, they didn't progress as fast as Simple Punch, but still. Especially Stamina, which grew the fastest whenever he kept practicing on low Vigor numbers, panting, his chest burning, his shoulders leaden.

He'd discovered two more icons. One was marked *Available Updates*; the other, *Technical Support*.

He tried both but received an identical message,

Impossible to establish connection with the updates server.

It appears to be unavailable.

Please check your universal information field connection settings.

A universal information field. Were they serious? Was this some kind of Internet of the future?

Having finished with the interface, Hagen

decided to practice some more. He switched the TV to some music channel, stood at the center of the room and began showering his imaginary opponent with blows. The opponent in question was in fact Mr. Goretsky.

He kept practicing until late at night. Exhausted, he took a shower, climbed into bed and slept like a log till Monday morning.

That had been his Sunday. On Monday, he visited the clinic, then returned to his practice. He pummeled the air like crazy, trying to develop speed. He did more of the same on Tuesday. On Wednesday night, he had an epiphany.

Hagen fashioned a punch bag out of a couch cushion and hung it on a hook on the wall. To do that, he'd had to remove the painting that used to grace the hook with its presence, namely, *Sunset over the Atlantic*. The painting appeared to be a collection of angular shapes in acid colors. Personally, Hagen had always thought it depicted a female gorilla in a hat and an evening dress. No matter how hard he'd looked, he'd never managed to see anything even remotely resembling a sunset, Atlantic or otherwise.

He soon discovered that by punching the cushion instead of thin air he could level up the skill much faster.

By the end of the week he'd made level 8 of Simple Punch. That brought damage to 1600 because his Strength had grown accordingly. At that point, he had another epiphany.

He had to go to a boxing gym.

Luckily, he knew one nearby, owned by an old Mexican guy.

Early Sunday morning, Hagen made his first appearance at Guillermo Ochoa's Boxing Club.

Mr. Ochoa didn't bat an eyelid seeing the puny individual who'd arrived at his gym's doorstep. His face didn't even twitch when this miserable excuse for a hobbit announced he wanted to train. But when his scrawny new customer had explained he intended to work out at least twelve hours a day every day, Mr Ochoa couldn't help it any longer. He exploded into laughter.

That didn't seem to baffle his new client. He didn't lower his intense blue eyes as he waited patiently for the old man to finish laughing without betraying his anger. Because he *was* angry, this weird customer. Mr. Ochoa knew enough about the human race to see that. Even when he snorted so hard laughing that snot flew from his large crooked nose, the young man didn't betray his impatience. He waited for the gym owner to finish laughing, then pulled a wad of crumpled bank notes from his pocket,

"Will this be enough to pay for the first

month?"

Mr. Ochoa grew serious. He counted the money and nodded. "That's enough for three months. And if you help me to clean the place in the evenings, I could make it six months."

He proffered his hand to the young man, 'Welcome to my boxing club- what's your name again?"

"Mike Hagen," the young man replied, shaking his hand. "But you can call me Mickey."

"Very well, Mickey. Welcome to my club. When are you going to start? If you'd like to-"

"How about now?" the hobbit interrupted him.

"*Now*?" Mr. Ochoa choked on his words.

"Yes, now."

The gym's owner looked him over, then swept his hand around the empty gym. "Help yourself. The locker room's over there."

Was it Hagen's imagination or had he noted a hint of respect in the old man's voice? It had never happened to him before. He actually might get used to it.

Five minutes later, Hagen was enthusiastically pummeling the punch bag. His enormous Hawaiian print shorts didn't do his matchstick legs any favors. His oversize T-shirt did little to conceal his feeble frame.

The punch bag didn't even budge under his

clumsy blows. His bright blue eyes, however, stared intently from under his frowning eyebrows. Little Mickey meant business, you could see that.

Which was why by mid-afternoon, Mr. Ochoa felt sorry for the boy and went to help him out with his technique.

✳ ✳ ✳

BY THE END of the second week in the gym, Hagen had felt much stronger, both physically and mentally. As it had turned out, his Premium account came with a triple leveling booster to all skills and stats. Hagen had found this out while perusing the Help section. The game's virtual assistant had proved much more advanced and efficient than its current analogs. It easily recognized any spoken questions and gave prompt and accurate answers.

That's how Hagen had found out that each of his combat skills gave him an additional ability every time it reached a factor of ten. For instance, level 10 of his Simple Punch gave him a 50% probability of punching through any block. At level 30, this probability turned into a 100% certainty.

Hagen had the chance to witness it by the end of his first week of training when he'd finally reached level 10 of the only skill he had.

Apart from several punch bags and a boxing ring, Mr. Ochoa's gym was also equipped with a few weights. On Hagen's second day, the old man had taken him there and shown him a few simple exercises for various muscle groups. This addition of weight training to his boxing routine — plus the fact that he was constantly ravenous now — had noticeably accelerated his Strength development.

These days, Hagen consumed beef, chicken and fish by the pound and finally bought a large pot of protein powder. Now he drank at least three protein shakes a day on top of his usual diet. The training left him permanently hungry, especially at night. He'd wake up, make himself a protein shake, drink it and go back to bed.

Logically, he'd gained several pounds in those couple of weeks. He'd actually grown a little.

By the end of his first month, his stats looked like this,

Mike "Crybaby" Hagen
Age, 29
Health, 9000 pt
Ratio of fights/wins 0/0
Weight, 134,2 lb
Height, 5'4"

Main characteristics,
Strength, 5
Agility, 4
Stamina, 9

He'd gained ten pounds and improved all of his stats. He was stronger now. His greater Stamina gave him better survival chances, allowing him more time to come up with a game-changing punch. Agility was the only stat that seemed to lag behind.

Hagen had decided against activating any more skills for the time being, investing all his time and effort into Simple Punch alone. If he managed to level it high enough, he'd be able to perform lightning blows his opponent simply couldn't dodge.

Simple Punch
Level, 16
Damage, 8000
+50% to your ability to penetrate any block
In order to improve the skill, you need to practice it.

These incredible damage numbers were the result of his Strength coefficient. Had his Strength still been level 1, he'd have had 1,600 pt. damage: a hundred per level. Now, however, you had to multiply 1,600 by 5.

And 8,000 damage was a power to be reckoned with! Despite his improved Stamina, he could have knocked himself out with a single blow. And as for the old Mike Hagen.... the new one would have made mincemeat out of him.

A month after he'd left the computer shop, Hagen walked over to Mr. Ochoa.

"I'm afraid, my time off is over," he said. "Tomorrow I'm going back to work. I'll see you in the evening."

The old man shrugged. "You come when you can."

"Thank you, sir. I think I'm finished for today-"

"Wait a sec," the gym owner pointed to a dark corner where a bronze-skinned guy with a plain, forgettable face was busy shadow-fighting. "Fancy taking on Juan for a bit of sparring? He's new too. He's been at it for six months already but he only comes here a few times a week if at all. He's not like you. All my other clients are serious athletes so I just can't find him a sparring partner."

Hagen shrugged. "Why not?"

He focused on his opponent.

Juan Manuel Guerrero
Age, 26

Level, 2
Health, 13000 pt.
Ratio of fights/wins, 7/2
Weight, 171,6 lb
Height, 6'2"

"Good. Wait here," Mr. Ochoa said, then headed toward his future opponent.

Juan turned and looked at Hagen. Oh. This wasn't going to be easy. The guy was tall with long arms and twice as much Health.

Still, Hagen had to start somewhere. Unless he wanted to attack old ladies on the street just to improve his stats, of course.

M. Ochoa waited for one of the sparring bouts to finish, then cleared the fighters away and called Guerrero and Hagen over to the ring. The two tapped gloves. Guerrero nodded. Hagen did the same.

"Ready? Box!" Ochoa signaled for the training fight to begin.

Guerrero circled Hagen, all the while leading with the left while keeping his distance.

Should he get closer, Hagen wondered. Too risky. Or should he wait for the other guy to attack? But would he be able to block his jab or dodge it?

Hagen circled on the spot, trying to stay face to face with his constantly moving opponent and waiting for his chance. He needed one single opportunity to strike which could be his only possibility in the whole bout.

"Get stuck in!" Mr. Ochoa encouraged them. "Come on! Get on with it!"

Guerrero went on the attack, feinting blows, ducking and weaving his body to confuse him.

At a certain moment, Hagen understood: it was now or never. Acting on impulse, he mechanically planted his fist in his attacker's face, simultaneously trying to block Guerrero's blow with his left. When he'd almost sensed the other's glove touching his, the contact was broken.

You've dealt damage: 8,000 (Simple Punch)
Your opponent's block has been penetrated

For several nights afterward Mike would dream about what happened next. His glove moved as if in slow motion, meeting Guerrero's badly placed block and penetrating it with a well-placed blow to his cheekbone. Guerrero's head flew back, showering droplets of sweat everywhere, as his opponent flew through the air.

This was how Hagen had found out that whenever a blow dealt more damage than 50% of the opponent's Health points, it meant a guaranteed knockout. And that had been a flying knockout all right.

A wave of pure orgasmic bliss flooded over Hagen. Even love making paled into insignificance next to this new feeling. That was the System's reaction to his first level gained.

Hagen stood embraced by a column of light, unable to hear what Mr. Ochoa was saying to him. He could clearly see a new system message,

Congratulations! You've defeated your opponent in an honest fight!
Defeating an opponent whose level is higher than yours doubles the XP received!
You've received +2 to your level!
Current level, 3

New system points of main characteristics available, 2
New system points of combat skills available, 2

On the advice of his virtual assistant later that night, Hagen divided the two characteristic points between Strength and Agility. At first, he'd wanted to invest both into Strength but apparently, you couldn't do that. Raising a stat more than 1 pt. at a time could be lethal. The

System was very unequivocal about that,

Warning! We've detected an abnormal increase of your Strength characteristic: +1 pt.
Your body will be restructured in keeping with the new reading (6) to comply with your new metabolism and chronotropy values.

Changes required: accelerated growth of muscle tissue, sinews and ligaments.

It went on and on, telling him about the changes made to his glycogen and intramuscular phosphocreatine levels, intramuscular and intermuscular coordination, etc etc.

But it all paled into insignificance compared to a small final notice in bold letters, framed in red. Which, in Hagen's opinion, they should have shown him even before offering him the *Accept/Decline* button.

Warning!
The restructuring of your body functions requires a considerable amount of nutrients. In order to avoid danger to your life, you're strongly encouraged to consume a minimum of 10 oz. animal protein, 3 lbs. of carbohydrates and 3 oz. of animal fats. A shortage of nutrients may result in body function failure.

Warning!
Artificial characteristic boosting of more that 1 pt. at a time is strictly forbidden! Severe danger of fatality!

A similar message appeared when Hagen tried to add an extra point to Agility,

Warning! We've detected an abnormal increase of your Agility characteristic: +1 pt.
Your body will be restructured in keeping with the new reading (5) to comply with your new motoric and coordination values.

Changes required: the restructuring of your central nervous system and the increase in elasticity of your muscle tissue, sinews, ligaments and joints.

It was followed by an identical requirement to consume copious amounts of protein, fat and carbs, with the addition of a couple gallons of water.

Hagen spent the next two hours consuming shedloads of fried chicken and pizzas, washing his food down with copious amounts of water. As he ate, he suddenly realized that the thought of having to confront Mr. Goretsky didn't scare him anymore. Now that his Strength had brought his damage up to 9,600, it was way more than the

50% of the guy's Health required to knock him out.

With that thought, he went to bed.

As he fell asleep, he smiled to himself. Tomorrow was a new day. The first day of the rest of his life.

He had to continue leveling up. That way, sooner or later he'd be able to sign up for his first all-in competition. And then... who knows? He too might hold the champion's belt above his head one day.

That was still a long way away, though. He'd have to think about it tomorrow. Because tomorrow-

Hagen smiled again.

Tomorrow he'd ask Lexa out.

TRANSLATED FROM RUSSIAN BY IRENE WOODHEAD AND NEIL P. MAYHEW

THE KHAKI-COLORED NOOB

A LITRPG SHORT STORY

BY EUGENIA DMITRIEVA AND VASILY MAHANENKO

HOME SWEET HOME! Or so they say. Personally, Sergeant Snegov couldn't have cared less. He hated going on leave.

He'd always found the seventy-five days of his hard-earned standby leave plus the extra fifteen days he received for being a veteran more depressing than a three-month stint in the rainy season in Congo where he'd served as a sniper in the 81st Detached Reconnaissance Battalion.

Sergeant Snegov didn't have much to look forward to leave-wise. At thirty-five, he was still single and commitment-free; even his parents had moved to the Moon to be closer to his younger sister, so he was looking at a long sequence of days only spiced up by an occasional one-night stand or a glass of wine in the thinning company of his civilian friends. The rest of the time he spent roaming around town or going on an occasional overnight mountain hiking trip.

That was pretty much it. Which explains why he hated going on leave.

If he could have had it his way, he'd have only used his veteran's days, purely to visit his parents and have a couple of BBQs with friends. Still, no one asked his opinion. Which was why every year Sergeant Snegov received his leave pay and his travel pass and was free like a bird to go back to wherever he'd come from, sporting his commander's footprint on his khaki-clad backside.

Now, too, he was facing another sad uneventful stretch he didn't really need. For the last seventeen years, the army had been the only life Sergeant Snegov had known: ever since the fateful moment when he, then a law student, had decided he'd had enough legal drudgery and enlisted. At the time, he'd naively thought he might spend his three years in some backwater garrison, then resume his studies.

Unfortunately, things hadn't quite gone according to plan. After his first eighteen months in the reconnaissance battalion, a number of composite peacekeeping forces were sent to Sudan to defuse yet another local conflict. Needless to say, their 81st Recon Battalion just happened to be amongst these said troops, complete with Private Snegov.

So it came to pass that after the initial three years, he'd re-enlisted — for five years this time — and was now nearing the end of his fourth stint in the army while civilian life — once so tempting to the eighteen-year-old idiot he had formerly been — had faded into total obscurity and insignificance.

"Morning," Sergeant Snegov grumbled a greeting to himself.

It was the eighth day of his leave. He'd just come back from a family visit to the Moon the night before. Now he was facing the insurmountable task of deciding what to do with himself for the remaining two and a half months.

This was admittedly a challenge which demanded full control of his faculties and had to be approached accordingly. Sergeant Snegov scrambled off the couch, gave his crotch a hearty scratch and staggered into the kitchen to get some beer.

Still not thinking straight, he tripped over the game capsule for the umpteenth time.

He cussed. The capsule was a birthday gift from some friends he'd received two years previously but had never gotten around to actually using. Sergeant Snegov hated computer games with a vengeance; still, disposing of a birthday gift wasn't a nice thing to do, was it? So the capsule had been sitting in his room gathering dust all this time, being shoved out of the way whenever Snegov happened to bump into it like he'd just done.

"Wretched piece of crap," he hissed, rubbing his knee and staring daggers at the unsuspecting machine. Giving it a wide berth, he reached the kitchen and opened the fridge.

He had good reason to hate virtual-reality capsules. All new recruits were obliged to use them in training in order to experience some of

259

the less savory details of warcraft, including death in action in every shape and form. If before that experience the young Snegov hadn't minded an occasional game of Firefly, the so-called "mental conditioning courses" (which was army speak for sophisticated mind torture) had completely turned him off computer games.

His parched stomach greedily imbibed the first beer, cheering him up and clearing his head somewhat. Snegov opened a new bottle, slumped onto a kitchen stool and rested his chin on his fist, not even realizing his own stunning resemblance to a khaki-clad copy of Auguste Rodin's *Thinker*.

Sipping his beer unhurriedly, he began contemplating his alternatives. He could, of course, hire an escort and take her on a week-long mountain hike. Or he could hire an escort and just stay in town. Alternatively, instead of hiring anyone, he could call a few friends and invite them on a fishing trip the coming weekend.

All three scenarios had their fortes and all three had to be considered carefully, so as not to repent at leisure — literally. Sergeant Snegov reached for his phone and ordered another pack of beer.

The doorbell rang almost straight away. Still, this wasn't the delivery man with a six-pack of liquid imagination booster. Instead, four of Snegov's few remaining friends stood there grinning in the doorway: a young and cheerful guy whom Snegov only knew by his online nickname which was Hamster Face; an equally young and cheerful Helen (nickname: Spitfire), and a married couple who went by the monikers of Shanamir and Morana respectively. According to the wife, she'd created a vampire character once, hence the nickname, and then she'd sort of grown into it.

"Aha," Snegov said, taking in his potential fishing trip team, "here's my constituency coming. Come in! I have an idea for you!"

He raised a meaningful finger to the ceiling, then stumbled back into the kitchen to put the kettle on. Snegov despised electric kettles and all other kitchen appliances, those heartless electronic devices which killed the taste of good food. This philosophy had earned him the reputation of being somewhat snobbish among his small circle of friends.

"Listen, guys," he struck up the moment his guests had seated themselves in his small abode, "fancy going on a fishing trip? We could have a quick barbeque on the beach, how about that? Fresh fish soup! I can't tell you how I missed proper Russian fish soup in that African jungle! They haven't got a clue how to fish! It's either a crocodile or some slimy wormy thingies that make your skin creep, bah! I've got a fishing rod. Don't worry, Shanamir, I'm not going to borrow yours."

Having blurted that out, Snegov leapt over the wretched capsule and headed back into the kitchen.

"You and your crocodiles!" Shanamir chuckled, ignoring his advances. "I'd love to go but unfortunately, I can't. I have this mad client who's already booked me a flight because he wants me to work on his project from his office! With no Internet connection, mind you. He thinks that way I can't copy the program and sell it to his competition. Paranoid? — you could say that. Still, the money is good. And once I'm back in a couple of weeks, I can go fishing with you anytime, for as long as you want!"

Helen sighed. "I'm sorry but I'm gonna pass. Don't forget I'm getting married in two weeks' time. My phone is about to explode with all the calls. Flower arrangements, caterers, seating charts... If it goes on like this, I might actually hold a fishing trip wedding. At least that will solve the menu problem: the guests will have to catch their own meal."

"If your guest list is too long, just tell me!" Snegov shouted cheerfully from the kitchen. "Eliminating people is my job. That might save you some money!"

"I'll think about it," Helen replied with a deadpan face.

"I'd love to come," Morana admitted, "but

I'd rather wait for Shan to come back."

"Likewise," Hamster Face agreed. "In two weeks sounds perfect to me. I already promised my old folks to help with their vegetable garden. It's the potato-planting season. Time to dig for victory!"

"So much for their genetically modified miracles," Shanamir added. "They're yet to make potatoes that can dig their own holes in the ground."

"I can't believe you, guys," Snegov said, bringing in a trayful of teacups. "You really want me to be stuck here on my own for two weeks with only beer cans for company?"

He expertly avoided another collision with the capsule and set the tray on the table. "Help yourselves."

The doorbell emitted a shrill tremulous whine.

"That's my beer," Snegov announced. "See what you're doing to me? I'm gonna drink myself into an early grave!"

Shaking a disapproving head, he walked out into the hallway. The others listened as he exchanged a few words with the delivery man. The door lock beeped as it shut. Snegov returned to the room with a pack of beer in his hand.

"What kind of life is this?" he demanded, setting it on the floor. "In Africa, you 're obliged to get sloshed, otherwise... ah, never mind. I come home — and I have to get sloshed again! Civilian life is a nightmare. It sucks."

"What you need is a wife," Morana said, eyeing the beer with contempt. "I have an idea. Fancy playing a bit of Barliona with me?"

"'xcuse me?" Snegov raised a sarcastic eyebrow. "Now why would I want to do something like *that*?"

"Well, if you're planning on getting drunk, you might just as well do it safely."

"There're some nice brothels in Barliona," Hamster Face gave him a wink.

"Well, thank you very much!" Snegov sniffed. "I think I'd rather drink alcohol-free beer and toss myself off. It's *way* more enjoyable than playing computer games. I mean guys, are you for serious?" he threw his hands in the air. "I'm on leave, for crissakes! I'm supposed to be enjoying myself! There's no way I'm climbing inside this sorry excuse for a coffin. You have to be kidding me..."

He heaved a sigh and ripped the beer pack open, producing a bottle of Gandalf.

"You shouldn't speak like that about Barliona, man," Hamster Face reached into the pack for two more bottles and handed one to Helen. "They have a new option now, allowing you to max out positive sensory sensations. Their food and drink are virtually indistinguishable from the real thing. Ditto for their brothels — but those never had sensory restrictions to begin with."

"I'm on a diet now," Morana explained. "Barliona is the only place where I can safely pig out. So that's what I'm gonna do while Shan's away."

"Now that's a thought," Helen perked up. "No need to skip desserts anymore!"

"You and your diets!" Shanamir chuckled.

"Please," Snegov finished the bottle in one gulp. "If I need a date, I can always get one in real life. That's not a problem," he reached for yet another bottle.

Probably, alcohol on an empty stomach hadn't been such a good idea. Or at least that's what Snegov told himself later, trying to find an explanation for what he did next. He screwed the cap off another beer, scratched his stubbly chin, then said, unexpectedly for himself,

"I suppose there's no chance of a space game instead?"

"Yeah right," Morana argued. "A space game! It'll take you two weeks just to work everything out. While in Barliona, I can show you around," she paused, contemplating his sorry state. "I suggest you try it for a couple of days. If you don't like it, we can always try a space game later."

"I suppose so," Snegov sighed, admitting defeat. "What exactly do I need to do there?"

He'd never been interested in Barliona. He knew, of course, that it was the latest fad, a breakthrough concept; he also knew that it was being used as the first virtual prison. That was the extent of it.

"Very well," Morana said. "Sit down and I'll tell you..."

✳ ✳ ✳

"*SWOBU*!" Snegov screamed in excitement, jumping up and down. "*Dabu*! *WAAAAAAAAAGH*! Where's my choppa? *Zug Zug*!"

He reached for the scabbard dangling from his belt and produced a massive weapon which looked like a cross between a butcher's hatchet and a cutlass. He launched it spinning in the air, then waited for its handle to drop obediently into his grip. "My life belongs to the Horde!" he screamed.

Morana winced. Snegov didn't even seem to care that his orcish antics had been borrowed from some totally irrelevant game worlds.

"Mordor and the Eye!" he hollered, whirling in place like an Afghan dervish.

It must have actually looked comical: the seven-foot green bulk of a monster swinging around like a chimp on steroids.

Snegov had chosen an orc, thinking that if he had to make a fool of himself, he might just as well do it in style. And just to make the effect complete, he made his orc a Hunter, of all things.

"He's green, isn't he?" Sergeant Snegov had explained his choice of character to Morana. " He'll blend in perfectly with the woods. What the heck did they need my ID for? Do they have age restrictions?"

"It'th Age Rating Fourteen," a female troll with a gorgeous red Mohawk cut lisped next to him. Her own skin was green with a lovely blue sheen. An impressive pair of fangs protruded from her jaws, which explained the temporary articulation problems of Morana the Awesome.

"Flippin' fangs," she cussed, managing an occasional clear phrase. "Wish I knew it when I joined Kartoth. Thuch a shame they don't allow race tethting."

Snegov already knew that she'd used the recently available opportunity to switch sides by joining Kartoss. New races, new quests, new dungeons and lots of new words whose meaning Snegov didn't even try to fathom.

"Would you like me to knock them out for you?" he politely offered, trying to live up to his new handle, Noghar the Slayer. Meeting her angry glare, he hurried to add, "Just trying to be helpful," he stepped back out of her range of fire just in case.

"You can't do it here. It'th gore-free. No blood; definitely no broken fangth," her voice rang with wistful regret. "Shit. Bathtard pathifists."

"So much for their authenticity," Snegov — or should we say Noghar the Slayer — tilted his head up, brought his cupped hands to his mouth and yelled at the sky, "Scammers!"

His thunderous roar made flocks of treetop-nesting birds take to the wing; their calls echoed over the woods as they rushed about overhead, panicking. Snegov grunted with satisfaction, poked his nose, wiped the finger on his short breeches, belched, then asked,

"What now? Are we supposed to just stand here discussing the state of your dental surgery?"

"No. We've got thome leveling to do."

"Leveling what?" he looked around, flexing his muscles in expectation of an area that needed flattening. He tried to strike a bodybuilder's pose but failed miserably, looking more like someone in the throes of constipation.

Contrary to his expectations, the mysterious leveling had nothing to do with ground works. They walked until they came to some miserable looking village where a scruffy troll doubled up with age explained to him how to use a bow and arrow, watched him shooting targets for a while, then sent him to the nearby woods with the task of bringing back some rabbits.

But if this part of the game was remotely

engaging — funny even, — Snegov's attempt to divine the gaming mechanics had failed miserably. Morana did her best to advise, showering him with vaguely familiar words which meant something entirely different — like "damage", "stats" or the mysterious "XP". Seeing as it hadn't helped him much, she repeated the same in a more human language.

By the time he'd made level 2, the information overload — all those numbers, stats and characteristics — had driven Sergeant Snegov decidedly mad. Even his own combat gear module back in the army was less complicated than this ridiculous toy. Why would they want to flash a *"You've received XP!"* message right in front of his nose just as he was taking aim?

"Shit and derision!" he shouted, slamming his bow to the ground after one such announcement too many. "What's all this now? First it's some fungi trying to scalp me alive, then I'm supposed to commit genocide on bunny rabbits, and all this with a constant running commentary! Is there a way of muting these wretched messages?"

"Wait a thec," Morana said. "Let'th see if we can change the thettings."

She raised her head from her needlework. Yes, you heard it right. A female troll sitting quietly on the grass doing some *broderie anglaise* — that's a sight to behold, I tell you. When

Snegov had tried to inquire about the reasons for such uncharacteristic behavior, she replied with a laconic and incomprehensible "Crafting quetht." He didn't dare expand on it, afraid for the state of his own mental health.

Guided by Morana, he somehow managed to change the settings, moving the annoying messages to the background of his vision. Finally, things got moving. He made the next five levels in no time, mainly thanks to the level-71 Priestess hovering in his wake. Still, he soon got pretty fed up with killing innocent critters. He tried to diversify the task by making some traps — a skill he'd learned in the army. He didn't dwell on the fact that the kind of traps he'd been trained to set were meant for a totally different kind of game: mainly sentient bipeds. Still, all these snares, nooses and trapping pits proved to work well against the forest inhabitants, too.

Immediately, the game offered him the choice of a new stat: Ingenuity, which allowed him to combine several items to create one new one.

"What's this about?" the green-skinned inventor turned to Morana.

"Firth time I hear about it," she admitted. "They've introduced a lot of new shit for this new fraction. Just take it! You can thort it out later."

Also, his real-life profession had allowed Snegov to receive two more additional characteristics: Accuracy and Camouflage. His ability to determine the direction of the wind, the type of ammunition and the right kind of foliage camouflage had proved extremely handy in his new virtual environment. And when his self-appointed "mentor" suggested he acquire and train a pet for himself, Snegov was beyond himself with joy. Now he spent all his quest-free time training and nourishing his *smilodon*[2], which had earned him his last available characteristic: Pet Control.

Now every new level garnered him less XP than the one before it. Finally, the two decided to make a move to another location.

"Aren't you fed up with your smilodon?" Morana grumbled, watching as he trained his pet to shake hands. By then, her enunciation problems had improved considerably. "It's a cat like any other! Their stats are very similar."

As a responsible animal lover, Snegov had taken the choice of pet very seriously. He'd even checked out numerous guides and manuals in order to study Barliona's available varieties. When he'd come across the smilodon, he was so excited that he even splurged on purchasing him a mate: a young female which received the proud moniker Grrreta Garrrbage.

"Demon, I'm bored," Snegov quoted the

---

[2] Smilodon: a saber-toothed tiger

words ascribed to the fabled Dr. Faustus, showing off his literacy and erudition while folding a length of vine to form a gargantuan-sized bow tie. "Also, provided the game developers based their fantasy beasts on real-world animals, smilodons should have a lot in common with today's lions — who live in prides and are therefore social animals who can be easily trained. Private Garrrbage!" he snapped at the animal. "Belay that!"

Hearing the familiar angry notes in her master's voice, Grrreta spat out the beetle she had caught, then dropped on her back, expecting a hearty belly rub for her obedience.

"I mean, there must be some practical point in this stupid game," Snegov concluded, pulling Grrreta toward himself by a front paw. The creature tried to protest but, having received a gentle flick on the nose, decided it best to comply.

"Well done, Private," Snegov gave the animal a good scratch behind the ear.

Grrreta closed her eyes, her purring strongly reminiscent of the noise made by a tank engine.

Admittedly, Barliona had surprised Snegov with its flexibility. He'd very soon discovered that virtually any idea, however unorthodox, could have a solution here. That allowed for a certain stretch of the imagination which in turn offered some relief from the boring predictable quests in the vein of "go and kill such-and-such".

During this first week in the game, Snegov had tried out a good dozen professions, from blacksmith to artist, but hadn't dwelt on anything in particular. "It's just so boring," he explained his indecision to Morana.

These days he was into Tanning. Logical, really: most of the quests he received demanded him killing particular animals. His frugal heart of a sergeant passionately protested against such waste, which was why he was now trying to process some wolf hides under the young troll lady's sarcastic stare.

"Them and their Middle Ages!" he wheezed, trying to scrape off some wax that sealed the stopper of a small pitcher of tannic acid. "Can you explain why they need to exercise such freakin' attention to detail like this stupid seal which I'm obliged to scrape off — while when it gets to real serious stuff, they create nothing but problems? All those spells, levels, the impervious bunny rabbits that you just can't hurt with an ordinary arrow..."

He set the pitcher aside and began counting, unbending his fingers, "Wolves here are better armored that some of the army vehicles I know. It's a good job they can's fire or launch assault groups! Eagles are worse than attack planes! I won't even mention bigger game. Am I supposed to push a ballista in front of me just on the slim chance that I might come across some of the local fauna? Or should I give my guys in the army a call and ask them to fetch me an anti-tank missile system?"

Snegov finalized his complaint with a complex four-letter figure of speech, then resumed his pitcher-opening exercise.

"That's because your leveling scheme generates mobs whose levels are higher than yours," Morana explained. "This way you can level up faster. It's not as easy, I agree. You need a higher-level partner to do that, otherwise it's too risky. That's why you're struggling with mobs' armor."

"Excuse me, ma'am," sounded the voice of a goblin mage known as Aryach the Useless. They'd met him a few days previously and grouped up with him straight away. The mage was polite to a fault and cost Morana nothing mana-wise. Now every time Aryach happened around, he'd approach Morana to get his share of buffs and heals.

"*Mobs, buffs...* what next?" Snegov kept grumbling. "Is human language not good enough for them?"

Finally, the stubborn stopper relented with a popping sound, surrendering to the power of human genius. Snegov cut his soliloquy short and brought the pitcher closer to himself. He set it in his lap and dragged one of the wolf skins closer.

That's when Grrreta decided it was the right moment to poke her curious feline nose into the pitcher. The odor escaping it made her hackles stand on end. Growling her disappointment, Grrreta upended the pitcher right into her owner's lap, then darted for the jungle.

"Grrreta! Come back, you sorry excuse for a toilet brush!" Snegov tried to jump to his feet but collapsed face down, scooping a mouthful of rotting leaves and offering his backside to the skies.

"Oh bummer!" he yelled, spitting out the leaves. "I can't straighten my legs!"

No wonder: the tanning acid had turned his leather pants rock hard, transforming this standard item of orcish gear into a piece of plaster cast.

"How interesting," Morana commented matter-of-factly, studying his pants' improved stats. "This is a Tanning debuff. Lots more points to Armor. Shame you can't use them."

As soon as she imparted this undoubtedly valuable information, the funny effect wore off, returning Snegov's pants to their initial condition.

"What a curious effect," Aryach agreed, "what a shame it doesn't last. Well, I'll be off, then!"

Aryach the Useless waved his farewell, setting off on yet another quest. He didn't live up to his misleading moniker, using every opportunity to level up, unlike Snegov.

Snegov heaved a sigh of relief and gingerly lowered himself onto his long-suffering backside. "I think I know now how the Tin Man used to feel," he cast a look over his shoulder at Private Garrrbage's guilty muzzle poking out of the shrubbery. "Grrreta, come here, kitty," he motioned the creature to approach. "Let's have a cuddle. Nasty humans! Giving my kitty some crap to sniff..." he took the approaching Grrreta in his arms and gave her a hearty scratch behind the ear.

The animal lay her head in her master's lap and blissfully closed her eyes, simultaneously kicking the wretched pitcher, as if accidentally, behind the log which still held the pile of wolf hides in need of tanning.

"Right, time to check my traps," reluctantly Snegov let go of his pet and rose to his feet, brushing Grrreta's hair from his pants. "You know, don't you, that had it not been for her, I would have quit a long time ago. It's just so boring! How can anyone find this entertaining?"

"You haven't been to the dungeons yet," Morana said. "Wait till the others are back, we'll go there together."

"But that's another week!" Snegov sighed and patted Grrreta's head. "You stay here, kitty, and keep an eye on Morana. Morrie, I'd like you to do the same. Keep an eye on Grrreta, please, and make sure she doesn't touch any more fish. I don't want any more incidents like the other day."

"As if she cares," Morana grumbled to his back.

Snegov wasn't listening: he was heading for the river.

The water felt just like real water. Admittedly, virtual reality had its advantages. Here, you could do some fishing from the comfort of your own home... and from what he'd heard, you could even make some fish soup.

"Hi, noob," a smug voice came out of thin air.

Snegov froze, casting wary glances around. "Hi yourself."

I'm an idiot, he thought. *So much for keeping my eyes peeled! I've served myself on a silver platter to whoever they are.*

"What do you want?" Snegov asked out loud, trying to sound goofy and careless.

"Are you aware you're trespassing?" the voice demanded.

"Am I really?" Snegov replied, slightly relieved. Some things never change, even in virtual reality. Been there, done that: "our block", "our street", "our territory"... Gang habits die hard even in the virtual world.

For some reason, the thought made him angry. Slowly he turned around, hands on his hips. "Well, if this is your ranch, mister, why didn't you put up a nice big fence all around it? Aren't you afraid of bunny rabbits ruining your carrots?"

"We're cheeky, aren't we?" the voice drawled.

Snegov sensed a light pain in his leg. Messages started flashing in the background, reporting incoming damage. A small icon appeared, similar to those that had appeared after some of Marana's spells. Buffs, that's what she called them.

"Next time I'll hit you properly with my dagger," the voice informed him pompously.

The air in front of Snegov rippled, revealing a new player: a certain Screwer the Awesome from the Kick Ass clan. His name glowed in fiery red letters. The number next to it denoted level 97.

What a face! During the character generation phase, Snegov had gotten a glimpse of zombies — but this one was admittedly repulsive even for his race. Part of his face was missing, his bare teeth grinning, his empty eye sockets gaping. His nose was reduced to two syphilitic holes. A measly tuft of hair crowned his head. His crumbling skull was held together by two strips of leather strapped crossways and secured with a tiny padlock just above his missing nose. Overall, it looked as if Screwer had just escaped from a necro BDSM party.

"Sorry man, I'm not interested," Snegov admitted. "Same-sex necrophilia isn't my thing."

With these words, he buried his fist in Screwer's ugly snout. He did it nice and proper, the way he used to do it in the street all those years back. Although he'd never become a proper martial arts expert (because they had to take real good care of his hands), still a punch like this was usually enough to end an ordinary fight.

Screwer's head rebounded slightly, but that seemed to be it. More messages flashed across Snegov's mental view. Their contents boiled down to two facts: that he'd failed to breach Screwer's defenses or deal him any damage.

The zombie guffawed, triumphant.

"Whatcha laughin' at, you dumbass?" wincing at the pain in his leg which now sported the Lameness debuff, Snegov stepped back and pulled out his "choppa". "Would you like me to make mincemeat of your gray cells? Here, enjoy!"

The shining blade traced an arc through the air and crashed down on the zombie's head without much effect. Screwer guffawed louder.

"Right, noob," Screwer announced when he could finally speak again, "I'm gonna kill you now. And once you're back from your respawn point, take my advice and mind your manners if you don't want to spend the rest of your time in the graveyard. Do I make myself clear?" without waiting for Snegov to answer, the zombie disappeared.

The next moment Snegov's back exploded in pain from several stab wounds. During the registration process, Snegov's real-life profession had made him exempt from the obligatory psychological evaluation, allowing him to switch off the sensory filters. He had set the pain threshold to 20% — and pleasure to 100% like everybody else. Because of that, the pain now was substantial but still bearable.

The world around him dimmed. A message popped up, informing him that due to his character's death, his access was blocked for the next twelve hours. A countdown timer appeared in his view.

Snegov pushed the capsule's lid open, threw his legs over the edge and sat up, resting his chin on his fist.

I fell for his trick like a greenhorn, he admitted as he searched his vocabulary for the right combination of four-letter words to describe his opponent's sexual preferences. Then he stumbled to the fridge to get a little more remedy for his wounded pride.

Half an hour later, when the drink had

improved his outlook somewhat, he gave Morana a call.

"You won't believe it," he blurted out the moment she picked up, "that piece of dead meat! He did me like I was still wet behind the ears!"

"Who — Screwer?" Morana asked grimly.

"Yeah! Wretched walking corpse! Why, do you know him?" Snegov sent the empty bottle sailing into the trash bin.

"Well, I saw you were dead so I went there to rez you and he was still there, the douchebag."

"He didn't hurt you, did he?" Snegov asked cautiously.

"What do you think? According to him, I was supposed to lick his stinking backside just for the right to play. And he wanted me to pay, too! Well, I told him where he could stuff it."

"And? Did he kill you?" Snegov asked, feeling guilty.

"He's not good enough," Morana's voice rang with pride. "Had he been good, he wouldn't have had to PK newbs in a starting location. I'm a healer, don't forget," she must have heard Snegov's puzzled chuckle as she hurried to explain, "I heal other players, cast shields, reduce incoming damage, do mana regen — I'm a pure healer, always wanted to be. Even with the level gap, Screwer just didn't have enough damage to kill me. Then again, I didn't have any weapons, did I? So he spent, like, twenty minutes trying to smoke me and then he just split. I've only just logged out. Come on and log back in so I can rez you. No good wasting twelve hours."

"Give me five minutes," Snegov polished off a further bottle, then climbed back into the capsule.

The countdown had disappeared, replaced by a new message: *Morana the Awesome would like to resurrect you.* Snegov pressed *Agree*.

The very next instant he was back in the game.

Nothing on the river bank reminded him of the recent fight. There was no blood; his own body was gone. The place was peaceful and quiet.

"I think it's time we move to some other location," Morana said, her troll's hulk towering way above him. "This crackpot won't leave us alone. Or," she offered after a pause, "we could join a space game, I suppose. You didn't like it here, anyway. You said it was boring."

"It was," Snegov replied. "Not any more. Grrreta, come!"

The pale ginger cat materialized soundlessly next to him.

"Track 'em!" Snegov commanded. "Find Screwer! Good girl!"

The smilodon obediently lowered her head to the ground, then dashed along the bank. Snegov and Morana could barely keep pace.

"I wonder," Snegov wheezed as he ran,

"Could she pull a loaded cart if necessary?"

"You'd better tell me what you're going to do once we find him."

"Nothing," Snegov replied. "We'll keep an eye on him. From a safe distance. Grrreta, stay! Come! Good girl!"

He flung his arms around the animal's bulbous head. "You see, this guy is too cheeky which means he knows the area really well. He knows the lie of the land. And we're gonna study him. Where he goes, what he does, where he hides. And once we know all that, we're gonna make him dance real slow."

"Well, if you think you can sneak after him, be my guest. I can't."

Indeed, between her height and her Mohawk, this troll lady was way too conspicuous for surveillance work.

"Aha," she suddenly said. "Aryach must have died here somewhere."

Snegov had already tried once to work out how she knew these things. Apparently — or so he'd divined from her cabbalistic explanation — a priest could detect a dead player's ghost at the place of his or her demise.

"I hope he's still in the capsule," she sighed. "I bet it's that scumbag's work!"

Snegov raised a strung bow, keeping a watchful eye on the undergrowth. "I suppose a medicopter is out of the question. Which means you're his only hope. Go ahead, I'll cover you."

Morana sniffed at the idea of a level-15 player defending her against a level-90 PK. Still, she chose not to argue, concentrating on the job at hand. Luckily for her, Aryach hadn't vacated his capsule yet. The moment she finished reciting the spell, he reappeared.

"Thanks," the goblin said, taking in his rescuers. "Would be a shame to lose all that time just because of some dimwit."

"Don't mention it," Morana waved a nonchalant hand while funneling a healing potion down his throat with the other. The goblin's XP bar began filling until it stopped at 100%. She then cast all available buffs on him and added, nodding at Snegov, "He killed Noghar too."

Snegov grinned. "Welcome to the club. Grrreta, this is Aryach."

The cat cast a pensive gaze over the goblin and sniffed. She then raised her hind leg high in the air and got busy licking her backside clean.

"Her manners still need some work," Snegov explained.

"I can see that," Aryach said.

He was about to add something when a familiar voice resounded from behind them,

"Aha! All present and correct! So what did you decide? Are you paying up — or do you need more encouragement?"

Morana instantly began casting shields:

first on the two lowbies, then on herself, while Snegov whirled around on the spot, scanning the area for the wretched zombie.

"What was the jail sentence for extortion last time you checked?" he asked while weighing up any potential escape routes.

Screwer scowled. "Please. This is a game, man. I have to act in keeping with my character. He's such a robbing bastard!"

"Too many of you around just lately," Morana murmured.

The next moment the space around Aryach filled with fireballs which floated in all directions while ignoring his group mates. One of the fireballs finally rammed into the PK, dealing him some insignificant damage while completely unstealthing him.

"I'm real scared," Screwer said with a sarcastic drawl. "Too bad. So what did you decide, noobs? It's pay or die!"

Snegov lowered his bow. "I think I know. This is your way of compensating for your real-life deficiencies. You're a loser, man. Just some corporate rat who can't afford real adventure. You're someone who could never live up to his dreams. I even feel sorry for you... a little," Snegov parted his fingers about half an inch, "this much."

"Are you trying to describe the size of your wiener?" Screwer retorted. "You may be a tough guy back in real life, but here in Barliona you're fair game."

To illustrate his words, he sprang toward Snegov, burying all of his daggers in his back. The shield's shimmering sphere heaved, absorbing some of the damage, while Morana began casting spells non-stop, trying to support Snegov in the uneven combat.

Aryach didn't waste time, either. He tried to set up some sort of cage surging with electric charges but failed miserably: the level gap was such that the cage disintegrated almost the moment it had appeared.

"You bastard!" Snegov thundered, recoiling. "Take this!" he raised his bow, showering the zombie with arrows.

This time their combined efforts allowed them to last slightly longer. Ignoring Snegov, Screwer attacked Aryach first. No amount of shields or overhealing could save the level-14 wizard. Snegov went the same route very soon after.

Five minutes later, he was already calling Morana again. Her number went to voicemail which gave him some hope that she was still holding the fort.

This time he had to wait all of fifteen minutes for his resurrection. Once back in the forest, Snegov discovered a new character standing next to Morana: a Drow Warlock going by the name of Jinx the Grudge Bearer. He cut a fine albeit sinister figure with his gorgeous robes and precious staff topped with an intricately carved demon's head whose ruby eyes seemed to glare at Snegov. Well, what else could you expect from a level-211 player and a member of the Dark Legion clan? Even though Snegov hadn't yet bothered to look into Barliona's clan system, you'd have to be deaf, dumb and blind not to know the name of Kartoss' strongest clan.

Aryach was the next to resurrect. "Thanks, dude," he said to the warlock.

"My pleasure," Jinx the Grudge Bearer replied, which pretty much explained his arrival at the newbie location as well as Screwer's prompt demise. "The guy's a pest. Next time I won't be so nice with him."

"Love the costume," Snegov said. "Shit, I really wanted to deal with him myself. Grrreta!"

The saber-toothed kitty materialized out of thin air and nudged Snegov's hand with her heavy head, cadging a cuddle.

"Good girl," Snegov said.

"Your enthusiasm is commendable," the warlock replied, watching Morana who got busy healing and buffing Aryach. "All you need is another fifty levels or so."

"Not quite," Snegov corrected him. "Leveling's got nothing to do with it. All we want is nail the motherfucker to the wall. That can't be too difficult."

"I'm afraid, the only way you can nail him to the wall, as you eloquently put it, is by inviting a high-level friend," Aryach joined in the conversation. "Which is exactly what I did. Thank you very much again," he bowed stiffly to Morana.

"I'm afraid he's right," Morana agreed. "That's gaming mechanics for you. Even if Screwer just stands there doing nothing, it might take you a few hours to kill him. And that's the best-case scenario."

"How about we play a trick on him?" Snegov squinted predatorily. "Can't we lure him into an avalanche or a rockfall? Or fell a tree on him?"

"That depends," Jinx looked at Snegov with some interest. "You seem to be thinking in the right direction. But to do that, you might need to level up Woodcutting first. Your idea is in fact quite time-consuming."

"I'd love to see that bastard being squashed by a tree," Aryach admitted dreamily.

Snegov twisted his ghastly tattooed face into a grin. "Guys," he said, pressing his paws to his chest, "you won't believe it. I'm not just good at everything to do with cutting and digging — I'm an expert! And when these skills are required in order to screw my neighbor, I'm a freakin' guru!"

Jinx chuckled and scratched his chin. "I offer a swap. My assistance in exchange for the video of the deed. I'll be around for a couple of days anyway rushing a friend," he nodded at Aryach, "or I might send a replacement. I promise I'll be watching that bastard and keep him on his toes. I can also lend you one of my beasties to protect you. Still, you need to understand that once I leave the location, this sorry excuse for an undead will be back straight away and will go on a PK spamming rampage."

Morana perked up. "Could you really do that? All the buffing and healing is on me. Email me, okay?"

"I'd rather use the communication amulet to contact you," Jinx offered Morana a strange-looking item Snegov had never seen before.

"Sorry," Snegov butted in, "I don't quite understand. He's not going to smuggle in a real PK, is he?"

For Snegov, a "PK" would forever stand for that trusty old general-purpose machine gun which was still in use in quite a few of the planet's hot spots.

"PK is gaming slang, man. It was created in the days when players spoke different languages. It stands for Player Killer."

"Roger that," Snegov's orcish paw scratched his bald green head covered in fancy Maori-like tattoos.

The tattoos were impressive. Snegov had a funny feeling that the game developers hadn't bothered to reinvent the wheel; they must have simply copied some ritual symbols borrowed from various extinct civilizations, randomized them, then offered them to the game users as "traditional Dark Orcish attributes". Another proof of this theory lay in the fact that the Light Elves' tattoo was an exact copy of the Incan Eagle.

In the meantime, the warlock got busy drawing some kind of geometric figures on the ground and placing various ritualistic ingredients onto them in an order that only he could fathom. Once he was finished, the drawing lit up with an ominous sickly-purplish glow.

A creature appeared at its center, best described as... as the result of an incestuous relationship between a dog and a snake. Yellow reptilian eyes glowed in a dog's skull; a forked tongue flicked between canine jaws; scales of deep orange covered a hairless body while the tail wasn't snake-like: it *was* a snake.

"Wow. First time I witness high level summoning," Morana admitted, studying the resulting creature in awe.

"This is a chimera of my own creation," Jinx said proudly. "It targets stealthed enemy. I've already set up auto attack. The moment he sees Screwer, he'll attack him first."

"Was it so necessary to ruin a dog?" Snegov asked grimly. "This beats even anime monsters — and those Japanese artists have some really sick imaginations!" he gave Grrreta a gentle pat on the neck and walked off, suddenly becoming interested in a bamboo copse.

"I've never seen a chimera like it," Morana said, trying to downplay Snegov's boorishness. Ticking off a top player and a potential ally for his lack of animal rights awareness wasn't a clever strategy. "How do we look after him? What does he eat?"

"He'll eat any flesh you happen to loot. Just throw him a bunch twice a day, that's it. Come on, Aryach. Time to move it."

Aryach nodded. He waved his goodbyes to everyone and left the group, then followed the warlock into the forest, apparently on a quest.

"So, mister AI animal rights activist, what's up?" Morana began.

A bamboo shoot snapped. Snegov came out, beaming like a cat, with a length of bamboo in one hand.

"Ever heard about Genghis Khan's bamboo trap?" he asked.

✳ ✳ ✳

THE NEXT THREE days flew past. Snegov couldn't even imagine that some measly computer game could turn out to be so complicated. His character development proved a real challenge, not to mention all the secondary and admittedly useless skills. Why would a hunter need to know Blacksmithing? Or Wood Carving? Turned out, he needed them in order to make arrows — so that he didn't need to spend his own hard-earned money buying new ones.

But now Snegov was grateful for the two days he'd spent mastering new crafting skills: his trapping pits were turning out just as he wanted them.

That created another problem, though. Had it been in real life, Sergeant Snegov would have smeared the spikes at the bottom of the trapping pits with plenty of excrement, just to make sure his quarry could enjoy the entire range of nasty sensations, including gangrene. In the virtual world, however, this wasn't an option.

Once again he had to pester Morana — who was already busy enough as it was making some ghillie camo suits for both of them, seeing as by then Snegov didn't have the time to level yet another skill.

Snegov learned a lot from her brief introduction lecture. Apparently, he could also study alchemy and make all sorts of poisons and nasty potions. He asked Morana to tell him more about the various ways of dealing damage to another character. The more he learned, the more questions he posed.

"Can one cast a spell on an item?" he asked, going through a mental list of possibilities that might open.

"If I try to select an item — say, this rock here, — I won't be able to do that," Morana admitted. "I can't heal an item nor can I cast a shield on it. But there're other ways. There's a profession called Enchantment which allows me to use certain ingredients in order to cast various effects on an item. That way this rock can receive a bonus to Armor or Intellect. Which is purely academic, as you can see. Weapons and armor are the only items one enchants, normally."

"Can you enchant a weapon to boost damage?" Snegov persisted.

"I did so already. I enchanted your bow, remember?"

"Think you can enchant these stakes for me?"

Indeed, that proved possible. Still, the choice of spells wasn't very big: a very minor damage boost, some fire DoT and an enchantment offering a paltry chance of stunning when dealing damage. Had Snegov had access to a top-level enchanter, he would have had more possibilities but as it was, he had to use what was available.

So Snegov kept sifting through the alternatives, pestering Morana with questions.

The first test run of the traps proved encouraging as well as disappointing. The wild boar which had fallen into the pit had received some additional damage as well as the fire DoT, but the main damage was laughable.

Morana hurried to his help. She sent word to Helen who'd just logged in, who in turn bought some top-level items from the vendors, from daggers to even a few spears. All of them had decent damage but the absence of additional stats and useful characteristics made those items really cheap and only good for resale.

For Snegov, however, it was exactly what the doctor ordered. Equipped with a few of those spears, his trapping pits could now make quick work of even a top-level player.

Having thus adapted various weapons to his own purposes and having sent Helen a lengthy shopping list, Snegov continued his experiments with his newly-acquired alchemy ingredients, murmuring something under his breath about Dr. Faustus and other famous real-life warlocks.

"It seems to work," Snegov commented on the efficiency of yet another concoction he'd smeared over a dagger blade. He turned to Morana who was busy writing something down on a sheet of parchment.

"What's that you've got there?" he sat next to her, poking his curious orcish nose into the manuscript.

"I'm making you some healing scrolls," Morana replied. "The Map-Making skill allows you to transfer spells to scrolls. This way you can recite the spell from the scroll which will then disappear while you'll get your heal."

"Can you recite it over an arrow?"

"Nope. Won't work. You can't cast a spell on an item, I told you that already. Had it been a fireball scroll, it might have worked. But why would you want to launch a fireball at an arrow? It'll just burn it, end of story."

"And what's gonna happen if you enchant the fireball scroll?"

"Oh. Never thought about it. Wait a sec, I'll make you a damage scroll."

Gradually, by way of scientific trial and error, Snegov worked out that enchanted scrolls could indeed affect items, applying various effects to them. Problem was, the said effects were highly unpredictable.

Once again Morana turned to her friends for help, receiving an armful of low-level spells of a variety of magic classes. That done, they got experimenting.

Or rather, it was Snegov who did most of the experimenting while Morana resurrected him after some especially unsuccessful attempts. A couple of times, the traps had activated in her hands just as she'd finished enchanting them, but the resulting damage was too low to do her any considerable harm.

"This is a million-dollar idea, I agree," Morana said thoughtfully, watching Snegov who was busy nailing together what looked like a sorry excuse for a birdhouse, "but I'm afraid, all this junk will never give us enough damage to smoke Screwer."

"And what if we buy some level-100 scrolls?"

"You know how much they cost? We don't even know if he walks into any of these traps. It would be cheaper to hire a bodyguard to follow you everywhere than to waste high-level spells."

"Bummer," Snegov set his handiwork aside, put two fingers in his mouth and whistled, summoning Grrreta and the chimera who'd received the name of Quasimuttley.

"Chow time!" Snegov barked. He took a heavy pot off the fire and began dishing out pieces of rabbit meat into wooden bowls (which he'd made all by himself). Much to his surprise, he'd discovered that food played an important role in a pet's development and that cooked meat worked much better in that respect than the carrion dropped by mobs.

"Such a waste," Morana commented, watching Quasimuttley as he wolfed down prime cuts of meat. "He's only a summoned pet. If he dies, they'll summon you a new one."

The two friends planned their day so as to comply with Jinx the Grudge Bearer's own schedule. Once he logged out, they would go to bed in order not to stumble across Screwer who'd never left the location anymore. His latest attempt to kill the obstinate noob had very nearly become his last: Quasimuttley had chased Screwer all around the location. Since then, he'd never dared anywhere near Snegov while Quasimuttley was around. The problem was, the chimera left the location whenever Jinx did, so Snegov didn't really have much choice.

Morana's quip had safely escaped Snegov's pointy green ears. She'd already noticed that her sergeant friend tended to have some sort of affinity with animals. If he could have had it his way, he would have amassed a whole menagerie of critters and set about tending to them, ignoring everything else around him.

"And what if we make a fake copy of our Quasimuttley here?" Snegov suggested, eyeing his pets with affection. "What's it called — a specter? That might help guide our test subject in the required direction."

"A phantom," Morana corrected him. "Well, I don't know. I need to look into it."

"Please do," Snegov poured the remaining rabbit meat into the bowls and returned to his handiwork, attaching enchanted spearheads to the wooden frame at different angles.

He showed the resulting piece to Morana. "Nice, eh?"

"Awesome," she replied wearily, finishing yet another camo net.

"Howdy, PK slayers," Jinx said as he materialized in the clearing. Aryach who was trailing in his wake nodded a greeting too.

The two teams had made an agreement to try and meet up at least once every gaming session in order to exchange buffs. Still, lately Jinx had been showing some interest in Snegov's inventions, to the point where he tried to linger a little longer every time, listening to his daily reports.

"Hi there, monster builder," Snegov grinned and began attaching yet another spearhead to the frame. "Fancy trying it on?"

Jinx cast a dubious glance at the contraption. "Not really. Is this your latest idea?"

Morana hurried to tell him about this newest of enchantment methods while Snegov offered a little demonstration. Both the wizard and the warlock were duly impressed. Jinx even asked Snegov's permission to see the entire building process.

Having watched it, he asked, "You sure it's your idea?"

Snegov chuckled. "Depends what you mean. The basic principle belongs to the Vietnamese. They've been using a similar thing for centuries. But it was Morana's idea to adapt it to the local environment."

"I just explained to him how gameplay works," Morana objected, unwilling to ride her inventor friend's coattails. "The idea is entirely his."

"Well done," Jinx said. To Snegov's surprise, Morana tried to conceal a contented smile.

He really couldn't understand the hero worship she seemed to have for Jinx as a top player. They couldn't be serious! Who cared about someone's success in a computer toy? Their achievements were a number-crunching exercise in futility. But these days, Barliona's successes sometimes made the real world's breaking news! Real-life people managed to earn their living by playing the game. Where was the world heading? If people were playing for fun as a pleasant distraction from real work, he could understand that. But this recent hysteria rendered him speechless.

"You wait till we get that bastard," Snegov cut Jinx' praise short. "Then you can commend us as much as you want."

"The results of your research are so interesting that I might make you a few top-level scrolls with warlock spells," Jinx said. "I'm curious how you're gonna use them. I might also ask a few friends to send you a couple of their own. Just promise me to film it."

Snegov shrugged. "That's not a problem. It won't be as spectacular and realistic as a Vietnam war movie, though."

"I don't mind," Jinx said. "It's a game, after all. When are you planning on making a start?"

"In an ideal world," Morana said, "we should be done with all the preparations tomorrow."

"See you tomorrow, then."

✹ ✹ ✹

SNEGOV LOVED the little mountain river nearby. Rapid and shallow, it reminded him of the boisterous streams of his own childhood, their narrow beds sandwiched between precipitous cliffs.

A giant tree trunk lay across the river as a makeshift bridge. One of the local simulators sent new players here to check their agility. Those who completed the quest were offered a nice albeit low-level prize; but those who failed it enjoyed a full-blown adrenaline boost from falling into the waterfall head first, followed by a well-deserved resurrection. That didn't happen very often: the tree trunk didn't harbor any tricks or secrets, but once in a while the desperate screams of yet another unfortunate klutz echoed from the local cliffs.

This time it was Snegov himself screaming his head off as he stood balancing on the trunk.

"You piece of undead meat, where do you think you are?" he shouted.

Morana sat on the opposite bank next to Grrreta, their facial expressions a motherly mixture of patience and skepticism.

Snegov suppressed a smile and continued teasing Screwer, "Come on, you wuss, show me what you can do! Or are you afraid of heights?"

Unhurriedly Screwer approached the "bridge", not even trying to hide. Judging by his name tag glowing red, he'd already killed someone somewhere else.

"Where's your mutt?" Screwer asked. "Not that you mean anything without him. Do you really think I can't keep my balance? Or do you think you're gonna push me in?"

Ignoring Morana, Screwer stepped theatrically onto the log, took a few light steps and disappeared.

"Boo," he barked victoriously into Snegov's ear, unstealthing right behind his back.

Clenching a little vial, Snegov flung it at the voice without taking aim. The crunching sound of breaking glass was followed by Screwer's furious scream as the tanning liquid turned his dandy set of leather armor into a trap as stiff as concrete. The effect only lasted three seconds, but that was well enough to do what Snegov had in mind.

"Number one, off you go," he commanded paratrooper-like as he kicked the zombie off the log. With a thunderous bellowing which momentarily drowned out the roar of the rapids, Screwer tumbled down the precipitous chasm.

"Birds fly low, prepare for a blow," Snegov commented, turning to his team.

"I got it on video," Morana told him. A small icon of a camera glowed next to her name tag. "I'm gonna upload it to the forum now!"

Their idea was as simple as can be. A video showing a top player being tricked and killed by a newb was bound to go viral, raising a tidal wave of ridicule and sarcastic comment. Screwer just wouldn't be able to allow such impunity go unpunished.

"What a scrub," Morana summed up when they'd finished watching the video.

"A scrub? What do you want me to scrub?" Snegov looked around in surprise.

"*He* is a scrub," she explained. "It's a word for clumsy players. Just like he is."

"Aha," remembering that he was an orc, Snegov reached under his shirt and scratched his belly, then emitted a thunderous belch. "In Congo, we used to call them *ambisinistrous*. Somebody who's a total klutz."

"Nice word," Morana nodded her approval, "but a bit of a mouthful. Too long to use on a raid."

She glanced at the waterfall destined to become Screwer's resting place for the next twelve hours and motioned to Snegov to follow her, "Time to do some leveling."

Eleven hours later, the timer went off, signaling the hour to start preparing for the murderous zombie's arrival. The two friends took their time completing the quest, then headed unhurriedly toward a "killing zone" that Snegov had lovingly set up in the forest.

"You and your video are popular," Morana chuckled. "Almost three million views!"

She read out a few of the juicier comments. On the video, you couldn't really see what it was that Snegov had hurled at Screwer. The whole scene looked as if the PK had simply allowed himself to be pushed down.

"We want him to get really angry," Snegov replied. "The more he winds himself up, the better."

The two revengeful friends took up their positions in the forest. Morana kept dog eye while Snegov made a show of training Grrreta, seemingly ignoring everything around him and generally behaving like an overconfident noob would, oblivious of any potential danger.

Screwer must have learned his lesson because this time he'd dropped his cartoon villain antics and attacked Snegov without a preliminary speech. Furious, he'd raced back all the way from the cemetery in search of the impudent noob who'd had the audacity to publicly humiliate him.

Without further ado, Screwer activated his microport, intent on killing the cheeky lowbie in one fell swoop. He got his wish, sort of. He did manage to port behind Snegov's back, that wasn't the problem. Still, his ruse didn't quite go as planned. Something snapped under Screwer's shoe, dragging him feet first into a trapping pit camouflaged with twigs and fallen leaves.

An indignant scream came from the trap as the daggers which studded the bottom of the pit sank into the zombie's skin, stripping him of the majority of his XP.

With a vindictive grin, Snegov unhurriedly produced his "choppa" and hacked through the rope which was attached to an enormous tree trunk, letting it hang above the trap. With a soft rustling noise, the trunk came loose. A wet crunching sound informed everyone of Screwer's demise, the second in one day.

"Our necrophiliac friend has made the Top Fails list," Morana said when Snegov logged back in.

Clad in Morana's ghillie suits, the two friends climbed a tree that offered an excellent view of the "killing zone" packed with more traps per square feet than the Congolese jungle. In real life, that would have been impossible so Snegov had taken full advantage of the new opportunities offered by gameplay.

"Prepare to launch a new movie star!" he guffawed, then shouted down into the wood, "Come out, dude, don't be shy! Audiences are waiting! You'll be happy you did!"

"You little shit," the familiar voice came from below, listing every indecent form of every punishment Screwer intended to inflict on Snegov once he got hold of him. And he fully intended to lay his hands on his enemy, that's for sure! It wasn't for nothing Screwer had been leveling up stealth, every PK's skill of choice. Now he patiently followed in Snegov's tracks, keeping his eyes peeled so as not to fall into another trap.

Unfortunately for him, Snegov never used the same trick twice. By tripping on a fine line laid in his path, Screwer triggered a high-level fireball spell. The next moment, the forest became a local version of Inferno.

"With compliments to our sponsor," Snegov said under his breath, forwarding the video to Jinx.

"Thanks a bunch. I've filmed it already," the warlock's voice boomed from above.

Morana and Snegov peered up, watching a flock of four gryphons circle the site of Screwer's ignominious demise. The fifth gryphon was already above their heads — complete with Jinx the Grudge Bearer astride it.

"Sorry, I couldn't help it," he shouted down. "I just had to see it for myself. I had a bet with my friends," he pointed at the other gryphons. "Now you need to win three more times so I can get my investment back."

"Why three?" Snegov asked.

"Because when the first video came out they said it was pure luck. And I said you'd be able to kill him at least five times in a row which can't be just pure luck in any way you look at it. My friends think that five consequent fails are too much even for an idiot like Screwer. So I might hit the jackpot provided you keep up the good work. Two kills down, three more to go."

Snegov scratched his head, pressed one finger to a nostril and blew his nose hard. "If you say so," he said. "Does that mean that you and your friends," he pointed skyward, "are going to watch us all the time?"

"But of course! We even made teleport scrolls! This is top class entertainment!"

Jinx waved a farewell and dug his heels into his gryphon's flanks, steering him toward the rest of the flock.

"I think you're right," Snegov said as the flying monsters disappeared in a perfect V-formation. "This game is disgustingly real. A petty war in the jungle and plenty of onlookers either getting their kicks from watching others die, or," he nodded at the sky, "getting rich quick by supporting the fighting parties," he shook his head. "Never mind. It's all academic. Time to do some work," he grappled with a dangling rope and slid to the ground.

This time the two friends didn't risk leaving their "comfort zone", rightfully expecting one of Screwer's buddies to come after them even before he respawned. They couldn't do any leveling, either, because Snegov's ability to receive XP was blocked for eight hours after every kill. They whiled away the time as best they could: Morana working on her Sewing and Enchanting skills, Snegov training Grrreta who was already two levels above him.

"Aha!" Morana raised her head to the sound of a falling tree somewhere in the woods. "Bummer. We should have filmed it."

"Let's take a look," Snegov suggested.

Warily the two friends stole toward the activated trap.

Unfortunately for them, it hadn't been Screwer's doing. Not quite. It was his warlock zombie friend Baratur who'd set his chimera loose in the woods. The creature had run far out in front until it had triggered the meticulously undercut tree barely kept straight with a complex system of trip wires. With a thump and a heartrending crunch, the chimera's body blinked and disappeared.

"Clever bastard," Screwer's voice came out

of thin air. "Wait till I get him."

"Relax, dude. We'll demine this place in no time," Baratur replied, laying out everything he needed to summon a new chimera.

Morana raised a surprised eyebrow. "Do all PKs play as zombies?"

"I don't care," Snegov sniffed, hearing the crystal sound of his broken hopes being shattered. "What's this new character, anyway? He'd better start praying to whatever gods he serves. If I catch him in real life, he'll be lucky if he gets away in one piece."

"I think we're done here," Morana summed up sadly, realizing that in a couple of hours they wouldn't have a single intact trap left. The summoned chimeras were nothing like hunters' pets: they couldn't be leveled up neither did they have any characteristics: they were disposable cannon fodder. You didn't have to be a mind reader to predict the results of this latest development: even Morana wouldn't be able to counter an attack from two PKs at once.

They were about to make themselves scarce when a flock of gryphons descended from above, expertly maneuvering through the tree tops. Five of them, carrying five of ex-"number Twos" — who actually were now #1 in the Kartoss Empire.

"You," a level-247 Death Knight known as Vader the Dark pointed his finger at Baratur.

"You should leave now."

"Why?" Baratur's voice rang with challenge. "I'm not breaking any rules! I'm enjoying a stroll in the forest, that's all. You aren't going to prevent me from exercising my gaming rights, are you?"

"I might," the Death Knight squinted at him. "If you're so smart I might exercise my own gaming rights by hunting *you*, how about that? We have a bit of a bet here and you're ruining it."

"All right, all right," Screwer butted in, unwilling to argue with top players, "we can always come back later."

"*You* aren't going anywhere," Vader said. "You can continue on your stroll... on your own."

"Why should I?" Screwer protested.

"Because I say so. You think it's your gaming right to take it out on newbs who can't even strike back? Very well. But you see, we have a bet whether this particular newb can kill you three more times in a row. Which means you should be on your own — purely for the sake of the experiment's integrity. You have three more tries to either find the newb and kill him — in which case you can continue with your old lifestyle — or the Dark Legion will make sure you'll never play in Kartoss again. Is that clear?"

The other four gryphon riders descended, allowing Snegov and Morana a glimpse of these Dark Legionnaires. Apart from their friend Jinx the Grudge Bearer, the group also included a Vagren priest nicknamed Fly, of all things, as well as a Dark Elf Druidess Clawsy and a thaurun Paladin Emperor PalPutin.

"They're funny," Snegov chuckled, pointing at Vader the Dark and Emperor PalPutin. "When I was little, I was absolutely crazy about that franchise, if you know what I mean. And the other one must have loved his school history lessons — he's even got a name to show for it!"

"In order to resolve the bet as quickly as possible," Vader continued, "we'll rez you every time you fail. If the newb wins, you will stay away from him, understood? You have three hours, otherwise you lose by default."

You'd never have thought a zombie's face was capable of conveying such a rapid succession of emotions, of which dismay was predominant.

"The newb isn't alone," he offered his last albeit admittedly weak argument. "He's got the priestess to help him."

"She won't be allowed to interfere," Vader decreed.

Jinx nodded. "I'll let them know of this change of terms," he produced his communication amulet and contacted Morana.

"We've heard it," she replied, elbowing Snegov by way of asking if he accepted the new terms.

Snegov shrugged. "Fine with me. We'd

better get on with it, then. No good just talking about it."

"We accept," Morana said. She wished Snegov good luck and joined the legionnaires.

Snegov was now on his own.

"Okay, let's do it," he said to himself before diving into the undergrowth.

Screwer's first death was admittedly stupid. As he stole through the forest, he saw a stake driven in his path. Mounted on it was a sign with a painstakingly drawn and very insulting message (courtesy of Snegov's entry-level Drawing skill).

The wretched newb had really done his best! Grinding his teeth, Screwer kicked the stake nice and hard, wishing it was his enemy's green orcish backside. Which was a fatal mistake, of course. Before Screwer had the chance to realize what he'd just done, a camouflaged net was already whisking him up to the skies toward his third death.

Now he was much more careful — but not careful enough not to disturb a complex system of a trip wires which triggered a confetti spell, enveloping the stealthed rogue in a cloud of colored bits of paper. While he was busy swearing, trying to brush off the revealing evidence, a heavy log came flying out of nowhere studded with spearheads like an organ roller with spikes and sending the wretch back to his resurrection point.

Each one of Screwer's deaths was accompanied by a thunderous laughter coming from the heavens, dooming him to a new attempt. Even his friends couldn't help laughing despite losing the bet as they watched the uneven contest.

Now that he only had one try left, Screwer had become doubly careful, unwilling to take any risks. He circled the thick of the woods where his enemy was hiding, trying to come up with a safe way of luring him out.

Finally, Snegov got fed up with it. Accompanied by Grrreta, he left the safety of his hideout and stepped into the clearing which he'd transformed into the gaming analog of a minefield.

"Come on, don't drag it out!" Snegov shouted, striking a picturesque pose with an enormous feline lying at his feet. "Let me kill you already so I can have my lunch! I'm fed up with your nonsense, creeping around with nothing to show for it!"

Snegov's cockiness was justified by two facts: firstly, that the clearing was completely encircled by traps and secondly, that he was way out of range of a thrown dagger which was a rogue's main distance weapon. In order to port behind Snegov's back, Screwer would first have had to cross two-thirds of the clearing which in this case meant certain death.

Still, Screwer couldn't afford to circle Snegov forever: he had less than an hour left in which to kill him. That could explain such brazen behavior on Snegov's part.

He'd forgotten one thing, though: he wasn't the only person who knew how to use scrolls. Unexpectedly Screwer reached into his bag, pulled out a piece of parchment and recited the spell out loud.

A wave of fire spread around him, consuming most of the clearing. Trip wires snapped, releasing the now useless spells and activating the traps; the camouflage of branches shriveled, exposing the trapping pits; the snare nooses burned before they could trip a careless foot.

In the blink of an eye, a well-fortified clearing had been turned into a scorched and perfectly defenseless desert. Snegov was still trying to grasp the significance of this when Screwer went for him, leaping over the exposed pits and traps, impatient to close the distance between himself and the hateful newb.

"Shit! Grrreta, run!" Snegov swung round and switched to the most effective secret mode of escape known to every recon man: cut and run. Luckily for him, the distance between himself and the resourceful zombie was just enough for him to make it into the thick of the woods where he still had a few traps left.

"I'm an idiot," he panted as he pulled a scroll out of his own bag, expecting his enemy's dagger to sink into his back any moment now. This piece of parchment was his last hope of winning. Still running, he turned round, selected Screwer as target and activated the scroll.

The Fear spell — a gift from Jinx — worked like a dream. Screwer — who was making truly Olympic speed — suddenly darted to one side, bug-eyed, and started thrashing around without looking where he was going. Predictably, on the fourth second of his throes he'd barged right into a trap which, if the truth were known, had taken many a real, non-virtual life. Two wooden structures shaped like doorframes and studded with charmed knife blades closed around Screwer, snapping through his body like the jaws of a giant predator.

"Holy shit," Snegov stopped with his hands on his knees, recovering his breath. Grrreta poked him with her head, looking anxiously into her master's eyes.

Snegov threw his arms around his kitty's neck. "Talk about newbs... that was close," he collapsed to the ground, still holding Grrreta's head to his chest, and stared at the sky where his gryphon-riding audience was unhurriedly descending. They seemed to be busy discussing something.

"Bravo!" Vader applauded as his gryphon hovered in mid-air just above the ground. "First time I see a newb with such a level gap win. That was clever! Are you going to apply to the Dark Legion? We could put in a word for you despite your low level. Consider it done."

The others nodded their approval.

Snegov shook his head. "I don't think so. I'm perfectly happy in my battalion, thank you very much. I'm not a big fan of all this mockery, anyway. I have plenty of adrenaline in real life to be goofing about in my spare time. This is the only good thing I've found here," he patted Grrreta on the neck. "Sorry, man. You'll have to do without me."

Vader nodded to Morana who hovered shyly nearby, "*You* should try, too,"

She smiled, flattered. "I need to talk to my husband."

There was no way she was joining anyone without Shanamir and in any case, she'd have to pass the initiation tests first. Still, just knowing the offer was there felt admittedly good.

With a curt goodbye, the legionnaires left our friends and ported away on some high-level business of their own.

"So, how about we go to town and get our reward for killing a PK?" Morana suggested. "We could do a bit of shopping and see what the forums say about our undead friend's demise. I bet the 'number twos' have already uploaded a video."

"Why not?" Snegov agreed. "I could use a new pair of pants. These ones need washing. But you know... I actually feel sorry for that idiot. He shouldn't have taken things so seriously."

"For some people, playing is the most vivid experience they'll ever get in their lives," Morana didn't seem too eager to share his belated bout of humanity. "Useless no-lifers. It's their choice and their problem."

THE NEXT MORNING, Snegov awoke to find that he was famous. A video depicting the sequence of Screwer's deaths had hit every top fail list in the game while Snegov's unorthodox tactics had become a hot topic in the forums. He didn't expect it to last, of course: give them a week, and they'd find a new subject for their heated discussions but at the moment, the orc Noghar the Slayer was a local celebrity. Which in fact annoyed him no end.

"So much for my leave!" the newborn 'star' grumbled, yanking a beer bottle open.

After a couple of gulps, he felt good enough to check his email. His box was bursting with all sorts of offers: from greeting cards and requests to deal with certain particularly annoying PKs to invitations to join clans and even gifts (which he wouldn't know what to do with).

And — surprise surprise — he had a letter from Screwer!

"Let's take a look," Snegov opened the file, then sighed, disappointed. This was a standard set of threats and insults, complete with promises to find him IRL. Exactly what Snegov — or 'the cheeky noob', according to the letter — had expected from a young thug like yesterday's opponent.

"What an idiot," Snegov summed up. He replied by sending Screwer his real name and address, then forgot about the incident entirely. He still had to get some decent clothes for Helen's wedding.

Two days later, Snegov was sitting in his lounge while cleaning his handgun which for some unfathomable reason was obligatory for all active combat servicemen on leave. There was a rumor that this tradition had originated with Israeli troops who in turn had had it ever since the times of the Israel Defense Forces when all soldiers were supposed to be armed while on leave.

Whether that was true, Snegov wasn't sure. No one he knew had ever had the desire to check the claim. It remained just what it was: a campfire story, while the handgun remained a handgun which demanded regular cleaning to ensure that spiders don't make webs in the barrel the way they did in their battalion pen-pushers' weapons.

The ringing of the doorbell distracted him from work.

"Who's that now, for Christ's sake?" Snegov asked himself, then answered his own question with, "Hell knows, Comrade Sergeant, Sir!"

"Too bad, Comrade Sergeant!" Snegov laid the frame of the gun onto a clean cloth spread on the table, then switched the monitor from the newsfeed to the intercom.

He was staring at three young men — two typical young hoods and a fat youth with an expression of contempt on his disdainful face.

"How can I help you, gentlemen?" Snegov inquired in slight bewilderment.

"Hi noob," a voice replied. "I told you I'd find you, didn't I?"

Snegov arched a quizzical eyebrow. With a malicious chuckle, he unlocked the door. He now had the rest of his leave completely planned out.

He had some drill practice to teach his new gamer friends. They could use a bit of training if he wanted them to pass the Army Physical Fitness Test.

TRANSLATED FROM RUSSIAN BY IRENE WOODHEAD
AND NEIL P. MAYHEW

SAVE THE DYNASTY

A TALE FROM REALITY BENDERS SERIES

BY MICHAEL ATAMANOV

TO UNDERSTAND what is happening, we must first go back a year and a half, to when the world we knew was forever changed by the coming of THE GAME. An intrusive advertising banner appeared suddenly before the eyes of computer users the world over, playing a video clip that quickly got on everyone's nerves. It showed a humanoid covered in thick fur like a sasquatch waving a clawed paw in greeting. With a very strong accent, this creature read the same text everywhere, though it was in different languages depending on the country:

People of Earth, by right of first discovery, the Geckho civilization declares its authority and jurisdiction over your planet. We will provide one Tong of safety to your world, but the fate of the human race will depend exclusively on what you do in that time. You have now made sufficient progress as a species, and may take part in the great game, the game that bends reality. So, come play and earn the right to take your place among the great spacefaring races!

That was followed by scenes of strange diagrams and blueprints, after which the fifty-second clip ended, and the popup window closed. A stupid practical joke? Some weird trick by elusive "Russian hackers," who it was now popular to blame for all kinds of failures? An intrusive advertisement for an upcoming computer game?

The truth turned out somewhat more shocking: it really was humanity's FIRST CONTACT with a highly developed interstellar civilization, the Geckho! The blueprints at the end of the video detailed how to assemble a device, which turned out to be a virtual reality capsule that allowed people to enter a mysterious virtual game. Actions and events in that game had an impact our real world. Technologies received in the game enriched the knowledge of humankind and devices built with in-game designs worked in reality just as well as in the virtual world. Meanwhile, if a terminally ill person created a character in the game that bends reality, their disease would be cured instantly.

But the problems in the game were also completely real, and one of them was that the people of our reality were apparently not the only ones who considered Earth their home planet. The Dark Faction was more technologically advanced and, unlike the humanity of our world, was not divided into different, frequently conflicting countries. But the most important thing was that, beyond advanced technology, their arsenal contained deadly magic...

This story offers a glimpse of the events of

the *Reality Benders* series of novels through the
eyes of the Dark Faction. These events take place
after the end of the first book, *Countdown*.

✳ ✳ ✳

PA-LIN-THU, CAPITAL OF THE FIRST DIRECTORY
PALACE OF THE CORULER THUMOR-ANHU LA-FIN
THE PRINCESS'S CHAMBERS

"THE BIFURCATION OF SPACE is a very rare and
metastable occurrence. We still don't even have a
near understanding of how our distant ancestors
managed to accomplish such a grandiose feat.
Beyond all doubt, it was extremely cost-intensive
in all senses of the word. However, we know the
perfectly well what compelled our ancient rulers
to do something so difficult and risky — fear and
hatred of the dull and uneducated masses, who
do not understand or accept anything in any way
connected with magic."

The old gray-haired wizard who said these
words was wearing a dark floor-length robe. He
stopped looking into the night sky with his nearly
blind eyes and decisively opened the window. The
formidable mage, who aroused horror in all that
saw him, turned around, wanting to make sure
his words reached the ears of his only listener, a
tall lithe girl in a form-fitting light-colored dress,

who was trying to tame a disobedient shock of her silvery white hair. The beautiful girl was clearly having a hard time holding the silver brush in her left hand, which was in a cast. She easily could have told a servant girl to do her hair for her, but Princess Minn-O La-Fin preferred to do it herself today.

The great wizened mage, one of the three corulers of humanity, could read the emotions of his beloved granddaughter easily: she was still angry at him, sulking about her broken arm and the death of her friends. The old man turned his gaze back to the cast on his dear granddaughter's arm and cringed in pain. Unfortunately, it had to be done. The "little dose of pain" was simultaneously a punishment, a test, and salvation for Princess Minn-O La-Fin. If her ruling grandfather hadn't rushed to prescribe this excruciating punishment, the Princess risked much more profound consequences. She needed to think about what she'd done: killing four Geckho in the game on a sea ferry? How could she even think of such a thing?! Attacking members of the great Geckho race, the most powerful masters and protectors of humanity in the game that bends reality, was an especially heinous crime. The potential response of the suzerains could have been extremely harsh and unpredictable, starting with extermination all members of the faction led by Thumor-Anhu La-

Fin in the virtual game, and ending with the complete destruction of all humanity in the real world.

He had been forced to take the lead in order to stymie the rage of the most powerful Geckho. Two servants of Minn-O La-Fin, loyal friends and lackeys of the Princess since childhood, who had also taken part in that attack on the Geckho, had already lost their heads in the real world, both as a punishment for the crime, and to shut the mouths of unneeded witnesses, thus cordoning off the coruler's granddaughter from harm. Minn-O La-Fin herself was present for the execution of her close friends, which was for the edification of the young Princess, and should have prevented the hot-headed girl from making such bad decisions in the future. Now, the official story, which the faction was sticking to in all conversations with the suzerains was this: "Minn-O La-Fin didn't know anything about her servants' actions and had nothing to do with the attack on the Geckho."

To be honest, there was one more witness of those bloody events on the ferry — a Surveyor called Gnat from the hostile Human-3 faction, a native of the alternative reality their distant ancestors had turned away from. This adversary had gotten mixed up in the affairs of the great mage before, and was becoming a greater threat with every passing day. So, tonight, Thumor-Anhu was trying to steer their conversation precisely to the topic of Gnat. But how to do that and not make it so obvious that Minn-O La-Fin would catch on?

Meanwhile, the Princess was thinking but still, noticing that her frightening grandfather had gone silent, turned and met eyes with him:

"Sorry, I got distracted. It's just that my arm hurts a lot..."

That wasn't true. The medicine, which had been injected right after the execution should have entirely precluded all sensations of pain. Also, when reading her emotions, the old man didn't sense any physical pain. All the same, it wasn't the right time to catch his granddaughter in a lie, and Thumor-Anhu La-Fin continued his speech:

"You aren't listening to me, Minn-O, but I'm trying to tell you about very important events of the distant past, which are now relevant in our time!"

All the same, the old mage's granddaughter elected to show her difficult character, demonstrating a complete lack of interest in the serious topic raised by her influential grandfather:

"Thumor-Anhu, if you want to tell me about the old splitting of the world into those with magic and those without, you already told me after the first time I met people from the alternative reality in the game. But I'll admit, I didn't understand why we have to continue that long forgotten animosity and go to war with the factions of the alternative Earth, and I still don't. So our distant ancestors got scared for their power and roped themselves off from people without magic, is that such an insurmountable barrier now?"

Those were dangerous words, bordering on heresy! They exploded the very basis of bases of human laws, which stated that only wise and just mages had been foreordained by nature to rule the uneducated and cowardly masses. If coruler Thumor-Anhu were hearing such things from someone he didn't know, he would turn that person to dust without a second thought! But in the case of his granddaughter, it was much more complicated and unfortunate.

The magical abilities of the very ancient La-Fin dynasty of hereditary mages and rulers, which had its roots somewhere in the unfathomable depths of eternity, had ended with Thumor-Anhu for some reason. None of his three children had inherited magical abilities from their great and powerful father. What was more, his two sons had died young during a military campaign to pacify a hunger strike in the Ninth Directory. Both perished without offspring.

The great mage of unearthly beauty had

one other child though, a daughter named Onessa-Rati La-Fin who, in the late stage of her pregnancy, had been seriously wounded by an act of terrorism in the palace of the coruler by a fanatical suicide bomber and anti-magic partisan. Despite the efforts of the best doctors and mage healers, despite the oceans of magical energy poured into her, and the rarest of healing elixirs, Onessa-Rati had passed away, managing to leave behind a prematurely born daughter, who she had named right before death: Minn-O, meaning "last hope." Thus, the only successor to the ancient magical La-Fin family was Princess Minn-O. By the age of eighteen, though, she had yet to show any predilection for magic.

The great mage Thumor-Anhu had long ago passed his one hundred seventieth year, but could only hope for Minn-O's future children, although the dream of another magical La-Fin grew more doubtful with each successive generation. Nevertheless, his only granddaughter, the last hope of the ancient dynasty in all senses, was valued by the severe old mage more than his own life. He loved her in his own way and protected her from any and all danger. And now, the old man didn't even raise his voice, despite the dangerous words of the Princess, and tried to clear up her confusion with patience:

"You're not right, Minn-O. The ancient mages were not afraid of some merely hypothetical threat to their power and authority. They faced a true danger to their own lives and those of their children. It was concern for those close to them that forced the most powerful wizards to 'cut off' the part of the world they controlled, 'cocooning' it and cordoning it off from the hostile rabble with an impassable wall. And it must be noted that their fears were not at all imaginary! The more we find out about the parallel world, the better we understand the ancient mages, who didn't want to have anything in common with that ghastly uneducated society. Human sacrifices, inquisitions, mage hunts, burning at the stake for the slightest suspicion of sorcerous abilities..."

"There was plenty of that in the history of our world as well," the Princess objected reasonably. "After all, the magical families only managed to hold onto their power by drowning every uprising in blood. They also tracked down anyone espousing the so-called 'heresy' that a person without magical abilities might be able to rule and cauterized the very concept with a red-hot poker. But I still haven't heard an answer to my question. Why can we not coexist with people from the alternative world in the game that bends reality? Why are we enemies by default, and don't even try to come to an agreement?"

The old man tried to let all the dangerous heresy go in one ear and out the other again, only at the very end of the Princess's speech shaking his head in reproach:

"You aren't listening carefully enough, Minn-O. I was saying that the bifurcation created by the ancient mages is extremely unstable, and the Universe is trying to bring our part of space back down to one reality, slamming the second shut into nothingness. Sure, once upon a time, our two independent nonintersecting worlds could exist, but after mankind encountered the Geckho and discovered the game that bends reality, everything changed. We have discovered a virtual world, which directly impacts both realities. And after studying the rules of the game and asking the wise Geckho about them, our mage analysts quickly realized that the version of humanity which gains advantage over the Earth in the game will be the only one to remain in the real Universe, while their opponents will be cast into the dustbin of memory, fairy tale and legend. And that is exactly why we cannot coexist with the Human-3 faction, or any of the others from the alternative world. Here, it's either them or us! And we must resolve this principal issue as quickly as possible, before the Tong of safety gifted to us by our suzerains passes, otherwise a divided humanity will not be able to repel the invasion from space by external foes."

The beautiful Princess had no other arguments against her sagacious grandfather and just turned away to the mirror, biting her lip in dismay as she thought. Thumor-Anhu La-Fin decided this was a convenient opportunity to raise the sorest part of his speech: his granddaughter's relationship with the most successful player of the enemy faction, a Surveyor by the name Gnat. With a significant degree of surprise, the old mage had discovered sentiments in the Princess's thoughts that were totally inappropriate to how he expected her to feel for a clear enemy: admiration, respect, gratefulness and even a bit of romantic intrigue. At any minute, it could reach tenderness, or even attraction! The day before yesterday, the old mage was so shocked by this discovery, that he couldn't find the strength to address it right away. For two days, Thumor-Anhu La-Fin had thought over this unexpected problem and prepared for this difficult conversation with the Princess. And now that moment had come.

"Minn-O, I don't see a particular reason to worry about the outcome of the conflict. Our faction in the game is progressing significantly quicker and more successfully than that of the alternative world. We already have twice as many players, and our average level is nearly as high as theirs. I'll allow that the enemy has many professional soldiers who honed their abilities and skills in the innumerable local conflicts of their harsh world, and that has a noticeable effect. However, we have better developed industry, a more stable economy, more advanced technologies and more lethal weaponry. The faction entrusted to me is quickly gaining strength and, soon, we will be able to crush the enemy. But only if one unpredictable factor doesn't interfere..."

The old man fell silent, not finishing his sentence and, in a totally predictable fashion, the Princess asked what "factor" her faction leader had been referring to.

"Gnat," the Great Mage answered significantly.

"Gnat???" The Princess asked in astonishment. "But Gnat has already left on a starship with the Geckho! Grandpa, you were outraged that he is the only person our suzerains let stay in the cosmos, while the others are refused, even for very large sums of money! Now, after you put such a high price on his head, I don't think he'll ever come back!"

"Nevertheless, the fact remains! Our trusted informant says Gnat is coming back, and not empty-handed. Last time, he brought a large number of valuable blueprints back from his trip to the stars, and a significant amount of space currency, which noticeably strengthened the Human-3 faction. And this time, according to our agent, Gnat will bring wealthy space traders to Earth, who are prepared to purchase valuable resources from our enemies, and sell them high-tech weaponry and components. If that happens, our whole strategy to isolate the Human-3 faction and obstruct their trade with the suzerains might go down the tubes. That must be prevented! And, Minn-O, I would like you to be the one in charge of the combat group!"

The old mage's granddaughter took some time to answer. But then, before saying if she agreed or refused, raised her eyes to her grandfather and inquired:

"Thumor-Anhu, you know perfectly well my record in battle against Gnat. I won't say I'm not confident in my own abilities but, in the past, Gnat has managed to get the upper hand on me every time. Moreover, he didn't simply win, but put me in an embarrassing and awkward position time and again. And when he captured me for the third time, Gnat, either joking or serious said that, if we meet again, he'll think I am trying to run into him on purpose to start a romantic relationship..."

As if the Great Mage didn't know that! The whole gaming career of his only granddaughter, a Cartographer by in-game profession, an excellent marksman, a great sentry and an unrivaled scout — had gone off the rails because of this enemy combatant. Not so long ago, Minn-O La-Fin was considered one of the most successful and effective players in her faction. She wasn't afraid of taking risks and had led many daring attacks deep into enemy territory, gaining extremely valuable information. But her first chance meeting with Gnat, still a green day-one Surveyor, had ended in the discovery of Minn-O La-Fin's secret observation post and the Princess being captured in great shame. After that, it was as if something had broken inside her, taking her former ease and swagger with it. Her lucky star had fizzled out, and the total defeat of the Great Mage's squadron in a battle in the Harpy Mountains was a totally unnecessary confirmation of that fact.

Gnat, on the other hand, feeling a hot streak, had behaved nobly with the wounded Minn-O, helped her and let the girl go free. After that came the ill-fated ferry... A firefight in a ghastly storm at night, four dead Geckho on board and a team of three perfectly coordinated soldiers against Gnat alone. And after the "unsuccessful double-cross," the Surveyor, who'd come out on top yet again, had been acridly condescending and kissed his captive among the bloodied Geckho corpses, promising that their romance would continue if and when they met again. That broke Minn-O once and for all, and she was no longer troubled even by the "little dose of pain," because she had lost confidence in her own abilities, which was a bigger concern.

"Minn-O, above all else, you need this. You

are the one who must defeat your troublesome rival, and then you will regain the wanton ease and courage that once distinguished you from all the other players of our faction."

The Princess considered it, then gave a distinct nod, accepting her ruling grandfather's suggestion.

"Now that sounds great! Our agent has already told us the precise location where the merchant starship will land, we also know the forces of the Human-3 ship that will meet it. Minn-O, I will give you enough soldiers to guarantee the success of this operation. Just don't rush it. First, let the merchant ship take off so no Geckho get hurt by accident, then you may begin! But remember your priority. It is not Gnat, but the very large sum of Geckho currency our enemies will receive for their goods. These millions must not reach their destination under any circumstances! And Gnat is merely a pleasant bonus, my gift to you. Try to take him captive. If you cannot, just kill him!"

VIRTUAL EARTH
"ANTIQUE BEACH" GAME NODE
LAND OF THE NPC CENTAURS

THE ENEMY APPEARED just a quarter hour before

the starship was scheduled to land, which was downright mockery on their part. Minn-O La-Fin's fifteen-soldier squadron, which had arrived the previous evening, camouflaged itself immediately and spent the whole frosty night and half of the damp rainy next day lying in cover, afraid of giving themselves away with a single unnecessary move. They had scanned for hidden surveillance apparatuses right when they arrived near the meeting zone and come up empty, but that was no guarantee there were no such devices here. The rocky surroundings of the mountain plateau meant it would be easy to conceal sensors, which would react to movement and sound, so any moving or speaking was strictly forbidden. There was no talk whatever of campfires or hot food. There was too much riding on this horse to expose themselves to elementary infrared radiation detectors or attract the attention of the aggressive centaurs that lived in this game node.

The high-tech thermal suits all the soldiers in the squadron were wearing adapted to the temperature of the environment, which made them entirely invisible to infrared devices. They didn't make the people inside the thin form-fitting suits any warmer, though. This time, safety had to come before comfort. It would also not be easy to see the hidden troops in the visible spectrum — they had chameleon capes that quickly changed color, blending into their surroundings. Minn-O La-Fin, before making a shelter for herself, personally checked every soldier's camouflage and was left very satisfied by what she saw — externally, they all looked like piles of rocks and pebbles just sitting randomly, in no way standing out on the backdrop of the surrounding landscape. Beyond technology, a certain role was played by the Stealth skill, which was necessary for all the characters in the Princess's team of commandos, who were of the Scout, Saboteur, Assassin and Sniper classes. Minn-O herself was a Geographer by profession, which offered not only increased vision radius, but also other game-class abilities like high movement speed and low visibility, so the Princess could hide among the rocks better than many of her subordinates.

But then, finally, the enemies arrived. On the even surface of the plateau, its thrusters humming in strain, a heavily armored *Peresvet*-class antigrav came up the steep incline. A half-flying-half-driving armored vehicle, the first one had been spotted in the Human-3 faction ten days earlier, which came as an unpleasant surprise to Minn-O's allies. Invulnerable to small arms, the highly mobile off-road vehicle had respectable firepower from a high-speed cannon mounted on a spinning tower and presented a great threat. Perhaps it was the introduction of the *Peresvet* that explained the vexing defeat in the Harpy Cliffs battle. But today, there was no discussion of underestimating the enemy forces — the strong and weak points of the *Peresvet* had already been well studied, and tactics for defeating them had been developed in the mass-scale bloody conflict in the Eastern Swamp.

Four First Legion troops jumped out of the motionless all-terrain vehicle — elite warriors of the enemy faction, they were professional soldiers and had noticeably improved their already lethal abilities by leveling combat skills in the game that bends reality. All four of the soldiers went in different directions and started looking around. At a certain point, one of them was just seven steps from the hidden Assassin of Minn-O La-Fin's squadron, but he still couldn't see the cloaked killer. The Princess's heart froze in fear, but the enemy soldier kept on his way, not having noticed his opponent, who was ready to throw himself on the man at a moment's notice.

Finally, the area was declared safe, and that very same enemy, blind as a mole, waved a hand, giving the signal. Another three emerged from the *Peresvet*, including a tall stately man in an armored suit, glimmering with a force field. The Princess knew him perfectly well. It was Ivan Lozovsky, an official diplomat of the enemy faction. His presence was completely expected — the diplomat was one of the very few people who understood the language of the extraterrestrial Geckho race, and the forthcoming negotiations with the merchants depended largely on him. But the two players accompanying him surprised Minn-O La-Fin greatly — a Gladiator boy and a Medic girl, and they weren't from the First Legion and were even of quite a low level. Who were these people and what were they doing here?

"They're friends of Gnat," the voice of Thumor-Anhu rang out in her headphones. "Hi, Minn-O. I decided to watch the operation myself from nearby with a magical support group. Don't pay us any mind — my mages will only intervene if your soldiers need help. I'm sure that won't be necessary."

The Princess tried not to act surprised, though that meant allied mages were not only observing the enemy, but also monitoring the thoughts of everyone present on the plateau. And probably, after all, every one of these mages, unlike those from Minn-O La-Fin's squadron, hadn't had to come here in stealth on foot through six game nodes, but had been dropped somewhere nearby from a flying antigrav. The girl suppressed the annoyance bubbling up inside her — that meant her soldiers also didn't have to crawl through swamps and forests for almost twenty-four hours, but could have been just flown right in?!

And meanwhile, only one gunman

remained inside the all-terrain vehicle, sitting at the high-speed automatic cannon, while the door to the vehicle was left enticingly open. All the other enemies were in her sights right now and it was possible...

"Stay on task, Minn-O! Your group's mission is not capturing enemy vehicles."

Her grandfather, in his impeccable wisdom, was right as always. She shouldn't be paying any attention to the *Peresvet* now! What was more, a strange sound somewhere between a whistle and a hum was now coming from above the gloomy cloud cover and building with every second. Soon, a bright spot appeared in the midst of the low gray clouds — the glow of starship engines. The merchants had arrived!

The space ship dove down from the low clouds, lowered its landing gear and very gently, with surgical precision, set down on the stone plateau. The strange narrow sleek vehicle bore no resemblance whatever to the Geckho ships Minn-O had seen in the space port.

Tiopeo-Myhh II
Miyelonian Long-Distance Interceptor

Miyelonian??? That was an entirely different space race, and even technically hostile toward the Geckho! What had brought them here?! Based on the intensive discussion that sparked up among Minn-O's opponents, they were occupied by the very same questions. But then the starship motors quieted down. They didn't turn all the way off, just went into a less intensive mode and the hatch at the tail of the strange flying device flew back.

Three beings came out of the opening: two short furry creatures that resembled large cats walking on their hind legs, and one man. Minn-O recognized him right away, despite the hundred steps between them. Gnat!!!

Gerd Gnat
Human
Human-3 Faction
Level-56 Surveyor

Fifty-six?! How? The Princess remembered perfectly that, on their last meeting a few days earlier, not only was he at level thirty, but also that that had been no impediment to his taking down three players, including Minn-O, who was at level fifty-one at the time. How rapidly Gnat had progressed since then! What was more, he now had the word "gerd" before his name, which meant "esteemed, respected." Minn-O herself was just level fifty-three and had no status. The girl's chest began to ache alarmingly from the bad presentiment... She now sensed that their fourth encounter might also not end in her favor...

"Don't turn mushy, granddaughter! Get yourself together! Order your soldiers to get ready. As before, the primary objective is the currency. Gnat is secondary. Don't touch the Miyelonians. I don't know what they're doing here, but we really don't need a conflict with a great cosmic race."

Meanwhile, the members of the Human-3 faction saw their long-absent player, and began shaking hands and embracing him. The diplomat bowed in respect to the high-status character, and the much stronger soldiers of the First Legion also expressed noticeably respect to the gerd. The medic girl threw herself around his neck and kissed her newly-arrived compatriot. Based on the warmth and duration of the kiss, Minn-O guessed these two were more than friends. Her heart was pierced with a needle of envy, although that was also strange.

At the same time, another two Miyelonians got out of the spaceship. Wearing armored space suits, they were armed and very tense. They squeaked out something, or more like meowed, and immediately Ivan Lozovsky walked up to them, accompanied by Gnat. Did he really know their language? As it turned out, he did not. The orange cat who had come out first with Gnat knew their language though, and her game class was even appropriate — Translator. She was also of quite a respectable level:

Ayni Uri-Miayuu
Miyelonian
Pride of the Tailed Star
Level-77 Translator

The negotiations didn't last long, and the people and Miyelonians soon began bustling about — six very heavy boxes were brought out and dragged to the starship. Some containers were also brought out of the starship and set down on the ground. The parties checked the contents and initiated the exchange.

"Our enemies are making part of the payment not in money, but weapons and goods," the senior mage explained to his granddaughter, also observing the negotiations with interest.

The goods were quickly loaded into their new vehicles, but Ivan Lozovsky and the Miyelonian continued talking through the fluffy-tailed Translator — clearly, they were either deepening their acquaintance or negotiating new deals. It seemed the moment of truth was near, and Minn-O ordered her soldiers to get ready. One of the Miyelonians counted out a whole handful of valuable large red crystals and handed them to the human diplomat. Lozovsky stood for a minute and clearly counted the theretofore unseen sum again, but then confirmed everything was right. Two of the Miyelonians hurried to the ship, but the other two were in no rush. What was this?

"I don't know either," my grandfather admitted. "Apparently, these two Miyelonians are going to stay behind, but I cannot understand in what capacity. As trade representatives of their race here on Earth? Hardly likely. After all, this is an exclusive economic zone of the Geckho, and our suzerains would not be glad to see smugglers of another race. Or were they hostages to guarantee the honesty of the next deal?"

Meanwhile, the starship turned its thrusters on overdrive and shot off like a bullet into the cloud-covered sky. The two Miyelonians were still there...

"Don't fall asleep, Minn-O! Lozovsky is walking toward the *Peresvet* with the payment. Don't let him get back into the armored vehicle!!!"

"Begin operation!!! Lay Lozovsky out! Don't kill him under any circumstances!" Minn-O La-Fin ordered.

Her precautions were unnecessary. Every person in the squadron already knew perfectly that the inventory of an enemy could only be cleaned out if they were immobilized or unconscious. But not dead. The game algorithms allowed only the "loot" that dropped to be taken as trophies from a corpse, which was not what we needed in this situation.

Her commandos started off with flying colors. The two Assassins used their ability to attack from a distance and knocked down the unsuspecting enemy. Then the Saboteur, who was instantly next to the fallen body, opened the loot window and loaded the valuable crystals into his own inventory before the paralyzed body of the diplomat even hit the ground. Done! The Saboteur took advantage of the confusion in the enemy ranks to quickly grab a couple more valuable items that caught his eye, after which he took out his laser pistol and shot himself in the temple. It was a calculated suicide. He would respawn later on his faction's territory together with the trophies. The main mission of the combat operation was complete!!!

The rest of Minn-O's troops didn't waste any time, opening fire on their commander's orders and shooting to kill. Two soldiers of the First Legion were sent to respawn before they even managed to raise their weapons. The Princess hadn't yet ordered them to touch Gnat, so she could try to take him alive at the end of the battle. However, it seemed that was a mistake.

No more than a second later, instead of the person in the standard Kevlar jacket half the enemy faction wore, a figure appeared on the battlefield in a strange black armored suit, encapsulated by a defensive forcefield. Two shots came from the fearsome Annihilator, which Gnat had also used on the ferry. Two hits, two corpses.

The two Miyelonians also armored up and equipped themselves with shimmering blades. The movement speed of these overgrown cats and the unpredictability of their trajectory came as a very unpleasant surprise for the Princess's squadron. They were living light-speed meatgrinders! And they were also joined by a Gladiator, who Gnat threw a shimmering curved blade just like the one used by the Miyelonians. But worst of all was the fact that the *Peresvet*, with its high-speed automatic cannon, and the two surviving First Legion soldiers hidden behind the stones, opened lethal and unbelievably accurate fire, by some miracle destroying the Princess's soldiers one after the next, including the far away and seemingly well camouflaged snipers. How???

"Surveyor abilities," said my grandfather, observing the firefight. "The turncoat told us Gnat's character has very high Perception, plus a bunch of leveled skills to help discover any and everything, along with the skill Target Detection. He's finding your gunmen and adding target markers for his allies."

In the ranks of the enemy, a medic girl had died, and the Princess's snipers had shot Lozovsky as he tried to stand up, but those were seemingly the last losses for the Human-3 Faction. The Princess had three surviving soldiers now, including Minn-O La-Fin herself, and they were taking so dense they couldn't even stick a nose out from behind their cover.

"Thumor-Anhu, help! I need magical help urgently!" the girl prayed in despair, understanding perfectly that, without magical support, the battle would be lost.

Taking a serious risk, the girl rolled behind another heap of rocks and loosed a series of laser pulses at Gnat, and finally also tossed a grenade at him. But it was no use. He had a well-leveled Danger Sense skill and easily got out of the laser rifle's field of fire, then the damage zone of the grenade shrapnel. How could he even be killed?! It was impossible! Was it not time to commit suicide as not to fall into enemy hands and just respawn on her own territory?

"Idiot! You can't see the most important thing! Look at your soldiers!" her grandfather ordered.

Minn-O turned her head sharply toward the huge pile next to her, where her last two surviving allies were supposed to be taking cover, and... turned to stone. Instead of continuing to fight the Human-3 faction, these two were fighting each other, grabbing at legs and punching!!! What the hell was this?!

Then, the Princess saw Gnat, standing without any cover in the middle of the plateau, pointing his balled-uup right hand toward the scuffling enemies. It was a very familiar scene...

Minn-O had seen her grandfather take control of the mind of either servants or enemies many times before. Did that mean Gnat... was a mage?! But how? After all, it was thought that no magic remained in the alternative world!

"That's exactly right, granddaughter, you've finally realized it."

The fight between the allies was already over, and both soldiers were dead. Gnat instantly lost all interest in them, turning his head unfailingly toward the hidden Minn-O and meeting gazes with her. The Princess's second of confusion was more than enough for him. The girl's hand, with a grenade squeezed in it, unclenched all on its own, and the dangerous object fell to the ground without being activated.

"Grandfather!!! Help!!!" Minn-O managed to mentally call out one last thing, but her desperate cry was left unanswered.

✵ ✵ ✵

FROM THE NEIGHBORING HILL, the still unseen old mage just watched indifferently as his only granddaughter was disarmed and tied up. Everything happened exactly as planned. The space currency they'd intercepted was a huge sum by any standards, so the enemy would surely feel it. Also, he could always buy back his beloved granddaughter at any moment with this money. But there was no reason to rush. After all, the true goal of this combat operation had only just now been achieved — Minn-O would be meeting with Gnat, who she liked quite a bit. Moreover, before her was a man with magical powers, making him quite a dashing perspective groom, morally preparing her for their relationship to progress to a romance. The wise mage had faith in the feminine wiles of his beautiful granddaughter and wished Minn-O success with his whole heart.

He suspected Gnat had magical abilities back on their first meeting, when the experienced psionic had tried to take control of the inexperienced opponent's mind and failed. Such a thing simply could not happen, considering the supposedly huge difference in Intelligence stats, which is what the probability of successful mental attack depends on. The list of all Human-3 faction players they got a while later from the turncoat, showing detailed stats on all characters, confirmed that Gnat shouldn't have been capable of reflecting the mental attack. But he had! Only one explanation remained. Any player potentially capable of magic, even if the chances were low, had defense against magical effects. Today, he great mage had seen he was right with his own eyes, and the enemy's magical abilities had grown stronger, now having become fully revealed.

Minn-O, still tied up, was loaded into the *Peresvet* and the armored vehicle rolled out toward Human-3 territory. There was nothing more to see here, and Thumor-Anhu ordered his servants to summon an antigrav to return home. The lower-rank mages accompanying him stayed in morose silence, clearly not understanding what was happening now, and why their powerful leader hadn't given the command to interfere in the battle and save the Princess. The old mage wasn't preparing to explain anything to them, because it was strictly a matter for the La-Fin family, and had nothing to do with the others.

According to the laws of their world, Minn-O could not take a mage from another great magical family as a groom and retain her high title and name as a member of the ancient La-Fin line. Gnat was another matter entirely. The experienced mage had read Gnat's emotions several times and understood that his granddaughter had always been to his liking. Even if it was impossible to bring Gnat to their reality, the omniscient Geckho said that a child conceived in the game could be brought into the real world under certain circumstances. And the prophets, who the respected coruler Thumor-Anhu La-Fin had been conferring with for the last two days gave an almost one-hundred-percent guarantee that a child born from such a liaison could be expected to have magical abilities.

Exactly what was needed to save the dynasty!

TRANSLATED FROM RUSSIAN BY ANDREW SCHMITT

Want to be the first to know about our latest LitRPG, sci fi and fantasy titles from your favorite authors?

Subscribe to our NEW RELEASES newsletter: http://eepurl.com/b7niIL

Thank you for reading *You're in Game-2!*
If you like what you've read, check out other LitRPG novels
published by Magic Dome Books:

An NPC's Path LitRPG series by Pavel Kornev:
The Dead Rogue

Reality Benders LitRPG series by Michael Atamanov:
Countdown

Dark Paladin LitRPG series by Vasily Mahanenko:
The Beginning
The Quest
Restart

**The Dark Herbalist LitRPG series
by Michael Atamanov:**
Video Game Plotline Tester
Stay on the Wing
A Trap for the Potentate

The Neuro LitRPG series by Andrei Livadny:
The Crystal Sphere
The Curse of Rion Castle
The Reapers

**The Way of the Shaman LitRPG series
by Vasily Mahanenko:**
Survival Quest
The Kartoss Gambit
The Secret of the Dark Forest
The Phantom Castle
The Karmadont Chess Set
Shaman's Revenge
Clans War
The Hour of Pain (a bonus short story)

Galactogon LitRPG series by Vasily Mahanenko:
Start the Game!

Phantom Server LitRPG series by Andrei Livadny:
Edge of Reality
The Outlaw
Black Sun

In order to have new books of the series translated faster, we need your help and support! Please consider leaving a review or spread the word by recommending *You're in Game!-2* to your friends and posting the link on social media. The more people buy the book, the sooner we'll be able to make new translations available.

Thank you!

Till next time!